LITTLE GOD BEN

Ben the tramp, a self-confessed coward and ex-sailor, is back in the Merchant Service and shipwrecked in the Pacific in this quintessentially 1930s comedy thriller.

Son of novelist Benjamin Farjeon, and brother to children's author Eleanor, playwright Herbert and composer Harry, Joseph Jefferson Farjeon (1883–1955) began work as an actor and freelance journalist before inevitably turning his own hand to writing fiction. Described by the *Sunday Times* as 'a master of the art of blending horrors with humour', Farjeon was a prolific author of mystery novels, with more than 60 books published between 1924 and 1955. His first play, *No. 17*, was produced at the New Theatre in 1925, when the actor Leon M. Lion 'made all London laugh' as Ben the tramp, an unorthodox amateur detective who became the most enduring of all Farjeon's creations. Rewritten as a novel in 1926 and filmed by Alfred Hitchcock six years later, with Mr Lion reprising his role, *No.17*'s success led to seven further books featuring the warm-hearted but danger-prone Ben: 'Ben is not merely a character but a parable—a mixture of Trimalchio and the Old Kent Road, a notable coward, a notable hero, above all a supreme humourist' (Seton Dearden, *Time and Tide*). Although he had become largely forgotten over the 60 years since his death, J. Jefferson Farjeon's reputation made an impressive resurgence in 2014 when his 1937 Crime Club book *Mystery in White* was reprinted by the British Library, returning him to the bestseller lists and resulting in readers wanting to know more about this enigmatic author from the Golden Age of detective fiction.

Also in this series

J. JEFFERSON FARJEON

Little God Ben

COLLINS
CRIME
CLUB

COLLINS CRIME CLUB

An imprint of HarperCollins*Publishers*
1 London Bridge Street
London SE1 9GF
www.harpercollins.co.uk

This paperback edition 2016

First published in Great Britain for The Crime Club Ltd
by W. Collins Sons & Co. Ltd 1935

A catalogue record for this book is
available from the British Library

ISBN 978-0-00-815597-1

Set in Sabon by Palimpsest Book Production Limited, Falkirk, Stirlingshire

Printed by Clays Ltd, St Ives plc

MIX
Paper from
responsible sources
FSC
www.fsc.org   FSC C007454

CONTENTS

Mainly About Knuckles

'Something's goin' ter 'appen,' said Ben, as the ship rolled.

'Well, see it don't 'appen 'ere,' replied a fellow-stoker apprehensively.

'I don't mean that sort of 'appen,' answered Ben. 'Yer feels that in yer stummick. I feels this in me knuckles. Whenever me knuckles goes funny, something 'appens.'

The fellow-stoker did not care much for the conversation. But they were off duty together, drawing in a little evening air to mingle with the coal-dust in their throats, and it was Ben or nothing. So he murmured,

'Wot's goin' ter 'appen?'

'I dunno,' said Ben. 'Orl I knows is that it is. It's a sort of a hitch like. Once it was afore I fell inter a barrel o' beer.'

'I wouldn't mind ticklin' a bit fer that,' observed the fellow-stoker.

'Ah, but it ain't always so nice. Another time it was afore a nassassinashun. I fergit 'oo was nassassinated. A king or somethin'. And another time I went ter bed and fahnd the cat 'ad 'ad kittens. I slep' on the floor. Yus, but they never hitched like this. Not the kittens, me knuckles. If somethin' 'orrerble don't 'appen afore midnight I've never seen a corpse!'

The fellow-stoker's dislike of the conversation increased. He preferred conversations beginning, 'Have you heard the one about the lady of Gloucester?' But Ben was a human anomaly, a man with a dirty face and a clean mind, and some error in his make-up had eliminated all interest in Gloucestershire ladies. It was unnatural.

''Ere, that's enough about corpses,' growled the fellow-stoker, 'and I'll bet you ain't seen none, neither!'

'Lumme, I was born among 'em!' retorted Ben. 'I spends orl me life tryin' ter git away from 'em. If there's a star called Corpse I was born under it! I could tell yer things, mate, as 'd mike yer eyes pop aht o' their sockets. I seed one in a hempty 'ouse runnin' abart—oi, look aht!'

The ship gave a violent lurch and threw them together. As they untied themselves Ben continued:

'It mide me run abart, too.'

''Ere, I've 'ad enough of you!' gasped the fellow-stoker, and hurried away to less gruesome climes.

Ben looked after him disappointedly. He hadn't meant to be gruesome. He had merely been relating history. He didn't like corpses any better than the next man, but you talked about what you knew about, and there it was. If Ben had lived among buttercups and daisies, he'd have talked about those, and would infinitely have preferred it.

He gazed at his knuckles. 'Somethin' orful!' he muttered. He stretched them, opening and closing his fingers. He shook them. The prophetic itch remained. He tried to forget them, and stared at the heaving grey sea.

It shouldn't have been grey, and it shouldn't have been

heaving. It should have been blue and calm, like the posters that had advertised this cruise, and stars should be coming out to illuminate sentiment. There was a lot of sentiment on the ship. Ben had spotted some of it, and had envied it in the secret labyrinths of his heart. They would be dancing soon up above. "Ow'd I look in a boiled shirt,' he wondered, 'with a gal pasted onter it?' But the Pacific Ocean often belies its name, and it was belying it drastically at this moment. Waves were sweeping across it in angry white-topped lines, indignantly slapping the ship that impeded them and sending up furies of spray. The wind was in an equally bad temper. It made you want to hold on to things. 'I didn't orter've come on this 'ere trip,' decided Ben. 'I orter've tiken a job 'oldin' 'orses!' Had he known the job to which the wind and the waves were speeding him, he would probably have shut his eyes tight and dived into them.

But he was spared that knowledge, and meanwhile the rolling ship and his itching knuckles were quite enough to go on with. It wasn't merely the itching that worried him. It was a vague sense of responsibility that accompanied the inconvenience. When you receive a warning, you ought to pass it on. 'Course, I couldn't 'ave stopped the kittens,' he reflected, 'but I might 'ave stopped the nassassinashun!'

The Second Engineer staggered into view. He, like the stokers, had come up for a little air, and was getting larger doses than he had bargained for.

'Whew!' he exclaimed. 'Dirty weather!'

'Yer right, sir,' answered Ben. 'Somethin's goin' ter 'appen.'

'*Going* to happen?' grinned the Second Engineer, as another fountain of spray shot up and drenched them. 'It's happening, ain't it?'

'Yus, but I means wuss'n this,' replied Ben, darkly. 'Me knuckles is hitchin'.'

3

'I *beg* your pardon?' said the Second Engineer politely.

'Knuckles, sir—hitchen',' repeated Ben. 'That's 'ow I knows. Yer may larf, but yer carn't git away from it, when me knuckles hitch, things 'appen.'

The Second Engineer was a good-natured man. He could retain an even temperament with the thermometer at 120. He had to. But superstition was one of his bugbears, and he always came down on it, particularly when the atmosphere was a bit nervy. He was aware of its disastrous potentialities.

'Now, listen, funny-mug!' he remarked. 'I know that itches are supposed to mean things. If your right eye itches it's good luck and if your left eye itches it's bad luck, and if they both itch it's damn bad luck—but knuckles are a new one on me! Shall I tell you what all this itching really means?'

'Somethin's goin' ter 'appen,' blinked Ben.

'No, you dolt!' roared the Second Engineer. 'It means you want a good scratch! So give your knuckles a good scratch and stop talking about 'em! Get me? Because if you don't, sonny, I'll give you a taste of *my* knuckles!'

Then he passed on.

'Meet yer when the boat goes dahn!' muttered Ben after him.

His retort increased his depression. It was the first time he had definitely focussed his fears. Of course, that was what his misbehaving knuckles meant—the boat was going down!

'Well, wot's it matter?' he reflected, catching hold of a rail as the ship heaved again. 'Am I afraid o' dyin'? Yus!'

The handsome admission completed his depression.

But Ben was never wholly absorbed in his own discomforts. An under-dog himself, he had a fellow feeling for other under-dogs, and the stokehold and engine-room were full of them. If they weren't particularly nice to him and kicked him about a bit, well, who was nice to him—barring, perhaps, the Second Engineer one time in three—and who didn't kick him about? He'd been born a football, and it was human to kick anything that bounced. And even the top-dogs did not arouse Ben's personal enmity. The world had to contain all sorts of people to make it go round, and he was a man of peace, though he found little. It would be a pity, for instance, if that pretty girl in the blue frock—the one the Third Officer had brought down yesterday to have a look at the engine-room—came to any harm. Nice hair, she had. And slim-like. She had smiled at Ben and had said, 'Don't you find it terribly hot here?' And when he had replied, ''Ot as ches'nuts,' she had laughed. Nice laugh, she had. And nice teeth. Yes, it would be a pity.

'And the Third Orficer 'iself might be wuss,' decided Ben, now he came to think of it. 'Corse, the way 'e looked at the gal'd mike a cod sick, but yer carn't 'elp yer fice when yer feels that way. Mindjer, some of 'em could do with a duckin'. That Lord Wot's-'is-nime wot's orl mide in one piece. 'E'd brike if yer bent 'im. And that there greasy bloke I seen torkin' to 'im. I'll bet 'e's a mess fust thing in the mornin'! If 'e was ter go ter the bottom, the bottom 'd git a fright and come up ter the top. But—well, Gawd mide 'im, so there yer are—'

A voice in his ear made him jump. He jumped into the chest of the Chief Engineer. The Chief Engineer's chest was the size of Ben altogether.

'What's the matter with you?' inquired the Chief Engineer, picking the population off his chest.

'Oo?' blinked Ben.

'Do you feel as green as you look?' demanded the Chief Engineer.

'Yus,' answered Ben.

5

'If you can't stand a bit of weather, why did you come on this trip?'

'Well, the doctor ses I orter 'ave a bit o' sunshine.'

'Don't be cheeky, my man!'

'Oo's wot?'

'I've had my eye on you for some time, and I'm asking you why you came on this trip?'

'Gawd knows!'

'Do you call that an answer?'

'Oh. Well, it was like this, see? Second Engineer engiged me. "Bill's ill," 'e ses. "Ben's 'ere," I ses. "'Oo's Ben?" 'e ses. "I am," I ses. "I shouldn't 'ave thort you was anything," 'e ses. "Life's full o' surprises," I ses, "once I fahnd a currant in a bun. Give us a charnce," I ses, "I've walked orl the way from the nearest pub." Mide 'im larf. That's the on'y way I can do it. Mike 'em larf. Like Pelligacharchi. You know, the bloke in the hopera. I seed it once. Lumme, them singers fair split yer ears.'

'Do you know what you're talking about?'

'No.'

The Chief Engineer stared at Ben very hard. Like many before him, he couldn't quite make Ben out.

'Have you ever seen a louse?' he asked.

Ben stared back and got ready for it.

'Not afore I see you,' he muttered.

The Chief Engineer's fist on Ben's chest made a deeper impression than the whole of Ben on the Chief Engineer's chest. Ben sat down and counted some stars.

'I *sed* somethin' was goin' ter 'appen,' he muttered, 'but it don't matter, 'cos this ain't it. You'll be goin' dahn, too, in a minit!'

'Oh! Will I?'

'Yus. The 'ole boat's goin' dahn. I knows 'cos me knuckles is hitchin'.'

'Of course, this fellow's mad,' said the Chief Engineer.

He took a deep breath. He was sorry he had lost his control for a moment, but he couldn't say so with four stripes on his sleeve. It was the nervy atmosphere. Everybody was nervy. He stretched out his hand and hoiked Ben up again, and something real or imagined in his attitude gave the little stoker a sudden and embarrassing disposition to cry.

'That's orl right, sir,' he mumbled, 'on'y it's true, see? I ain't kiddin' yer, and some-un orter tell the Captain afore it's too late.'

'Tell the Captain?' frowned the Chief Engineer.

'Yus.'

'Tell him what?'

'That me knuckles is hitchin'.'

The Chief Engineer shook him.

'If they go on itching, report to the Second Engineer, and ask him if you should report to the Doctor. Meanwhile, get some stuffing into you and remember you're a bit of the British Empire!'

'Yus, a lot the British Hempire's done fer me!' thought Ben, as the Chief Engineer departed.

Report to the Second Engineer? He had already done that. Report to the Doctor? No, thanks! If you weren't ill what was the use? And if you were ill you died of fright knowing . . .! But what about reporting to the Captain?

As Ben stared at his knuckles, which were not even soothed by the portions of ocean that periodically splashed on to them, the audacious idea grew. Report to the Captain—direct! Give *him* the red light! And then, when the ship had been saved through the warning of a little stoker whom everybody

7

trod on, perhaps people would stop treading on him, and they might even erect a statue of him over the Houses of Parliament.

'Little Ben on top o' Big Ben!' reflected the lesser of the two. 'Coo, that'd put the hother sights o' Lunnon in the shide!'

He glanced furtively around him. Nobody about. He glanced towards the companion-way that led for'ard up to the boat deck. He shook his head.

'No!' he said.

Then he thought of the pretty girl in the blue frock. 'Fancy 'er torkin' ter me!' he reflected. '"Doncher find it 'ot 'ere?" she ses, and then I ses, "'Ot as ches'nuts," I ses, and then she larfs. Nice larf. It'd be a pity . . .'

He moved towards the companion-way. It is to be remembered that Ben believed implicitly in his knuckles.

2

Something Happens

To walk from a well-deck to a Captain's quarters is ordinarily quite a simple job, but the difference between a journey you may make and a journey you may not is abysmal. The latter is ten times as long, and ten times as difficult.

Ben's difficulties were increased by the unusual rolling of the ship. Although he had spent many years in the merchant service he had never permanently discovered his sea legs. Sometimes they obeyed the oceanic instinct, at other times they did not, and this was one of the other times. Twice before he completed the first stage of the journey to the companion-way he shortened his left leg when he ought to have lengthened it, and thrice he lengthened his right leg when he ought to have shortened it. The result was dislocating to joints, and he arrived at the companion-way playing for safety, with both legs shortened.

Then he paused. A hurrying figure appeared on the ladder above him. Still squatting, he watched it descend and materialise into the Doctor.

'Are you the fellow who's come out in spots?' demanded the Doctor brusquely.

'No, sir,' replied Ben. 'That's Jim—but they ain't nothing.'

'How do *you* know?'

''E 'as 'em in 'ealth.'

'Thanks for the information, my man, but I'll do my own diagnosing, if you don't mind.' Ben didn't mind. He had no idea what diagnosing was, but it sounded nasty. 'What are *you* supposed to be doing?'

'Eh? Oh! Restin'.'

'Ah—*not* practising a Russian dance! Well, take my advice and rest under cover, or you'll be washed overboard!'

The Doctor proceeded on his way, and Ben proceeded on his. But at the top of the companion-way he shot into another figure. Lord What's-his-name, the man who found it difficult to bend. As they regained their breath they regarded each other from opposite angles. This was the first, and least strange, of many meetings, although neither of them knew it.

'You appear in a hurry,' observed the lordly obstacle, refixing his monocle.

'Yus, I got a messidge,' mumbled Ben.

'In that case I must not detain you,' replied Lord What's-his-name. Other people knew him as Lord Cooling. It was a name that had appeared on many glowing company prospectuses, the prospectus usually being more glowing than the company. 'I trust we may meet again one day in less urgent circumstances. Good-evening.'

Then Ben escaped to the second companion-way leading from the main deck to the saloon deck. The higher he got the more anxious he grew. He was permitted on the main deck, provided he did not linger and merely used it as a passage from the quarters where he slept to the quarters where he worked, but the saloon deck was taboo, and he hoped there would be no more awkward meetings. Fortunately for this hope the weather had driven most of the passengers inside, and apart from slipping on a step, tripping over a rope, hitting a rail, and nearly being shot into a ventilator, he passed safely through the next few seconds. But just as he was about to ascend the third companion-way to the boat deck he heard voices; and, still being near the ventilator that had just failed to suck him down into the unknown region it ventilated, he slipped behind it. The manœuvre was necessary since one of the voices he recognised as the Third Officer's.

'You'd better go in, Miss Sheringham,' the Third Officer was urging.

'It's certainly blowy,' came the response, and then Ben recognised that voice also. It was the voice of the pretty girl in the blue frock. But now she was wearing oilskins.

'And it's going to get worse,' answered the Third Officer. 'Nothing whatever to worry about, you know, but it's pleasanter inside.'

'Why did you say there was nothing to worry about?' asked the girl.

'Because there isn't,' returned the Third Officer.

'Or because there is?'

The Third Officer laughed.

'That's much too clever for me! I've been through gales that make this seem like a sea breeze, but—'

'But it's a jolly good sea breeze!' Now the girl laughed too. 'Won't the dancing floor be wobbly tonight? I wonder how many will be on it!'

'If you're on it, I expect you'll be dancing a solo.'

'I have a higher opinion of British manhood, Mr Haines! I shall certainly be on it. I rather like the idea of trying to do a slow fox-trot up a moving mountain—'

'Look out!'

Ben accepted the warning as well as the girl, but none of them ducked quickly enough. The sudden fountain drenched all three.

'Really, Miss Sheringham, I wish you'd go in!' exclaimed the Third Officer, after the drench. He made no attempt now to hide his anxiety.

'I think I will!' gasped the girl. 'I'm soaked! But how did you know I was out?'

'Well—I've eyes.'

'Jolly quick ones! I hadn't been out two minutes before you pounced on me!'

'We try to look after our passengers.'

'Beautifully put! Still, you're quite right—I'd no idea it was so awful . . . I say, what's that?'

'What?'

'Over there! Towards the horizon—where I'm pointing!'

There came a short silence. The wind rose to a shriek, then died down again. Ben could only hear the voices because the gale was blowing in his direction.

'I can't see anything,' said the Third Officer.

'Nor can I now. That mist has blotted it out. It was dark—like a whale. If I saw it at all.'

'And that isn't mist, it's rain,' answered the Third Officer briskly. 'It'll be here in a moment and drown you! Go inside at once. It's not a request this time, it's an order!'

Ben heard a little laugh, and then the voices ceased. Footsteps sounded, and faded away. Ben was alone again.

He waited a second or two. The long terror through which he was to reach the strangest salvation he had ever known began to grip him. He didn't like his memory of the Third Officer's tone. He had studied tones. He knew whether 'That's

12

all right' meant that it was or it wasn't and whether 'Come here' meant a kiss or a kick. He knew that the Third Officer's 'That's an order' meant trouble.

This, however, was not the entire cause of Ben's new anxiety. He had an instinct for the tone of a gale as well as the tone of a human being. The instinct was now informing him that the gale was 'behaving funny.' Possibly not another person on board received the warning in precisely the way Ben received it. As though to compensate in some degree for his colossal ignorance, he had been granted an uncomfortable sensitiveness to certain impending occasions. The sensitiveness was variously expressed in various parts of his anatomy. Itching knuckles—that meant general danger. Twitching knee-caps—that meant personal danger. A sort of tickle in his nose—that meant cheese in the vicinity. A violent throbbing of his ear-lobes—that meant the wind was about to behave funny. You couldn't get away from it.

Well, no matter how one throbbed and tickled and twitched and itched, one could not remain behind a ventilator for ever; and so, creeping from a concealment no longer necessary, he skated—first uphill and then downhill—to the rails. He wanted to know whether he could see what the girl had thought she had seen, and devoutly hoped that he wouldn't. The hope was so devout that at first he searched with his eyes shut. Then he opened them.

'Vizerbility nil,' he murmured. 'I don't see nothing!'

Nothing, that was, beyond the most unpleasant ocean he had ever gazed at. It seemed to be in a kind of white fright and to be attempting to escape from the low clouds and the tearing wind, but the wind was chasing it mercilessly, emitting sounds that clearly came from some elemental madhouse; and the rain was in its wake. In a few moments the rain would add its stinging dampness to the starboard bow.

'Lumme, we're goin' ter git it!' gulped Ben.

He turned to complete his interrupted journey. Perhaps it seemed a little footless now. The Captain on his bridge did not need the information of a fireman that the weather was not fine! But, having started on his ridiculous mission, Ben wanted to finish it. He had detached himself from normal, sensible routine, and he was like a bit of homeless, wind-blown chaff. Things beyond his power were buffetting him about, and he would have to go on being buffetted about until he was buffetted to rest.

He might have hesitated, however, if impulse had not caused him to turn his head for one more glance over the starboard bow, towards the oncoming rain. In that glance he saw what the girl had seen; and because it was closer, and because his eyes were more experienced, he interpreted it before it was wiped into oblivion again.

''Eving 'elp us!' he gasped.

And he sped up the third companion-way to the boat deck.

As he did so the Junior Wireless Officer emerged from the wireless-room aft and began walking hurriedly towards him. The Junior Wireless Officer had a T T T message in his hand—a message which ranks second in importance to an S.O.S.—but Ben did not know this, nor would he have paused if he had. He paid no attention to the approaching officer, or to the notice that warned passengers and unauthorised persons away from the Captain's deck, or to the unspeakable transgression of mounting the ladder without permission to the bridge. In a flash he was on the Captain's deck and clambering up the ladder. The Junior Wireless Officer saw him, stopped dead for an instant, and then came forward again at increased speed.

The Captain also saw him. He was standing on the bridge with the First Officer, and he was looking very grim. His grimness increased tenfold as Ben's head popped amazingly into view below him.

'What the hell—!' bawled the First Officer, speaking the Captain's thoughts.

'Something ter report, sir!' Ben bawled back.

As his head rose higher the First Officer seized it and spun it. Ben felt like a top. He had not finished spinning before he received a fresh impetus from below, and found himself projected towards the starboard cab. It was the Junior Wireless Officer, mounting the ladder at express speed.

The Junior Wireless Officer's voice, however, was contrastingly composed. The wireless-room permits itself pace, but never panic.

'Navigation Warning, sir,' said the Junior Wireless Officer, saluting and holding out his envelope.

The Captain took it and opened it.

'Hallo—floating wreckage,' he exclaimed, glancing at the First Officer. 'Latitude—'

'Lattertood 'Ere and Lojitood 'Ere!' bellowed Ben. 'Unner the surface—water-logged—I jest seed it orf the starboard bow!'

Then the starboard bow got it.

3

The Fruits of Panic

Ben never learned what happened immediately after the submerged wreckage struck the ship, for the impact toppled him over to the deck just beneath the bridge, and the suddenly descending rain pinned him there with the effectiveness of a vast moist weight. He never learned that, although water poured through the wound in the ship's side, flooding it with devastating rapidity, shifting cargo, bursting fresh cracks, and eventually sending the ship to its doom, not a single life was lost. That was another story, not Ben's; and, incredible though it was, Ben's story was the more incredible. Indeed, since Ben was destined like the rest to continue life, no one could have predicted the circumstances that coupled his continued existence with such enduring ignorance.

Above him, as he lay on the edge of his biggest adventure, the Captain was staggering to his feet. The Captain, the First Officer, and the Junior Wireless Operator had also been bowled over, and the two former had only one thought in their minds. The Captain was the first to regain himself and act upon it. He staggered towards the lever that worked the water-tight doors. He was too late, however. His half-blinded eyes watched the indicator move to 'Quarter-shut' and 'Half-shut'—and there it stopped. 'Three-quarters-shut' and 'Shut' were unattainable goals. Something had jammed.

Below, human pandemonium joined the pandemonium of the elements. It is perhaps less discreditable than is popularly imagined by critics in comfortable arm-chairs that certain people should develop panic during the first moments of a wreck. In this case the damage had occurred with nerve-shattering suddenness, and quite a number of folk lost their heads. It was during this preliminary period, which would have spelt complete chaos had it endured, that two incidents occurred beyond the control of a ship's discipline.

The first incident occurred at one of the boats. There was a mad, unintelligent rush for it. A few people scrambled in. The Third Officer, followed by Ruth Sheringham whom he had been conducting inside when the crash occurred, did his best to stem the rush, and then to organise it. 'Yes, get in, get in!' he shouted to the hesitating girl. As she climbed she stumbled, and he lurched forward to her assistance. The mad crowd behind him carried him forward with her. The ship heaved, the boat swung outwards, partly through the violent movement of the ship and partly through the insane work of clumsy, frenzied hands at the davits. Something gave way. The boat slid down, and the ocean rose dizzily to meet it. As the boat smacked the water, and the Third Officer endured the worst moment of his life, he bawled. 'Unhook! Unhook! Release the hook!' He was releasing one as he bawled. He told Ruth Sheringham later that she had unhooked the other, but she had no memory of it. The great, wounded ship towered over them. It shot away from them. Somebody was sick . . .

That incident was noticed, and served as an awesome example to quell the panic on board and substitute a sense of numb discipline. The second incident was not noticed. The same violent lurch that had sent the little boat down also sent Ben down. In perfect, unprotesting obedience to the laws of gravitation, Ben rolled along the sloping deck, bounced, and shot into the Pacific.

He sank like a log. He rose like the Great War. The sudden immersion somewhat anomalously brought him back to life, and his arms and legs worked as arms and legs had never worked before. He was unable to swim but he had an excellent sense of self-protection, and it told him that he would not sink so long as he kept every part of him moving at the same time. Possibly the sea held him on its surface for a while out of sheer interest. It did not often receive such astonishing gifts, and he was passed from crest to crest for moist examination. But at last it wearied of him and began to draw him down. Ben, after all, was very small fry for so large a host.

His mould was not that of the hero who dies but once. He was the coward—and the first to admit it—who dies many times before his death, and he now added another demise to his unfinished record. In the space of five seconds he died, went up to heaven, was thrown, went down to hell, was thrown up, wondered who wanted him, decided to speak to God about it, climbed a golden ladder, told God it wasn't fair, asked if he were going to receive the same treatment in this new world that he'd received in the last, asked why it was so wet, asked why it was so cold, asked why everything was bobbing up and down, asked whether he were on a blinkin' dancing floor, thought of the girl in the blue frock— and then found the girl in the blue frock looking at him. Of course, it was impossible!

'Oi!' he sputtered. 'Wot's 'appenin'?'

'Sh!' replied the impossible vision.

'Yus, but I ain't 'ere!' he protested.

Another voice answered him.

'We picked you up. Stay still, and don't talk.'

It was the Third Officer's voice. Quiet and commanding. But a shower of water spilling over a great watery wall was more effective in securing Ben's obedient silence.

He gave up trying to work things out. He was in a boat. The boat was racing up and down mountains. That was enough to go on with.

Time passed. The boat continued to race up and down mountains. He lost count of both time and the mountains. They seemed endless. He also lost count of himself. He had been through a number of shattering evolutions and his saturated form was full of bumps and bruises. If one detached one's mind from the past and the future—particularly the future—and regarded oneself as a sort of tree-trunk, it was pleasant to remain inactive and do nothing. Ben's spirit drifted while his body tossed.

Grey became dark grey. Dark grey became black. In blackness, Ben opened his eyes again.

'Oi!' he mumbled. 'Wot's 'appenin'?'

'If you ask that again,' replied the Third Officer, 'I'll scrag you.'

'Any assistance you desire in that line,' came another voice, 'will be gladly offered.'

That was Lord Wot's-'is-name. So he was in the boat, too, was he?

''Oo's arst wot agine?' murmured Ben.

'Every time you open your eyes,' Lord Cooling informed him, 'you ask what is happening. This, I think, is the tenth occasion. It becomes slightly monotonous.'

19

Ben had no recollection of the other nine times.

'Well, wot *is* 'appenin'?' he inquired.

'Can't someone keep that fellow quiet?' groaned a man at the other end of the boat. He was a film star, who concealed his modest origin under the name of Richard Ardentino. The public would not have recognised his voice at that moment. In a film of a wreck it had been very different.

'Don't excite him, don't excite him!' exclaimed another sufferer, who had never attempted to change his own modest name of Smith. 'If you do, he'll only upset the boat!'

The reference to excitement produced the condition. Smarting under a sense of the world's injustice, Ben suddenly became emotional.

'Why ain't I ter be told nothin'?' he cried. 'One minit I'm on the Captin's bridge—nex' minit I'm on the deck—nex' minit I'm in the sea—nex' minit I'm 'ere! Corse, that don't matter! It ain't int'restin'! And if nex' minit I find meself on top o' the Hifle Tower, that's orl right, I mustn't arsk no questions, carry on!'

He had raised his head to offer this protest. Now he sank back, coming to roost—though in the dark he did not know this—in the lap of the girl. The Third Officer replied, quietly:

'Take it easy, sonny. I expect you've been through worse than the rest of us, but we're none of us having a picnic. What's happened is that the ship has been wrecked and that we have been saved, so let's all be grateful and leave it at that for the moment, eh? As a member of the crew, you'll know I've got a job on, and that I need discipline to carry it through.'

'Sorry, sir,' muttered Ben. 'Blime the bump on me 'ead.'

The boat slid down into a watery trough, took a dose,

climbed to the next crest, shivered, and slid down again. Ben was forgotten.

Then passed a succession of hours that were devastating in their varying hopes and fears. If this were a saga of the sea, each hour would be described in detail. If it were a treatise on psychology, the effect on each separate nerve-centre would be analysed and ticketed. But our tale does not aspire to be a classic or a work of reference. It is merely an amazing adventure, which did not separate itself from other adventures and gain its own individuality until a night and a day and then another night had passed, until storms had been endured (one, during the second night, of special violence), until winds, tides and rain had driven the boat across countless miles of unknown ocean, and until the terrifying monotony of the hazardous voyage came to a conclusion.

It came to a conclusion just before dawn on a dark, unseen beach. Though unseen, the beach was heard, and the Third Officer's eyes—the only eyes that had never closed—strained fruitlessly to pierce the booming blackness. 'This is the end!' he thought. But he did not relinquish his efforts. For thirty-six hours he had kept the boat right side up, and now he steeled himself for the stiffest test of all. He gave a few quiet orders as the boat rushed onwards. A black mass rose and missed them by a few feet. He managed to avoid another by inches. Rock scraped the boat's bottom. The boat shivered, then lurched forward again. Ahead were more black masses, and a shouting white line. The boat raced through the line, hit something, staggered, swung round, reared and kicked. It could advance no farther, but the kick shot its human contents towards the goal it could not reach . . .

Ben descended in a shallow, sandy pool. 'Now I *am* dead—proper this time!' he decided, as the pool shrieked around

21

J. Jefferson Farjeon

him. Finding that he wasn't dead, he rose with a bellow and scrambled forward. Did someone pull him along as he went, or did he pull someone along? He did not know. All he knew was that the five oceans were after him, excluding the considerable portions he had swallowed. Those were with him.

Then he tripped over something and fell flat.

4

What the Dawn Brought

Ben had something of the ostrich in him. When he fell flat he remained flat, hoping that trouble would pass over him. He remained flat now.

Nothing happened. This, in a world where nine-tenths of the happenings were unpleasant, was satisfactory. A condition not to be disturbed. He stayed where he was till he forgot where he was, and drifted into a series of entirely new adventures. The only one he remembered when he returned from them to consciousness was a unique journey in a boat made entirely of cheese. This should have been agreeable, since he liked cheese and was very hungry, but every time he ate the cheese he made a hole in the boat and the sea poured in. It was the sea that woke him up. Dampness slid round his boots and along to his knees. The cheese, on the other hand, vanished, and in its place against his mouth was sand.

He turned over and sat up. Around him were vague forms, enjoying the lethargy from which he had just emerged. In the dim light of dawn he counted them. Six wet little heaps. With himself, seven. He, the seventh, was the most conspicuous but the least complete. Recent rigours had deprived him of all garments above the waist, betraying the tattooings of a regretted youth.

The heap nearest to him was Lord Cooling. His leg was only a few inches away, and the once-immaculate trouser was rucked up, revealing a sodden sock and suspender. Another heap, almost as close, was Ruth Sheringham. She, also, showed more leg than seemed to Ben respectable. He wondered whether he ought to do something about it. The other heaps were not, to him, identifiable; but we may identify them, and compare them with their normal attitudes.

One was the film star, Richard Ardentino; his normal attitude was splendidly erect, with face raised to the light. One was Henry Smith; his favourite attitude was under a suburban rose-arch (he grew the best roses in Wembley), or playing cards in the 8.59 to Broad Street. One was Ernest Medworth, whose more familiar attitude was poring over Stock Exchange figures to discover whether, scrupulously or otherwise, they could be turned to his advantage. And the last was Elsie Noyes. Her attitude was best expressed at the head of a line of girl guides . . .

'Yus, but where's the Third Orficer?' wondered Ben suddenly.

He should have made an eighth little heap.

The absence of the Third Officer began to worry Ben even more than the absence of skirt over Ruth Sheringham's leg. He rose slowly to his feet, and peered beyond the heaps.

He could not see much. Just a misty, creepy dimness. A grey veil that screened—what? Away to the east, beyond the wicked breakers and across the heaving sea, faint light began to illuminate the horizon, but here the grey veil still reigned supreme, concealing all but the nearest objects.

'It's narsty,' thought Ben.

Nevertheless, he stole forward, slowly and uneagerly, stepping carefully among the mounds and envying them their immobility. He had been much happier before he had ceased to be a mound himself. But somewhere through that grey veil, Ben decided, was the Third Officer, and if he'd got into trouble—well, somebody would have to find him, wouldn't they?

As he advanced, turning his back upon the shore, the dimness became more creepy. It seemed to be full of ghostly slits, and he did not know whether the darkness in front of him were cliff, wall, or forest. Something ran over his foot. By insisting it was a crab he just saved himself from screaming. But even crabs weren't nice. Some of these Pacific blighters had claws that . . .

'Wozzat?' gulped Ben.

He leapt, and then stood stock still, while another panic passed. The new oppression had seemed like a figure. Not the Third Officer's figure. A figure twice as tall, if not three times; standing motionless. But where was it now? A figure that size couldn't come and go without a sound! The only sound Ben heard was the thumping of his heart.

'I better git back,' thought Ben unsteadily. 'Yer wants two at this job!'

He turned. The sensation that the giant was now behind him caused him to take a header over a large stone. He dived into two arms. They were the arms of the Third Officer.

'Lumme!' gasped Ben.

'Can't you stand?' asked the Third Officer, trying to make him erect.

'My knees is funny,' explained Ben.

'All of you's funny,' replied the Third Officer.

25

'Well, yer give me a shock!'

'The shock was mutual.'

'Oo's wot?'

'Never mind. Where are you going?'

'I ain't, I'm comin' back.'

'Where *were* you going, then?'

'Ter look fer you, like.'

'Very nice of you,' smiled the Third Officer. 'Well, now you've found me like. Did you find anything else?'

'Yus,' answered Ben, with unpleasant recollection.

'What?'

'Bloke twen'y foot 'igh.'

'What are you talking about?' came the sharp demand.

'Bloke twen'y foot 'igh,' replied Ben. Then he added, 'Mindjer, I ain't sure wot I seed 'im, but if I seed 'im, that's wot 'e was.'

The Third Officer frowned, then regarded Ben searchingly.

'Anything left in the bottle, sonny?' he inquired.

'If I 'ad a bottle, there wouldn't be,' said Ben.

'Where did you see this Gargantuan creature?'

'Oo?'

'Where did you see this giant?'

'Be'ind me. 'Ave a look. I've 'ad mine, and one's enuff.'

'Most kind!' murmured the Third Officer, and stared over Ben's shoulder.

Then, Ben gazing east and the Third Officer gazing west, each man saw an interesting sight.

Ben saw the sun rise. It slipped into view over the rim of the world, at first the tiniest curve of gold, then a gradually developing disc. The sea threw off its shroud and woke up. It became a madly dancing expanse of water, with a wide, shimmering path stretching from horizon to shore.

The Third Officer saw what the sun rose on. He saw a forest awaken. He saw the tops of great trees catching the first upward rays. He saw the amber light flow down. He saw Ben's giant . . .

'Wozzer matter?' jerked Ben suddenly.

The Third Officer did not reply immediately. Then he said: 'Turn round and see—but take it quietly.'

It has been mentioned that Ben had an instinct for interpreting tones. He knew by the Third Officer's tone that when he turned he was going to witness a peculiarly unpleasant sight, and for this very sound reason he did not turn immediately. But at last the operation could no longer be postponed with credit to the Merchant Service, and he twisted his neck round, though not his body and his legs. You need those to run with.

The sight that met his anxious eyes was definitely unpleasant. It was, in fact, the giant. Ben had over-estimated the giant's height, which was nearer ten feet than twenty; even so, it was sufficiently above the average to be impressive. There were, however, other features more disturbing still. The giant's staring eyes had large white rings painted round them. His great mouth extended almost from ear to ear in a humourless grin. His nose had three nostrils. Ben counted them several times, very rapidly, and there was no mistake about it; he wondered, even in the grip of terror, whether they all functioned.

The one satisfactory thing about the giant was his perfect immobility. He was standing on a pedestal, carved in rock.

'Coo!' muttered Ben.

'In the language of Shakespeare,' answered the Third Officer, 'you have said it.'

Then Ben made another discovery. The giant was merely

one member of a little family party. The other members—there were four in all, but there surely should have been five, since a fifth pedestal was empty—were of varying sizes. They were all equal in ugliness, however, and they were all staring unblinkingly towards the rising sun, standing out with uncanny brilliance against their background of dense foliage. The points that stood out most brilliantly were the staring optics themselves. They were not of rock. They were gold.

Ben did the only obvious thing. He shut his own eyes very tight, counted ten, and then opened them again. The family party was still there.

'Yes, I tried that,' murmured the Third Officer. 'It doesn't work.'

'Lumme!' whispered Ben. ''Ave they come dahn ter 'ave a bathe?'

A voice behind him made him start.

'Excuse me,' said the voice, 'but *do* you both see what I see?'

A sadly shrunken Lord Cooling stood behind them.

'We do,' replied the Third Officer, 'and we are just discussing theories. My friend here suggests that they have appeared for their morning dip.'

'Well, tastes vary,' commented Lord Cooling. 'Personally, I have lost my enthusiasm for the water. What is the alternative theory?'

'Fairly obvious, I think,' said the Third Officer.

'Yus, Guy Forks fact'ry,' suggested Ben.

'These flashes of rare intelligence are a little overpowering,' observed Lord Cooling, attempting to preserve his dignity by screwing in his monocle. He had saved his monocle, though he had lost nearly all else. 'May I have your own thought, Mr Haines?'

'Well, sir—the island's inhabited,' answered Haines.

'Ah! And would you call that an advantage, now—or not?'

'It does rather depend, sir, on the inhabitants.'

'Exactly. But are you sure? These examples of art *may* belong to a pre-Epstein Age? For instance, I understand they exist on Easter Island, which is no longer cannibalistic?'

''Ere! Wot's that?' jerked Ben.

Haines threw Lord Cooling a warning glance.

'I haven't suggested that these inhabitants are cannibalistic,' he said.

'I will accept that, with a private reservation,' smiled Lord Cooling. 'Perhaps my mind moves rather fast, but I agree that, in any case, one must fit one's words to one's company.'

'Just as well, sir,' nodded Haines. 'All the company isn't present, either.'

'True, Mr Haines. While I was trying hard not to wake up a few minutes ago, I thought I missed your own company?'

'I dare say, sir.'

'Where were you?'

'Mouching around.'

'Have you done any mouching in that unpleasant forest?'

'Not yet. Our stoker is the real pioneer—though he returned from his pioneering rather hurriedly. I was trying to find bits of the boat.'

'Any luck?'

Haines shook his head gravely.

'The bits I did find were quite useless. It's the provisions we want.'

'Very true. We may not quite appreciate the—er—native fare. Which brings us back to the natives. You've not seen any, of course?'

'No.'

29

'Then let us assume the race is extinct.'

'We can't, sir. I came upon a footprint or two—and that's why I'm not too keen on *those* things!' He jerked his head towards the statues. 'Still, we'll get through this all right. I—I hope, sir, I can count on you for optimism?'

'I am a company promoter, Mr Haines,' replied Lord Cooling. 'You can count on my optimism implicitly.'

But Haines had suddenly ceased to listen. His eyes gazed beyond Lord Cooling towards the beach. The other little heaps were stirring, and the heap he was most interested in had risen and was coming towards them.

As Ruth Sheringham approached, her sodden blue dress clinging to her pathetically but in no way, Haines considered, detracting from her charm, her lithe body stiffened, and she stopped. But she only paused for a few seconds. She came on again without any visible signs of panic.

'Well done, Miss Sheringham,' said Haines.

'Did you think I was the fainting kind?' she retorted. 'Aren't they pretty?'

'Go on!' muttered Ben in astonishment.

Lord Cooling regarded Ben with growing disapproval.

'Historians of the future may deduce that Miss Sheringham did not quite mean what she said,' he suggested with frigid sarcasm, 'and they may also record that a stoker who talked too much was presented as a peace offering to a cannibal chief!'

'Well, ain't *you* torkin' too much?' retorted Ben, with a boldness he would never have shown on the ship. 'We sed we was goin' ter keep mum abart them cannerbuls!'

'Cannibals?' repeated Ruth.

'*Will* you shut up?' Haines exclaimed to Ben.

'Well, why does heverybody sit on me?' answered Ben. 'I was born sat on, and I'm fair sick of it, that's a fack!'

Lord Cooling sighed.

'If you will give me your name and permanent address,' he said, 'I will write you a letter of apology and post it in the nearest pillar-box. Meanwhile, here come the others. It appears to be a tortoise race—with, I notice, our film star an easy winner. Well, perhaps their voices will be a little more useful than our own—'

He stopped abruptly, gazed at something on the ground, stooped, and picked it up. It was a small white object.

'What's that?' inquired Haines, arrested by the other's rather ominous interest.

'I *hope* a beef-bone,' murmured Lord Cooling.

Haines stepped nearer Ruth. In spite of her tight hold on herself, she had given a little shiver.

'Cold, isn't it?' she smiled. The sunlight, gaining in intensity every minute, gave her the lie. 'In these wet things, you know.'

'Yes, I know, Miss Sheringham,' Haines smiled back, reassuringly. 'And I know something else—there's nothing whatever to be worried about.'

'Course not,' nodded the girl. 'Everything's just too lovely to believe!'

Then the four other little heaps drew up and stared at the hideous statuary. It was Elsie Noyes who, forgetful of the discipline of a girl guide captain, expressed the common emotion by exclaiming:

'Oh, my God!'

If she forgot her part, so did Ardentino and Henry Smith, whose faces would not have been recognised in Elstree or Wembley Park. Ernest Medworth, on the other hand, soon reverted to type. He found himself staring at the golden eyes, and wondering what they were worth.

'Someone's been busy here!' he commented.

'Yes, I don't imagine these things came up from seed,' answered Cooling.

'Ha, ha, very funny!' laughed Smith, uneasily. 'That's good, that is! They're not exactly roses!'

He laughed alone. The fact depressed and annoyed him. Dash it all, did they think he *felt* like laughing? But one had to try to put a cheerful face on things—one had to be British, and all that. Pity there weren't a few of his train companions here to help keep the old flag flying.

He tried again. 'Well, you've got to say it's pretty here,' he remarked. 'Take away the waxworks, and it's a bit like Rottingdean before they spoilt it.'

'Don't make us home-sick, Mr Smith,' pleaded Lord Cooling, cynically.

'The fellow's an idiot!' grunted Medworth.

Smith's cheeks flamed. 'What's the matter with everybody?' he snapped. 'Can't one make a passing remark?'

'The sooner *your* remarks pass, the better!' retorted Medworth, rudely. 'This isn't the time for reminiscences!'

'Now, now, we mustn't lose one's temper, that's the first thing one mustn't do!' cried Miss Noyes, quoting from her book of rules. 'If these—these heathen gods or whatever they are mean that the place is inhabited, well, we know where we are, that's something, and we must organise against them—organise!'

She was hardly the best tonic for frayed nerves. Smith was the only member who was grateful to her. She had at least diverted attention from himself.

'I suppose that *is* what they mean?' inquired Ardentino, glancing towards the Third Officer.

'That this island's inhabited?' replied Haines. 'Yes, there's not much doubt about that.'

'Well—er—we want it to be inhabited, don't we?'

'Depends upon the inhabitants,' answered Medworth.

'Yes, we only move among the best people,' added Ruth. 'What happens if they're not in Debrett?'

The question was not answered. Somewhere in the forest, a twig snapped.

Personal differences were forgotten. For ten seconds eight people stood motionless. The gods themselves were not more still. Then another twig snapped.

'I think,' suggested Lord Cooling quietly, 'we swallow pride—momentarily—and take cover?'

'I don't think—I *know*!' muttered Medworth.

'Nah fer the runnin' race!' said Ben.

And led it.

5

Behaviour of Mr Robert Oakley

Ben led the race at the start, but he had to share honours at the end. The result was a dead heat between himself and four others, and there was considerable crowding at the large rock of concealment that formed the winning-post.

The losers were Ruth Sheringham, Tom Haines, and Lord Cooling. They had started late, and with a little diffidence. Lord Cooling, although he had been the first to suggest retreat, did not like turning his back on an enemy. Many charges would be brought against him when he met his Maker, but not that of cowardice. An ancestor of his had fought at Crecy. Haines shared his distaste for running away, and was by no means certain that it was good strategy; but the sight of Ruth, standing beside him and waiting for her cue, had made him gulp down his pride, and he had suddenly seized her arm and rushed her to the rock. Lord Cooling, bringing up the rear, had endeavoured to mingle dignity with haste until a new sound had urged him to shed the dignity. 'After all,' he reflected, as his feet sped faster than they had sped since Eton, 'if one is going to run, one may as well run.'

The new sound certainly provided plenty of excuse. It was a mournful chanting.

At first the chanting was wholly eerie. It drifted forward from the forest, a depressing dirge that lacked the slightest gleam of hope. 'Sahnds like a corpse singin'!' thought Ben, and it was not a bad description. The slowness of the corpse's approach added to the painful tension.

But, before the chanter appeared, the sharpest brains—not Ben's—became conscious of a curious psychology. There was something elusive in the chanting, something vaguely at war with itself. Did it represent religious fervour, or sheer boredom, or a combination of both? The words, when at last they became decipherable, afforded no clue. They were, as far as could be determined:

> 'Waa—lala,
> Waa—lala,
> Oli O li,
> Waa—lala.'

This doleful sound was repeated, with occasional pauses, until the chanter emerged from the forest through a narrow track and came into sight.

His appearance was even more arresting than his song. He was a complete anachronism. On his head was a wreath of feathers. In his hand was a gruesome receptacle formed out of a painted skull suspended from three short chains. But, instead of the nakedness or partial nakedness that should have accompanied these primitive indications, soiled ducks encased the chanter's rather stout body. Soiled? Let us be frank and admit that they were filthy. Even Ben's low standard of cleanliness was startled.

Obviously British—his atmosphere of dry resignation was characteristic of his race—he appeared to have 'gone native' through local necessity rather than through any acquired enthusiasm for native ways. His bored expression indicated quite plainly that he was merely performing a duty forced upon him.

The duty itself carried on the strange story. Reaching the first of the effigies, the chanter stopped his chanting, took from his pocket a handkerchief that matched his ducks, dusted the effigy, and knelt before it. Then, with bowed head, he repeated:

> '*Waa—lala,*
> *Waa—lala,*
> *Oli O li,*
> *Waa—lala.*'

Rising, he glanced back towards the forest, took out his handkerchief again, blew his nose, moved to the second effigy, and repeated the whole performance, but with a slight variation. This time the dirge ran:

> '*Waa—lala,*
> *Snowden and Bala,*
> *Ochy Och-aye,*
> *Waa—lala.*'

This version stamped him so definitely as a Briton that Haines made a movement to leave his concealment; but Lord Cooling stretched out a detaining hand. 'Let us hear the rest of the performance,' he whispered. 'One only learns a bird's habits while it is unconscious.' Haines nodded.

But the rest of the performance was mere repetition, adding nothing to their knowledge until the fifth pedestal was reached. The one that was empty.

Then, for the first time, the chanter's face registered something akin to emotion. He stared at the pedestal, rubbed his eyes, stared again, and exclaimed:

'Purple blazes!'

He stooped. His hands groped in the tangled undergrowth. They brought up the head and shoulders of a fifth statue. The fifth statue looked, even allowing for distance, the smallest of the group, and it was obviously broken.

'Now I'm for it!' said the chanter, as he dropped the portion back into the undergrowth. 'Orate pro anima Oakley!'

He smiled rather sadly. He was taking the situation well. But he took the next situation even better, for when he raised his eyes and saw eight figures emerging from behind a rock, he might have been reasonably excused for leaping out of his skin. Instead, he merely stood quite still and counted them.

'That the lot?' he inquired politely.

The absurdity and inadequacy of the greeting delayed the response. The shipwrecked party had yet to learn the peculiar mood and temperament of Mr Robert Oakley. His next remark was even more unexpected.

'Who won the last Cup Tie?' he asked. 'Dear old Arsenal?'

Then Ben became practical.

'Look aht!' he exclaimed. ''E's looney!'

Ben's curiosity, which often got him into difficulties, had drawn him a little ahead of the rest. He had a remarkable faculty for rapid movement, retreating in a straight line and advancing in a curve. He wondered now, as their queer host's eyes fastened on him, whether the moment had not arrived for another straight line. The eyes gave him a very odd

37

sensation. He had likened Oakley's chanting to that of a corpse, although strictly speaking he had never heard a corpse sing. These eyes, also, looked somehow dead, and in their solemnity lay a defunct smile . . .

'Looney?' repeated the subject of the theory. 'Shouldn't wonder. I've no means of tellin'. It's so long since I had anything sane to compare myself with. But quite harmless, believe me—quite harmless. Despite old Yorick!'

He swung the skull he was carrying towards Ben, and Ben retreated into the chest of Lord Cooling. Lord Cooling cleared his chest and then his throat.

'When you have finished babbling, sir,' he said, '*would* you mind informing us who the devil you are?'

'I asked my question first,' replied Oakley. 'Did Arsenal win the Cup?'

'What the deuce does that matter?' rasped Cooling. 'Do you play football here?'

'Not matter?' blinked Oakley incredulously. 'Not *matter*? You *are* English, aren't you?'

Haines and Ruth exchanged smiling glances. Terror lay behind them, and more terror lay ahead of them, but for the moment life was almost amusing.

'Derby County,' said Haines. 'Jolly good match.'

'Thank you, brother,' answered Oakley, and then repeated, as though he were repeating the name of his sweetheart, 'Derby County!'

Ernest Medworth swore.

'How much more rope are we going to give this fellow?' he demanded. 'Enough to hang himself I don't mind, but is this delay going to hang us?'

'Would you like *me* to try to deal with him?' suggested Smith.

'What he needs is discipline!' declared Miss Noyes.

'Or a charge of gun-powder,' proposed the film star.

'I can tell you what *you* all need,' observed Oakley unruffled. 'Patience and calmness. It's the only thing that gets you anywhere on this island. I've had three years of it, so I know. What is going to happen is going to happen, and no amount of agitation will alter it.'

'Yus, but wot's goin' ter 'appen?' asked Ben.

'That,' returned Oakley, waving a hand towards the statues, 'is literally in the lap of the gods. By the way, one's got knocked over. Did you do it, by any chance?'

'Wot, me?' exclaimed Ben.

'Yes, in a fit of jealousy. Oomoo looks something like you.'

''Oo 'oo?'

'Oomoo. Our little God of Storms. I rather like Oomoo. Something almost human about him. But the others—the larger ones—well, let me introduce you. Hojak.' He waved towards the tallest. 'He's the God of Fire. I've never quite got over my distaste for the feller. Mooane. The chap with the toothache. God of Water. Kook. God of Earth. Gug. Both g's pronounced hard, as in chewing-gum. God of Eatables. H'm.' He paused. 'We don't much care for Gug. And, finally, Oomoo, who appears to have been demolished last night by one of his own storms.'

The introductions did not have a soothing effect.

'And who are *you*?' inquired Lord Cooling. '*Not* for the first time of asking?'

'Who am I? Oh, yes. Well, I *was* Bob Oakley before I got washed up here three years ago. What I am now I've never quite found out. I think it's a sort of Low Priest. If that sounds good, forget it. A Low Priest is an office boy to a High Priest. You must meet our High Priest—he's a dear chap. One of my duties, as you may have noticed, is to do the Caruso stuff to the Ugly-Mugs and dust 'em on Fête Days—'

'Fite Dyes?' interposed Ben inquiringly.

'Same thing,' nodded Oakley. 'I'm supposed to sprinkle 'em, too, with the contents of Yorick, but there's been so much rain during the past forty-eight hours—has it been the same in London?—that I gave the wash a miss. No one was looking—apart, of course, from yourselves.'

'No doubt about it,' growled Medworth, 'the fellow's stark staring mad.'

'That is my devout hope,' Lord Cooling admitted. 'I am hoping that Mr Oakley got such a bump when he arrived here three years ago that he has been suffering from delusions ever since. But in any case, Mr Medworth, we have no other source of information at present, so—with your permission—?'

'Carry on, my lord,' grunted Medworth. 'You're the spokesman.'

'Thank you.' Cooling turned back to Oakley. 'You mentioned a Fête Day. Is this one?'

'Always, after a storm,' answered Oakley.

'What happens on Fête Days, in addition to the—spring cleaning of the gods?'

'We eat and thanksgive.'

'Eat?'

'Eat.'

'What do you eat?'

'Well,' said Oakley, 'you haven't been thrown up on a Eustace Miles Restaurant.'

'Ah,' murmured Lord Cooling, dropping the little white object he had till now retained. '*Not* a beef-bone!'

As a good girl guide, Miss Noyes attempted to quell certain signs of panic.

'Now then, my man!' she exclaimed sharply. 'Don't try to frighten us with any nonsense!'

Oakley gave one of his rare faint smiles.

'*You* needn't be frightened, ma'am,' he assured her. 'They don't care for Cochran Young Ladies. Prefer 'em round and Victorian. I say,' he added suddenly, 'are there still Cochran Young Ladies?'

Miss Noyes having failed in her mission, Haines now made an effort.

'Mr Oakley,' he said, 'we are trying to bear with you, but please realise that—in your sense—we are novices. Are you really and truly serious in all you're saying?'

'And what about Noel Coward?' asked Oakley. 'Has he written anything since *Private Lives*? Dashed good! Oh, and is the Income Tax still five bob? That's one thing you'll be spared here.'

'Damn it!' exploded Medworth. 'We've been *wrecked*!'

'Well, I didn't suppose it was a train accident. Did somebody ask me something?'

'Yes, I asked you whether you were really and truly serious,' repeated Haines.

'Abart the grub,' explained Ben, ''cos if yer are, I'm tikin' the next boat 'ome!'

'I like you, Little Tich, 'pon my soul, I do,' said Oakley. 'Oh, yes, quite, quite serious. I've come to believe this last month or two that I'm being quietly fattened.' He held out an arm and regarded it. 'Getting a bit too meaty for my pleasure. But they're not bad fellers, really. Not comic opera villains, you know. Real pukka chaps. There's one little girl . . .' He stopped and shrugged his shoulders. 'Treat 'em right, and—according to their religion—they'll treat you right.'

'They sound perfectly delightful!' observed Ruth.

Oakley looked at her. He appeared to be noticing her definitely for the first time. Something crept into his eyes. Haines was quick to remark it. But he also remarked that the something was instantly quelled, and that Oakley's eyes had resumed their protective moodiness when he replied.

'That's the idea,' he nodded. 'Just simple and primitive. Never known any different—poor blighters.'

'Tha's right,' said Ben.

In the little silence that ensued, while apprehensive glances were directed toward the silent forest, Ben wondered why he had said it. He did not know that it was the dawning of an instinct destined to determine vital issues on the island and to bear astonishing fruit. *Were* they poor blighters? If they'd never known any different, well, there you were, weren't you? And that little girl—she'd probably be black, like the rest—but he'd like a squint at her. He'd seen a picture of a little black girl once in a magazine. She hadn't looked so bad. Of course, she *had* been black. But she'd been smiling. What did black girls smile at? Same things as white girls? Had the photographer said, 'Now, then, when I say "Three," watch out for the little mouse' . . .

Miss Noyes's voice, thin and precise, brought him out of his reverie.

'But, surely,' she was saying, 'there have been some missionaries?'

'What for?' inquired Oakley. 'To teach them about the jolly old slums?'

'Tha's wot I calls a good 'un!' grinned Ben.

'You like it?' inquired Oakley, regarding him with interest.

Before Ben could reply, Lord Cooling froze him through his monocle.

'We are intensely interested in what you like and what you do not like,' he said, 'but I think we *can* exist without this information!' Then, turning to Oakley, he continued, 'But your own information, Mr Oakley, is more important. Before I finally rid myself of the hope that you are a raving lunatic, will you kindly explain to me how it is that you can talk of—of being fattened as though you were merely discussing the weather—how you can speak of football and Cochran and Noel Coward at a moment like this—and—'

'Yes, and why you weren't surprised to see us!' interrupted Smith, deeming it time for Wembley to get in a word. 'That wasn't natural, was it? Why, if you meet a pal in the tube, you say, "By Jove," or something!'

'Quite right,' agreed Medworth.

'There you are!' cried Smith, warming under this approval. 'Shall I tell you what I call it? Fishy! I believe the whole story's spoof! Where are these cannibals? Yes, and what's more, I believe he made these damn statues himself! Now, then, sir, no more lies—let's have the truth, this time!'

He was not used to making speeches. He turned, flushed, to Miss Noyes. She nodded in agreement. He turned to the Third Officer.

'I am quite sure Mr Oakley did not carve these statues,' said Haines rather shortly.

'And *I* don't know what Mr Smith means by *fishy*,' added Ruth. 'Does he mean that Mr Oakley wasn't surprised because he arranged the wreck and expected us?'

'Let us confine the present charge to lunacy,' interrupted Lord Cooling frigidly as Smith subsided, 'and suggest that

43

three years alone on this island have—slightly?—turned Mr Oakley's head!'

Oakley maintained the uncanny composure that was being complained of till the voices ceased. Then he looked at Lord Cooling thoughtfully and remarked:

'My reactions disturb you?'

'You don't appear to react at all,' answered Lord Cooling.

'I see. Well, might this explain it? For the last three years I have lived on a cannibal island where the Chief has twenty-one wives—God help him—where the High Priest drinks out of his predecessor's skull, where twins are sacrificed, when they occur, to the new moon—fortunately, they occur less often than the new moon—where the word "Holalulala" means "Take his eyes out" and "Lungoo" means "Fried knuckles," and where there is a Temple of Gold that would make the Bank of England's mouth water.'

'What's that?' exclaimed Medworth sharply.

'So, after all, perhaps it is natural that my bump of surprise has got a little blunted,' went on Oakley. 'And you can take it from me. I have done everything in my power to assist the blunting process. If that sounds good, forget it. There are two ways of going mad. You can get raw and feel everything, or you can get numb and feel nothing. I've got numb. As soon as I begin to feel anything, I knock it on the head. Course, one gets caught a bit sometimes.' He paused and glanced towards Ruth, then turned to Lord Cooling again. 'It would give me the greatest pleasure, sir, to smash that monocle out of your blasted eye. I wouldn't mind squashin' the feller who called me fishy under my foot, though I've a notion he'd feel slimy. If I kissed that pretty girl over there—first I've seen of my own race for three years—I would probably recall a very pleasant sensation. But I only allow little emotions. The infants in arms. Big 'uns—taboo. So you're safe from me, the whole damn lot of you. Note—from *me*. As for t'others, why worry? Think of yourselves, and then compare yourselves with the stars. Millions. Billions. Trillions. It's just amusin'.'

One man, at least, was uninterested in the philosophy of Mr Robert Oakley.

'Pardon me,' said Medworth, 'but would you mind repeating that about a Temple of Gold?'

The next moment everybody was uninterested in Mr Ernest Medworth. A faint sound was beginning to disturb the silence of the forest. The slow and distant beating of a drum.

'The Campbells are coming, hurrah, hurrah,' observed Oakley unemotionally. 'Well, good luck, chaps.'

He turned to go, but Medworth seized his arm.

'Wait a minute—where are you off to?' he demanded. Medworth's voice contained plenty of emotion.

'Pity about your complexion,' answered Oakley. 'Try and do something about it.'

'Shut up, you fool, and answer my question!'

'Certainly. I'm off to report.'

'Do you mean you're going to tell them about—us?'

'That's exactly what I mean. The presence of you and the absence of Oomoo. They're apt to be a bit over-excitable when they're not prepared for surprises.'

Medworth let his arm go and turned to the others.

'What do you think about it?' he exclaimed. 'Don't you think he ought to stay?'

'It doesn't matter what they think about it, old chap,' replied Oakley, as the distant drumming grew louder. 'I've got to go. I'm part of the Lord Mayor's Show. Of course—if any of you would like to come with me?'

There were no volunteers.

'Just one final question, Mr Oakley,' said Lord Cooling. 'When the—er—Lord Mayor's Show arrives, what attitude do you advise?'

'Don't start hitting about,' answered Oakley. 'Just be nice and obliging. Like me.'

Then he turned again, and a few seconds later had disappeared like an impossible dream into the forest.

'Oi!' muttered Ben, with a gulp. 'Me knuckles is hitchin'!'

6

The Resuscitation of a God

'Well, ladies and gentlemen,' said Lord Cooling, after a few moments of silence broken only by the distant beating of the drum. The fact that it was still distant was the sole bright spot in the situation. 'Do we adopt Mr Oakley's advice, and wait?'

'I don't see any alternative,' answered Haines.

'Nor do I,' added Ruth.

'No, not now that the fool's gone off to tell 'em,' muttered Smith, nervily. 'Who let him go? We ought to have kept him, the blasted idiot!'

'Well, I *do* see an alternative,' exclaimed Ardentino. 'At least we can put the ladies into safety!'

'Where's that?' inquired Ben.

Lord Cooling smiled acidly.

'Yes, where is your safe spot?' he asked. 'Find it, Mr Ardentino, and I have an idea the ladies will not be the only occupants. Yourself, for example?'

'Are you insinuating anything?' demanded Ardentino angrily.

'No—suggesting,' replied Lord Cooling. 'I am suggesting that the only reason we don't all climb trees is because we don't see any with convenient branches low enough. Personally, I think this is just as well. Eight representatives of King George found by a band of naked savages at the tops of eight trees would not be the best advertisement for the Union Jack.'

Ruth gave a little shriek of laughter. Smith looked scared, and Ardentino frowned.

'You may think this the moment for humour!' he snapped.

'It is certainly not the moment for panic,' responded Cooling.

'Who mentioned panic? Or trees, for that matter? Well, I'm going to have a look round, anyway—'

'And I'll join you,' interposed Miss Noyes, with sudden efficiency. 'You're quite right. What we need is to organise a base. And then someone can come out from it to—to parley with them. Don't you agree, Mr Smith?'

'Eh? Yes! I must say that sounds sensible,' answered Smith. 'Now, then. Base. Let's find one.'

He ran towards a mass of rocks, like a lost dog. The film star and the girl guide captain followed him with only a fraction less dignity. The drum was growing considerably nearer.

'Let them go, let them go!' grunted Medworth. 'They'll be caught with the rest of us, and meanwhile we've got something more important to talk about!'

'And the whole day, of course, to talk about it,' commented Lord Cooling.

'Well, we've got a minute, haven't we? . . . Hallo! What's that?'

The drum had abruptly ceased. The cessation was even more unnerving than the sound.

'I expect Oakley's met the Lord Mayor's Show,' said Haines, 'and is telling them the good news.'

'So now is our last chance to hear yours,' suggested Cooling, to Medworth. 'What is this important thing we have to talk about?'

Medworth glanced towards the forest, then drew close to the others.

'That Temple of Gold,' he answered, in a low voice. 'Rather—interesting, eh?'

Lord Cooling readjusted his eye-glass and stared through it fixedly.

'This is a time for statements, not hints, Medworth,' he said.

'Then here's my statement,' replied Medworth. 'If there's gold on this confounded island, let's see that we leave with a little!'

'Why a little?' inquired Lord Cooling. 'Why not a lot?'

'Your idea's even better than mine,' grinned Medworth.

Ruth and Haines frowned at each other. It was Ben, however, who put their thought into words.

'Wouldn't that be stealin'?' he blinked.

'Oh, shut your mouth!' exclaimed Medworth. 'No one's asked your opinion!'

'No, but yer gettin' it, see?' retorted Ben. 'I bin in quod once, but it wasn't fer stealin', it was fer 'ittin' a copper wot 'it me fust!'

'*Would* you mind not wasting valuable time—?' began Lord Cooling.

'*I* ain't wastin' vallerble time, *you* are,' interrupted Ben, with desperate boldness, 'torkin' abart carryin' away gold pillars when they'll be 'ere any minit! Wot's the good o' that? *I* gotter nidea better'n your'n. Put this 'ere Oomoo back,

49

see? Tha's where the trouble's goin' ter be. Yer could tell that by wot that bloke sed. Pick up the blinkin' bits, and when they comes and finds 'e's 'ere agine it'll put 'em in a good 'umer. 'Ow's *that* fer sense?'

He did not wait for an answer, but dashed to the vacant pedestal. As he began groping in the undergrowth, the drum sounded once more.

The minute that followed was one of the most confused—and also, as matters transpired, one of the most vital—in Ben's bewildering experience. He was never able to sort out the details afterwards. The closeness of the drum filled him with a terror that would have sent him leaping towards the sea if he had not been on his hands and knees among the tall, coarse grasses. He did make one jump, but was unnerved by the discovery that he had the god's head in his hands, and when he dropped the head he lost his own, and fell down flat on top of it. There he lay for a few horrible seconds, while the drumming from the forest grew nearer and nearer. He was doing the ostrich trick again, praying that trouble would pass over him. The grasses were high enough to conceal him temporarily. But as he lay, communicating his palpitations to the foliage, a new thought struck him. Struck him with such force that it brought him to his feet. There was no concealment for him here. The procession would stop at this very spot, and if he were found among the broken pieces of the god he might be held responsible for the catastrophe, and reduced to broken pieces himself. He tried to run. The panic he had striven valiantly to avoid had got him by the throat. It had also got him by the feet. They felt weighted with nightmare lead.

Vaguely he saw the figures of his companions. Four were stationary. Three were running. Whether towards him or away from him he could not say, and he certainly did not care. The drum was now shouting in his ear, and other sounds came out of the forest. Murmurs. Chanting. Tramping. He felt like a caught mouse, and waited for huge heads to peer and leer at him.

Then suddenly out of the chaos came to him his mad, insane idea. He acted upon it before he knew that he had got it. He leapt on to the vacant pedestal and, staring heavenwards, struck a godlike attitude.

The murmurs increased. The chanting rose. The tramping thudded. The drum beat with the force of a sledge-hammer. Then, all at once, every sound ceased. The world seemed to have stopped rotating.

'Wot's 'appenin'?' wondered Ben, his eyes still fixed glassily on the tree-tops.

The next instant a great voice rose, a voice charged with stupendous emotion.

'Oomoo! Oomoo! Oomoo!'

There was a sound as of an army crashing. A hundred natives fell flat on their faces before the human representation of their Little God.

51

7

Alias Oomoo

The success of Ben's ruse was not merely startling. It was terrifying. For the moment he had duped these natives and was being taken for the God of Storms. The dusky, prostrate backs glimpsed out of the corners of his motionless eyes, the strange chorus of awed murmurings that rose from the ground, and the constant repetition of the word 'Oomoo,' proved that. He was receiving the island's worship! But what would happen when the moment passed? When it was discovered that he was not a god but a miserable scared-stiff mortal? When he sneezed, say—he felt the desire rising as the alarming thought occurred—or when his knees gave way and he wobbled from the pedestal?

Then the worship would be transformed to wrath! He would be seized and torn to bits, and these humble murmurings would change to howls of primitive rage! Ben pictured himself being torn to bits and, in his too lively imagination, watched his limbs being tossed high into the air.

'Well, wot's goin' ter 'appen is goin' ter 'appen,' he thought, 'on'y I 'opes it 'appens quick!'

In spite of the hope, he did nothing to expedite the happening, but continued earnestly to emulate a Madame Tussaud waxwork.

The moments slipped by. The murmurings continued. The dawning sneeze was wrestled with and temporarily conquered. But Ben's limbs began to ache. His pose, not unlike that of Eros, was difficult to hold.

''Ow long's this goin' on?' he wondered.

Then the native nearest to him rose to his feet. His head, large and perspiring and not in the least attractive, loomed up into view from a black hell. Two arms, also large, rose above the head, and two black thick lips spoke.

'Vooloo? Vooloo, Oomoo? Vooloo?'

'Wot the 'ell does that mean?' thought Ben.

''Ad I better answer 'im, or pertend I ain't int'rested?'

He pretended he wasn't interested, and while the native waited for the answer that did not come, the unresponsive god noticed another figure edging quietly towards him. It was Oakley.

Now the native, evidently a man of some authority, turned his body, and waved his arms towards Ben's companions. Four of them—Ruth, Haines, Cooling and Medworth—had not moved since the appearance of the natives, and were awaiting the end of the astonishing episode with tense curiosity. The other three, having failed in their unheroic attempt to escape, were being closely watched by half a dozen giants with spears.

'Holalulala?' cried the native spokesman.

Only by the upward inflexion did Ben gather that this was not a statement but a question. Hadn't he heard the word before? Memory stirred uneasily.

'Moose?'

He knew he hadn't heard that one.

'Lungoo?'

Ben remembered Lungoo. Oakley had mentioned that it meant 'Fried knuckles.' Was this fellow inquiring whether Ben, alias Oomoo, would like his companions' knuckles to be fried? 'Lumme, I can't git away from knuckles!' thought Ben. Then, in a sudden flash, he remembered Oakley's interpretation of Holalulala: 'Take his eyes out.'

'Nah, then, I must do somethink!' reflected Ben, hoping that gods were permitted to perspire. 'Orl I gotter decide is, wot?'

Oakley evidently shared Ben's opinion that something must be done. He had been quietly edging closer and closer, and now he stood only a few feet away. His lips moved softly, as though still urged by prayer, and the prayer ran:

> '*Waa—lala, Make-a-sign lala,*
> *Holdi-tongue, li,*
> *Waa—lala.*'

If this was the strangest injunction Ben had ever received, it was also the most welcome. It was, in fact, exactly what he needed, providing him with a method of postponing further the dreaded moment of discovery. Yes, of course, that was it! Make a sign! Gods didn't speak—not, anyway, in Ben's voice—but they did make signs, and Ben knew a lot of signs. Which one should he choose? A slow, solemn wink? One of these new-fangled continental salutes? Something in the thumb line? Or could he kill two birds with one stone by bringing his nose into it and settling a tickle?

While these alternatives were flashing through Ben's mind, the decision was taken out of his hands by the spokesman.

'Chehaka!' he roared, like a despairing animal, and his great arms once more shot upwards.

Startled into activity, and misinterpreting the intention of the arms, Ben raised his own arms to ward off an expected blow. The effect was instantaneous. Instead of attacking Ben, the spokesman clasped his fingers together and bellowed seraphically:

'Oomoo poopoo! Oomoo poopoo!'

'I've pooped,' thought Ben.

Then another silence fell, faintly broken a second later by Oakley's low chanting again:

> '*Waa—lala, Wave-your-arms lala,*
> *Hurry O li,*
> *Waa—lala!*'

Ben waved his arms. He waved them slowly and solemnly, like a windmill in a gentle breeze. His impulse was for quicker motion, which would have been more in keeping with the beating of his heart, but the intelligence of Oakley was having an effect upon him, and he was doing his best to emulate it. Oakley's mind working to save Ben's skin supplied the one faint ray of hope.

The spokesman—he was, as Ben learned later, the Chief of the tribe, though not the actual ruling spirit—stared intently at the godly motions, trying to interpret them. Failing, he turned to Oakley and muttered:

'Kwee? Kwee?'

It was the moment Oakley had played for. He realised before Ben did that immediate danger was past, and with the realisation came a totally novel sense of power. The sense would have elated another. It might have produced a feeling of drunken joy, but Oakley remained calm. He was beyond joy or misery. He accepted what came with the same passive exterior and almost the same emotion, or lack of it. All he experienced now, as he found the Chief's inquiring eyes upon him, was a feeling of vague comfort.

The comfort was not shared by the other white folk. The three who had attempted escape were too near six sharp spears, and Ardentino was wondering whether to make a second attempt; while the four who had stood firm were perilously near the snapping point. Ruth's fingers were gripping Haines's sleeve, though only he of the two knew it, and Medworth was in ripe condition to shriek. Cooling, unhampered by the altruistic anxiety infused into Haines by the pressure on his sleeve, was the least mentally perturbed. He disliked pain intensely, and was ready to go to considerable lengths to avoid it, but even if his knuckles were destined to be fried, he would not lose his sense of superiority. He even smiled when he found that Oakley was looking towards him.

Medworth, on the other hand, rebelled.

'What the hell are you staring at us for?' shouted Medworth suddenly bursting. 'If you think—'

Oakley raised his head sharply. Ben followed suit. The Chief's expression grew as black as his skin. Medworth subsided. Then Oakley turned to the Chief again, made a little gesture towards Ben, and gave his interpretation of slowly-moving arms when revolved by the will of a heathen god.

'Sula,' said Oakley.

The Chief nodded eagerly.

'Domo,' went on Oakley.

The Chief nodded again.

'Toree,' concluded the interpreter.

The Chief nodded a third time. Then he fell on his face at the feet of Ben and muttered with reverence, 'Hya! Hyaya, Oomoo! Hya!' Then he leapt up again—for a large and fleshy man he had wonderful agility—swung round, and screamed to his people, 'Oomoo poopoo! Sula! Domo! Toree!' Then he made a sign, and two of the natives jumped to their feet and disappeared into the forest.

The rest of the natives now also rose from the ground and began softly murmuring to each other. Their voices made an eerie buzz. A pause had evidently been reached in the proceedings, and Lord Cooling, after a glance at Haines, cleared his throat and ventured an inquiry.

'Of course, Mr Oakley,' he said with ironic politeness, 'all this is intensely interesting and instructive, but personally I have always objected to studying a language without a key. May we know—with all due deference to the great god Oomoo, on whose rise from the coal-dust to fame let me be the first to congratulate him—may we know what precise bearing the entertaining conversation we have just heard has upon—*us?*'

'Yes, and may we know where those two black blighters have gone?' added Medworth. 'If you think, just because we've—we've stood here quietly we're going to allow any nonsense, you'll find out your mistake!'

The Chief's eyes blazed, but Oakley stepped to him quickly and whispered in his ear. The whispering continued for several seconds, and was accompanied by glances and gestures towards Ben. When at last the Chief shrugged his shoulders and folded his arms, Oakley turned from him and spoke in a sing-song voice that contrasted oddly with his words.

'Listen, Oh, unwise white worms!' he said. 'The Chief of this island has agreed, since I have assured him that it is

Oomoo's will, that the situation shall be explained to you, but let me remind you that if you are not careful your blasted impatience will land you in the soup-tureen—and that, dear brothers, is no mere figure of speech on this island. Got that? Good. Then now to the translation. And remember that the Chief's present interest in listening to our strange foreign sounds will not last for ever. Sula means trial—'

'What's that?' interrupted Medworth.

'Yes, you really are a pitiable white worm,' replied Oakley. 'Interrupt me again, and I shall be obliged to make a very unpleasant suggestion to our Chief. It will be "Moose," and it will cost you that trifle, your head.'

Lord Cooling smiled. There were moments when Oakley's lugubrious sense of humour quite appealed to him.

'To proceed,' continued Oakley. 'Sula means trial. Domo means tomorrow. Compare *demain*, French for the same thing. And Toree is the place where the trial will occur tomorrow. The Temple of Gold.'

Once more Ernest Medworth forgot himself.

'Temple of Gold?' he exclaimed. 'Do you mean—we're all going *there*?'

'To be tried,' Oakley reminded him grimly. 'I hope you will like it.'

'But for what crime are we to be tried?' asked Cooling. 'Gate-crashing?'

'Gate-crashing is an undoubted offence here,' answered Oakley, 'but you are more likely to be tried for the crime of being white.'

'A crime we are criminal enough to be proud of,' murmured Lord Cooling, screwing his monocle more firmly into his eye and regarding the Chief, who had drawn a little closer as though fascinated by the incomprehensible voices of

58

his prisoners. 'And who,' queried Cooling, 'is going to be our judge?'

'Who but Oomoo, since it was Oomoo who ordered the trial,' replied Oakley.

'I see. And—er—you will interpret the judgment of Oomoo?'

'If the High Priest permits me. He may have his own ideas on the subject.'

'Let us hope they will be nice ideas, Mr Oakley. Meanwhile, what is happening? This stage wait is a little trying—and most of all, judging from his expression, to Oomoo. Can you do anything to shorten it? I fear our god will not last.'

The fear was shared by Ben himself, whose god-like mien was now being violently invaded by the increasing tickle on his nose. But before Oakley could answer, the Chief suddenly issued a new instruction, and pointed to Cooling. The instruction ran:

'Karamee valogee O lahala laholee. Vooloo malooloo karamo sula somo domo toree. Gala majeela O wooleeja, cloom lungoo—huh?'

'Meaning?' murmured Cooling.

For an instant all eyes were on him. Oomoo seized the instant, and scratched his nose with a thoroughness and rapidity that created a record in nasal history.

'Meaning,' translated Oakley, 'that the Chief is taking a special interest in you and that your voice gives him a sort of spinal pleasure. For this reason—and also, I think, because he is attracted by your eyeglass—he desires you to address him personally, and to give him a sample of the defence you will put up tomorrow before Oomoo in the Temple of Gold. Of course, he will not understand it. A word of advice. Make it snappy.'

'It cannot be too snappy for me,' retorted Cooling, retreating a little as the Chief grew uncomfortably close. 'I suppose you couldn't call the fellow off, could you?'

'Kwee?' said the Chief, pointing to Cooling's monocle, and continuing to advance as Cooling backed.

'I beg you to keep your distance,' answered Cooling, doing his best to wave away the traffic. 'If you come too close I may forget myself and make your face even less beautiful than it is at present, and thus achieve an impossibility . . . Yes, sir, this is an eyeglass. One day, if you are a good little boy, I may buy you one, but meanwhile let me inform you, sir, that you are going to receive a surprise at the trial domo in your toree. Your little god, to whom these words are addressed as much as to yourself—kindly note that, little god—is going to pronounce a verdict that will considerably surprise you . . . Yes, yes, I have told you before, this *is* an eyeglass . . . Believe me, sir, Oomoo will find some way—he will indeed, be instructed to find a way, and will receive the precise instructions later—to recompense me and my companions for the indignity you are putting upon us. Oh, and to recompense himself, also, of course—'

'One per cent,' muttered Medworth.

'We might make it two,' suggested Cooling, 'and two per cent of the gold in his temple will buy quite a lot of things in dear old Leicester Square. Yes, Mr Chief, our price is going to be a stiff one, a damned stiff one, and you will pay it because if you disobey your little god he will send a storm that will sink your confounded island to the bottom of your confounded ocean—AH!'

The abrupt termination of the speech was caused by the Chief's hand, which suddenly shot out and snatched the eyeglass from the lordly optic. Delighted with his prize the Chief sprang

60

back, and held the glass before his own optic. The next moment he gave a shout of terrified rage and sent the monocle spinning through the air.

'Hooja, hooja, hooja!' he howled.

For a few seconds pandemonium existed. Gazes were riveted on an island chief having spasms. Even the six stalwart guards with spears forgot their duty of guarding the three most restless of the white folk, and Ardentino, suddenly finding the chance he had been seeking, slipped away and bounded round a rock. Then a fresh diversion was created. It came from the forest.

The two natives returned. They carried a golden litter. Behind them, chanting and dancing, were a score of dusky girls. The Chief ceased foaming at the mouth, made a sign to the procession, and waved towards Oomoo.

'Wot's this?' wondered Ben. 'A revoo?'

He fought a strange embarrassment. The dusky girls were undoubtedly attractive, but they were hardly decent. Then the embarrassment changed to new alarm as the procession made a bee-line for him. Reaching him, it stopped. The golden litter was raised to his level. The dusky girls fell below his level, and flopped down on their faces.

''Ere! Am I ter git on it?' thought Ben. 'It ain't sife!'

He tried to glimpse Oakley without moving his eyes. He failed, because Oakley had moved out of his direct line of vision. This was a nuisance. He had the sense to realise that if he openly appealed to Oakley, revealing his dependence on him, his authority would vanish like smoke, so he rolled his eyes round majestically. At the most easterly point of their circular tour they found Oakley. Oakley was nodding quietly, with the unobtrusive skill of a conjuror's confederate.

'Well, there ain't no fare ter pay,' reflected Ben resignedly. ''Ere goes!'

He stepped on to the litter. As soon as he was on it, it began to move again. It moved so suddenly and swiftly that Ben lost both his balance and his head, sat down promptly, and ejaculated:

'Oi!'

'Oi!' repeated the natives, with awed reverence.

The divine word echoed through the forest as the gasping god was borne into it.

8

The Village of Skulls

The journey that followed was the most extraordinary of Ben's extraordinary existence, not even excepting a funeral procession in which he had once taken the principal part. It was so extraordinary, in fact, that for a while he didn't believe it. 'I've eaten suthink,' he decided, 'and this is wot's 'appened.' There could be no other possible explanation of the impressive golden litter beneath his less impressive frame, of the two giants who were bearing him along, of the fat Chief who strode by his side, of the chanting, dancing girls with their impossibly naked bodies. Why, even in a musical comedy, girls wore more clothing! 'Yus, that's wot it is,' insisted Ben. 'I've eaten suthink!'

The forest itself added to the impression of nightmare. The trees were higher than trees had any right to be. As the procession advanced they grew thicker and more luxuriant, and great coils of foliage wound round them like bursting snakes. Some of the trees had been struck down by the storm, and lay prone upon the ground or slanted at angles that gave them a queer resemblance to long forest guns. One tree lay directly across their track, and as the procession clambered over it the Chief began mumbling. Ben gathered he was apologising. The apology was necessary, for the process of negotiating the obstacle nearly shook Ben off his perch.

'Wunner wot'd 'appen if I give a big shout?' reflected Ben. 'P'r'aps I'd wike meself up like?'

He refrained, although he longed to wake up like. It had been bad enough on the pedestal, but it was worse on the litter. Now there were no white faces around him to remind him of home, and he felt terribly lonely. His sole crumb of comfort resided in the probability that his companions in distress were forming some other part of the procession, assumedly in the rear; but a crumb of comfort you cannot see is of small use.

Presently the trees became a little less dense, and the track forked into two. There was a pause. The front part, including Ben, then took the right track, and the back part, including the rest of the white party with the exception of Ardentino, took the left track.

We will follow the right track. It led to a large clearing. Now, instead of trees, were bamboo huts. Outside the huts sprawled babies and squatted old men. A long perpendicular pole protruded through the top of each hut. Some of the poles were barren, others bore skulls. The barren poles were preferable.

Women and children issued from the huts like variously-sized black dots to watch the procession pass by. They all stared at Ben, and some of them flopped on their faces. It surprised the unhappy god to notice that many of the children were quite pretty. One in particular nearly made him forget his sanctity and turn his head. 'Fancy findin' a kid like that 'ere!' he thought. 'Wash 'er black orf and she'd be orl right at a party!' He hoped vaguely that he would see her again. Fortunately for the moment, he had no prevision of the conditions in which his hope was destined to be fulfilled.

The procession wound through the bamboo village without halting. The ground began to rise. A rocky peak appeared above a distant belt of trees, a peak on which something gleamed. Ben fixed his eyes upon the gleaming thing. Then the procession stopped with a jolt, and he found himself before another bamboo hut which evidently marked the conclusion of their journey.

This hut was considerably larger than the others. It was of the same bee-hive shape, and appeared to follow much the same pattern, but an impressive bamboo wall encircled it, and the hut formed the central point of a big enclosure. Three long poles, instead of the usual one, rose gloomily from the roof, and on each were three skulls.

'I s'pose this is where Old King Cole lives,' thought Ben. 'Well, there's no accountin' fer tiste!'

A brief consultation was proceeding below him. He had been carried shoulder high throughout the journey, as though closer proximity to the ground would contaminate him, and he was still being held at the same elevation. He thought he heard Oakley's voice. Then he was carried through an opening in the palisade, across the wide space between the fence and the hut, and into the hut. The 'front door' was a very thick greenish curtain formed out of several layers of heavily plaited rushes.

At first Ben could see nothing inside. The transition from external sunlight to interior dimness temporarily destroyed his vision. Other eyes could see, however, if his could not, and he was carried onward without pause. He seemed to be travelling through a dark vastness. His head, surely, ought to have struck the roof, but the roof was a distant dome above which, he suddenly recalled, were nine skulls. This lent enchantment to the distance.

His eyes were becoming accustomed to the dimness when the procession, now considerably diminished in size, made its final halt before an enormous chair. It was fixed to a raised platform, and it was of painted wood. The artist who had painted the chair appeared to have exhausted his entire paint-box, for if any hue was absent from this seat of state, Ben had never met it. It was the Chief's throne, resigned for the occasion to the Chief's most distinguished visitor.

'Ain't I never goin' ter walk agine?' wondered Ben, as he was lifted from the litter to the throne. 'Don't gods need no exercise?'

But a more important question was becoming urgent in his mind—or, more correctly speaking, in his stomach. Did gods eat?

He placed his numb hands upon his numb knees, and while he did so the procession melted away. He was conscious of more murmurings, and more prostrations. The Chief's big bulk lowered itself once more before him. Then the Chief also melted away, and there came a blessed stillness and silence. Allowing his eye to rove a little, he noticed that one figure still remained. His heart nearly turned over in gratitude. It was Oakley.

'Oi!' whispered Ben.

'Shut up!' Oakley whispered back. 'Wives coming.'

'Wot—on land?' mumbled Ben.

'Wives, not waves,' murmured Oakley. 'To be presented. But only a dozen of them.'

'Do they 'ave clothes on?' asked Ben. ''Cos if not, I ain't goin' ter look!'

'Shut up, shut up!' muttered Oakley. 'You're doing fine. Don't spoil it.'

'Yus, but don't fergit I'm gettin' 'ungry!' whispered Ben. Encouraged by Oakley's praise, he readjusted his features into a ghastly grin and prepared to wait.

'Don't look so jolly,' came the low admonition.

'Gawd, 'oo's jolly?' growled Ben, and changed his expression to the nearest he could find to a dying haddock.

A long bamboo wall, extending from floor to roof, separated the outer chamber, or throne room, from the inner quarters of the hut, and at the end farthest from the throne was a thick rush curtain similar to that which stood for the front door. The rushes now rustled apart and the Chief returned followed by twelve of his wives. Oakley had originally mentioned twenty-one, so Ben deduced that the balance of nine were on holiday. These twelve, apart from the foremost who was bursting with over-exposed flesh, looked as though they could also have done with a change. The Chief's taste in femininity was not good.

The Chief stood aside. The twelve wives approached Ben in single file. One by one, they went flat before him, murmuring 'Oomoo!' as they did so. The last one—last and least, for she was the sorriest of the crew and looked thoroughly wretched and browbeaten—tripped, and the Chief hissed in anger. Just in time the little god restrained his impulse to leap down to her assistance and help her up.

Ben was always sorry for people who fell down. He knew what it felt like.

'Never mind, I'll do suthink fer yer if I can,' thought Ben as the miserable creature scrambled to her feet. 'Yus, why shouldn't I? I am a god, ain't I?'

And then an amazing idea flashed into Ben's mind, carrying him dizzily beyond his own needs and the needs of his companions. If he were really destined to continue his strange dominance, why shouldn't he use the power for the benefit of others on this island? Why shouldn't he do something for other creatures as well as just for this one frightened woman? For that jolly little child he'd noticed, for instance? For the dancing girls—get some decent clothes on them? Even, perhaps, for the Chief himself, whose notions of diet might be improved with proper direction?

The amazing idea grew. Behind the expression of a dying haddock dawned conceptions undreamed of by haddocks in their hey-day! A god ought to do good. He should not stoop to stealing gold—especially for a paltry two per cent. of the profit! If Ben was only a little god, he might be able to teach these black people about the Big God—make them switch over, like—which would have the ultimate advantage of releasing Ben from duty. 'Course, yer really wants a bloke like the Third Officer fer this kind o' job,' reflected Ben, 'but it's too late ter swop with 'im nah . . .'

A voice broke in upon his reverie.

'You can come out of your trance, old son,' said Oakley. 'But keep your voice low.'

'Eh?' jerked Ben.

His mind snapped back from the future to the present. He and Oakley were alone again. He had been so absorbed in his beneficent vision that he had not noticed the wives returning to their quarters. His last memory was of the twelfth wife tripping.

'Have you ever been a god before?' inquired Oakley. 'This seems almost too good for a first performance.'

'Stop kiddin'!' muttered Ben.

'Believe me, I am not kidding. Your mind seemed to be on Olympus.'

'Where's that?'

'Oh, just a little hill.'

'Well, see, I was thinkin'.'

'A mistake, take my word for it. Never think on a cannibal island.'

'Yus, but that's wot I was thinkin 'abart!'

'What?'

'Cannerbul island. I'm the blinkin' gawd 'ere, ain't I? Well, then, why can't I stop the cannerbul part?'

Oakley regarded Ben with interest.

'Is your head turning, old sport?' he asked.

'Fair spinnin',' returned Ben. 'Jest the sime, mite, I'm seerious.'

Oakley glanced towards the rush curtain through which a Chief had just gone with a dozen wives. He smiled with the grim pain of knowledge.

'Of course you can't stop it,' he said.

'Why not?' insisted Ben. 'Me bein' a gawd—and you standin' by like ter 'elp with the lingo?'

'Of a hundred reasons, I will mention two,' answered Oakley. 'First, the peculiar composition of gods. Gods are made in man's own image. Do you understand what I am talking about?'

'No.'

'Then let me put it in another way. Gods are created for man's convenience. They think the things that the individual or the community want them to think. In the Great War, the English God said we were right. The German God said the Germans were right. The Japanese God said the Japs were right. The American God said, Say, Boy, the Americans are right. Do you think any country would have acepted a God that had put them in the wrong? And you'll find it the same here. Oomoo believes in cannibalism. Oomoo believes in hanging up skulls like inn signs. Oomoo believes in sacrifices. If Oomoo didn't—good-bye, Oomoo. So if you want to turn this black island white, old sport, forget it. All we can do is to try and save the white that's on it.'

Ben looked depressed.

'But the second reason is equally forceful,' went on Oakley. 'It is the High Priest. Your present host is merely the figure-head. It's the High Priest who pulls the strings, and the High Priest is quite the nastiest bit of work ever achieved by Creation. Not that I mind him. I don't mind anything. Why worry? Yes, really and truly, sweetheart, why worry? Bernard Shaw once said—by the way, is the dear old fossil still alive?—he once said that we were all born with the death sentence. Quite true. It's just a question of how, when, and where . . . Just the same, when I first came here, the High Priest used to give me the chilly shivers. See *him* giving up his pound of flesh!'

'Ere, that's enuff abart 'im!' interposed Ben.

'As you like,' replied Oakley. 'And, after all, time's going, and I must get practical.'

'Yus, afore Old King Cole pops back agine,' agreed Ben. 'Where's 'e gorn?'

'He has gone to pray. I told him you desired him and his wives to repeat the Storm Prayer ten times in the kitchen. Each time takes a minute, and they're probably about half-way through.'

'Wot 'appens when they're orl the way through?'

'Food will be brought to you, and placed before you.'

'Wot sort o' food?'

'Is that a wise question?'

'I ain't goin' ter eat no knuckles!'

'You will not be offered knuckles. At the moment, I happen to know, there are no supplies. It will probably be a smelly vegetable called Wooma. The best way to avoid being sick is to eat it very slowly while thinking hard of something entirely different. Choose your own subject. I always choose Welsh Rarebit.'

'Yus, well, s'pose I'm sick any'ow?' asked Ben. ''Ow'll that be fer givin' me away?'

'You must not be sick anyhow,' ordered Oakley, 'but even so it might not give you away. There will be no one by you when you eat.'

'Owjer know that?' demanded Ben, relieved that he was not going to be watched.

'Because I arranged that,' replied Oakley. 'When you and your pals get back to London—with gold or without—you'll have to thank me for some pretty rapid thinking. And now, if you don't mind, I'll do a spot of rapid talking as well, because I reckon the Chief must now be entering the seventh lap, which only leaves three more. Here are the other things I have so far arranged for you. Listen, mark, and digest. Item, that you must be alone when you eat. Gods do not actually eat—they spirit food away, and it is a very private performance. Item, you like solitude. Gods have to get through a great deal of pondering, and Oomoo, the God of Storms, has to decided which seas he shall whip up and which he shall calm down. Thus, you will be visited periodically, but never—we hope—for long sessions. Item, you are not to be touched. That was an easy item to arrange, for they are as afraid of you here as you are of them.'

'Go on!' murmured Ben incredulously.

71

'Item,' continued Oakley, after a glance towards the inner curtain, 'if a situation gets beyond you, or if you feel your nerve snapping, lift both your arms and place your hands upon your head. That will imply that you are falling into a divine trance and that you must have immediate solitude. In other words, it will mean, "Scoot!" Admit I am doing all I can for you.'

'I'll leave yer me skull in me will,' answered Ben.

'Item, remember that gods never move off their pedestals or seats. Not in public, anyway.'

'Yus, but I'm gettin' stiff,' said Ben.

'You must suffer the penalty of greatness,' answered Oakley. 'It will only be, we hope, for twenty-four hours. Item, do not take any risks or play any tricks. In other words, don't "get funny." One false move may ruin everything.'

'Wot's the hitem if I sneeze?'

'The hope that it will be interpreted as godly wrath. Possibly it may be safe to sneeze here, in the Chief's house. In the Temple of Gold, it will be more hazardous. In fact,' added Oakley, with uncomfortable significance, 'it is in the Temple of Gold that our real trouble will begin. The Chief is fairly simple. Any clever sharper could play the three-card trick on him. The High Priest is a very different matter. Now I must go.'

'Oi! 'Arf a mo'!' gasped Ben as Oakley began to move. 'Wot 'appens if 'Is Nobs comes 'ere?'

'His nobs?'

'The 'Igh Priest?'

'Oh—that's not very likely,' replied Oakley. 'He's an exclusive old fellow. He hardly ever leaves the precincts of the Golden Temple.'

'Yus, but s'pose terday is one o' the 'ardly evers?'

'In that case, you must certainly not sneeze.'

'Wot's 'e like?'

'A description of him does not exist.'

''Ave a shot!'

'Well—how about a tall skeleton thinly covered with yellowish flesh?'

'Lumme!' muttered Ben miserably. 'I wish I could go 'ome.'

'I'm doing my darndest to get you there,' Oakley reminded him.

'Tha's right,' nodded Ben. 'I ain't fergettin'. But where are yer goin' now?'

'To see the others who share your wish.'

'Well, give 'em Oomoo's love, and doncher be gorn long. I feel like a ship wot's lorst 'er rudder when you ain't 'ere. Oh, and 'ere's another messidge fer 'em. Tell 'em ter fergit that there gold, see? It ain't ours, and gawds don't steal. See?'

Oakley had turned to go, but now he turned back for a moment, and peered into Ben's solemn face.

'You're a queer blighter,' he remarked. 'I can't recall ever having met anything quite like you before. I'll give them your message, but I don't imagine they'll pay any attention to it. After all—they're human.'

'Well, so are the black johnnies, ain't they?' answered Ben. 'I mean ter say—well, ain't they?'

Oakley smiled gravely.

'I've an idea you're going to be a bit of trouble, Ben,' he said.

'If yer goin' ter git trouble, yer might as well give it,' replied Ben. 'Fair's fair!'

9

Wooma and Gung

'Well, Miss Sheringham,' said Tom Haines, 'how do you like pleasure-cruising?'

They were sitting on a slab of rock. Around them was a tall, encircling palisade of the inevitable bamboo, similar in design to that which, at the same moment, encircled Ben; but the hut it enclosed, and which formed their temporary indoor quarters, was smaller and less imposing. It was, in fact, the island prison.

'I prefer a cruise that sticks to its programme,' replied Ruth, after a pause. 'This wasn't advertised on the posters, you know.'

'Yes, you've a case against the Company,' smiled Haines.

'I'll ring up my solicitor first thing after breakfast,' she smiled back.

They were the only two who seemed able to smile. On another rocky slab a little way off, Smith and Miss Noyes were sitting side by side in doleful silence, while Lord Cooling and Ernest Medworth were inside the hut, gloomily examining its dimensions and dirt draughts. A couple of native spearmen, hovering around them with suspicious curiosity, added to the discomfort.

'And, talking about breakfast,' added Ruth, 'do we get any, do you suppose?'

'Bound to,' answered Haines, optimistically. 'If our gaolers forget, Oakley will probably come along and remind them.'

'Expect so,' she nodded. 'The question is less if we'll get any than if we'll want any! Do you know, I feel so far from civilisation already that I can hardly believe people are sitting down to coffee and ham and eggs at this very moment!'

'To Oakley, after three years, they must be entire theories.'

'What do you think of our Mr Oakley?'

'I can't help rather liking him.'

'Same here—only—is he bats?'

'I don't blame him, if he is.'

'Rather not. If we stay here a week, we'll all be bats by the end of it.' She dug her heel into the ground and regarded her bedraggled shoe. Had this disgraceful footwear once tempted her into a shop in Bond Street? 'But meanwhile, Mr Haines, it won't add to the comfort of the island if we find that our Mr Oakley's brain *is* wonky.'

'He talked some good sense.'

'I believe most of them do between their spasms. But in spite of his sense, he seems to me to be mentally—upside down. While he's talking I get a queer feeling that, if some-body came along and cut him in half, he'd just go on talking and saying it didn't matter. Ugh!' She gave a little shiver. 'I'm glad you're here, anyway. If you weren't, I'd—'

She paused, and stared at her shoe harder than ever.

'Well, I am here, Miss Sheringham—and I'm glad I'm here, too,' he answered. 'So that's that.'

75

'I've got a suggestion,' she said after a moment. 'My first name's Ruth. Suppose you use it? It won't mean that we're going to marry each other and live happily ever after—just that it'll seem more friendly. I say, am I getting hysterical?'

'Not a bit!' he laughed. 'I think you're wonderful. And I agree with you. My name's Tom.'

'Hallo, Tom!'

'Hallo, Ruth!'

She giggled. She *was* on the verge of hysterics. She had been hugging on to herself for hours, and during that grim march through the forest she had nearly collapsed, though nobody had known it . . Now, suddenly, she heard herself giggling, and stopped abruptly while she could.

'Don't worry,' she said in response to his anxious glance. 'I'm all right. Only we mustn't get sentimental, or you'll see a strong woman weep. What do you suppose the others are talking about?'

Haines turned his head. Smith and Miss Noyes were not talking about anything. They were still sitting side by side in moody silence. Cooling and Medworth were just issuing from the hut.

'Shouldn't we all have a confab or something?' asked Ruth.

'Not much good, till Oakley comes along with some news,' replied Haines.

'Suppose he doesn't come along?'

'He's promised to. He told me he'd have to go with the major part of the procession when it split. I should think that, at the moment, our little stoker needs his assistance even more than we do.'

She nodded, and her face grew grave.

'Poor little stoker!' she murmured. 'What on earth is going to happen to him?'

'I'm fairly good at riddles,' replied Haines, 'but that one beats me, Ruth.' She smiled slightly as he pronounced her name. But one thing's certain. If Oomoo can't save us, we've got to save Oomoo.'

'Carried unanimously,' she answered. 'There's something about that funny little fellow that—that makes me want to tuck him up in bed and put him to sleep.'

'I'm not sure, though, that Ardentino isn't the one we ought to be most anxious about,' Haines went on frowning. 'He was an idiot to bolt off like that. He'll probably get it hot when they catch him.'

'Perhaps they won't catch him?'

'In the long run they're bound to. This is an island, not a Continent with frontiers!'

He rose as he spoke. The rock on which he had been sitting was at the foot of a little mound. He began to climb.

'What are you doing?' exclaimed Ruth sharply.

'Going to have a squint over the prison wall,' he answered. 'I can get a view from the top.'

'Be careful!'

'It's quite safe. Come along, too, if you like. Maybe we'll see our film star hanging on to the top of a tree!'

She jumped up and joined him. It was an easy climb, but he took her hand in case she slipped. That at any rate was the excuse he gave himself. Below them their companions watched, and Cooling and Medworth approached the mound. The two spearmen consulted, but did not interfere.

'What's the idea?' called Medworth.

'To improve my knowledge of the geography of the island,' Haines called back.

'Well, when you've improved it, come down and talk to us,' said Medworth. 'We're going into conference.'

'Waste of time without Oakley,' replied Haines as Ruth glanced at him.

'Opinions differ!' retorted Medworth, looking at Cooling. 'Oakley's going to do what we tell him!'

'Let us hope,' Cooling corrected dryly. 'Meanwhile, kindly give us a geographical report.'

The two climbers reached the top. They were now several feet above the height of the fence, and a considerable portion of the island came into view. They saw the dark forest through which they had been marched, sloping gently towards the sea. The shore was invisible from where they stood, but a great expanse of sea glittered with almost unnatural brilliance to the horizon, and above rose the blue dome of the Pacific sky.

'Wonderful, isn't it?' said Haines.

'I prefer the Outer Circle of Regent's Park,' she returned.

'Perhaps, though that would make our position a bit zoological. I feel rather like a baboon as it is! Well, do you see our friend clinging to a tree?'

They strained their eyes. There was no sign of Ardentino. Then they turned, and gazed in the opposite direction. The gradual rise continued for a distance, then became a stiff climb through more forest country to a high peak. Studying the line of the sea horizon, and following it round to its two visible limits, Haines deduced that unless the island were considerably longer than it was broad the sea could not be far beyond the peak, and that the ground must drop sharply into the ocean.

Near the foot of the stiff ascent could be seen the unprepossessing roofs of the village of skulls. His keen eyes easily identified the gruesome objects on the poles, and he hoped that Ruth's sight was not quite so good. But his main interest was a point of light that gleamed from the peak. The sun's rays had caught something there, and was turning it into a little golden eye.

'What are you staring at?' cried Medworth. 'Must you keep it to yourself?'

'You can come up and stare, too, if you like,' said Haines. 'I imagine it's the Temple of Gold.'

'By Jove, is it?' exclaimed Medworth, and made for the mound.

Smith and Miss Noyes advanced, also. They had shaken off their stupor, and had joined the group. But a sudden voice behind them made them turn. A stout native bearing a long, troughlike vessel had entered the compound and was demanding their attention.

'Wooma!' he cried, as though he were announcing a distinguished visitor. 'Wooma! Wooma!'

He placed the trough on the ground and pointed to it.

'Wooma!' he repeated solemnly.

Lord Cooling, sighing for his lost monocle, advanced towards him.

'Do we understand,' he inquired, with a sarcasm entirely lost on his audience, 'that this evil-smelling concoction is Wooma?'

'Wooma,' said the native again, and thumped his massive chest.

'I think we may take it, ladies and gentlemen,' observed Cooling turning to the others, 'that this is Wooma. Wooma, moreover, that our chef has killed, caught, grown, or stunned himself. You will note that he is beating his chest with a sort of gastronomic vanity. Our next question is—*what* is Wooma?'

He bent over the trough, held his nose, and examined.

'I record, with relief,' he reported, after the examination, 'that Wooma appears to be one of the very lesser vegetables, happily unknown in the British Isles. This brings us to our final question. Assuming that we eat Wooma—possibly a rash assumption—*how* do we eat it? It is evidently a communal dish. Do we say, "One, two, three, go!" and then fall upon it with our naked fingers? Or do we descend on all fours, and devour it like puppies? How lost one feels here without Mr Oakley!'

'Very humorous, his lordship, isn't he?' murmured Smith miserably, to Miss Noyes.

'And very wise,' Miss Noyes murmured back with equal misery. 'They say it was our sense of humour that won the war.'

The chef now turned and darted away. A few seconds later they saw him returning with another trough.

'Good God!' exclaimed Lord Cooling. 'Is he bringing us more? Are we going to have one each?'

The suffocating theory was pleasantly dispelled by the contents of the second trough. It was filled with fruit, some of which they almost recognised. Placing it on the ground, the native shouted, 'Gung!' and once more thumped his chest, implying this time that he had picked the gung. Then he pointed from the trough to his mouth. Then he seized a piece of fruit, rubbed it rapidly along his teeth, and threw it back. Then he cried, 'Sweeze!' and did it all over again. His attitude was quite friendly, and he was clearly doing his best to help.

'Thung,' said Lord Cooling.

It was a mistake. The native's friendliness vanished. He leaped into the air, his eyes rolling. The spearmen shook their spears. Then the native rushed from the compound howling. His howls were echoed by the other natives outside.

'I hoped it might mean, "Thank you,"' sighed Cooling. 'Thung for gung. Evidently, it did not. Well, let us eat. Personally, I shall go direct to the second course.'

Ruth and Haines had descended, and now six hungry mortals ate the strangest breakfast of their lives. Its strangeness was not decreased by the fact that the spearmen joined them.

10

The Shadow of the High Priest

Oakley did not arrive for an hour. When he came his expression was grim.

'I don't like your face,' said Lord Cooling.

'I was never too fond of it myself,' replied Oakley. 'Let's go into the Ritz and talk about it.'

'Ritz?' murmured Smith uncomprehendingly.

'Well, pigsty, then,' corrected Oakley, jerking his head towards the prison hut. 'We'll be quieter in there. These natives can't understand our lingo, but we might as well keep 'em outside in case any of you faint or anything.'

'I applaud your suggestion, Mr Oakley,' said Lord Cooling, 'but how, exactly, does one "keep 'em outside"? According to my short experience, when they are least wanted they possess a positively leech-like habit.'

'Like this,' responded Oakley, and turned to the spearmen. '*Choo!*' The spearmen wheeled round and withdrew to a distance, though they seemed a little sad about it. 'Cannibal for "Buzz off." You can remember it by thinking of the last half of a sneeze. I've written out a little conversation guide, by the way, to help you with some of the choicer expressions. I'll give it to you later.'

'Do they do everything you tell them to?' inquired Haines, as they moved towards the hut.

'No, only the little things,' answered Oakley. 'Going away and coming back, and stunts like that. But they'd pull their own ears off if the High Priest issued the instruction.'

'I don't think I'm going to like the High Priest,' commented Cooling.

'I know you're not,' observed Oakley, 'but when he comes do your best to look pleasant.'

'Eh? When he comes?' exclaimed Medworth.

'Yes—that's one of the pretty tit-bits I've got to tell you about.'

They entered the hut. It was dim, and had a vaguely vault-like smell.

'*Hardly* the Ritz!' murmured Ruth with a little shiver.

'My sleeping quarters are hardly the Savoy,' said Oakley, 'but that's what I call 'em. Passes the time. However, if you're keen on accuracy, we'll christen this the Bastille. Well, sit down, children, while Papa tells you his bedtime story. Oh, I say, do they still have bedtime stories? I used to rather like those Uncles and Aunts.'

'Try to keep your mind from straying, Mr Oakley,' suggested Cooling. 'The point that immediately concerns us is seating capacity. What do we sit on?'

'Ourselves,' replied Oakley and squatted.

One by one, the rest followed suit. The days of luxury, even of simple comfort, seemed very long ago.

'Well, here goes,' began Oakley. 'We'll take things in their order. First, our jewel, Ben. He is seated at this moment—I devoutly hope—on the Chief's throne in Buckingham Palace.

The Chief's first twelve wives—this year's rating—have all done their salaams, and I have told the Chief that Oomoo wishes to be disturbed as little as possible—'

'That is probably a correct interpretation of his wish,' murmured Cooling.

'—and that he and his wives are to remain in their own half of the bee-hive.'

'Bee-hive?' queried Smith.

'Buckingham Palace—the Chief's hut—is shaped like a bee-hive,' explained Oakley kindly.

'Thank you,' muttered Smith. 'If you spoke plainly, p'r'aps we understand you!'

Oakley smiled dryly. There was a lugubrious quality in his rare smiles that acted on spirits like blotting-paper. The same quality impregnated his tone and his grim and mirthless humour.

'There will be plenty of plain speaking before long, Mr Smith,' he answered. 'Meanwhile, be grateful for all you do not understand.' He turned back to the others. 'Oomoo will remain where he is until he is conveyed to the Golden Temple. I am doing my best to ease his agonies.'

'It seems to me we all owe you a great deal, Oakley,' said Haines.

'Hear, hear!' added Ruth. 'How is the poor little man standing his agonies?'

Oakley paused before replying. Ruth's loveliness disturbed him. When he looked at her he felt like a man who had decided to die in a ditch and whose decision was weakened by a cool and refreshing breeze. She made him *feel* again—slightly. And he had done with feeling. He was an observer, recording his own vanishing history with detached complacency; a fatalist, watching and waiting for the inevitable; dead already, in so far as individual physical effort was concerned, and alive only in his queer mental attitude. He mustn't feel. Quite definitely, it would be dangerous and fruitless to feel. So he rested his eyes deliberately on the beautiful face to prove to himself that his sluggish blood was not quickening.

'What are you staring at me like that for?' Ruth challenged him, suddenly reddening. 'I don't think I like it!'

'Then girls have changed since my time on earth,' responded Oakley. 'I was testing my heart-beats. Quite steady, thank God! You asked me something. Oh, yes. You asked me how Ben was standing it? To be quite honest, I'm not sure. At one moment I think he's going to shriek the show away, at the next he comes out with some piece of quaint philosophy. Enigma, that chap. Baffles me. Scared stiff, of course. Frozen. But he hangs on, and still manages to function. And—those bits of philosophy—'

'Damn it, man!' exclaimed Medworth, interrupting abruptly. 'Do you think we want to waste time on his philosophy? What's his philosophy got to do with it?'

'His philosophy is going to have the hell of a lot to do with it, if I'm any judge,' replied Oakley calmly. 'It may even upset your gold cart. But don't you want to know what I did when I left Ben?'

'Oh, carry on, carry on!'

'Thank you. You'll be interested. I received an order from the H.P. to go and report at the Temple of Gold. You gather, I take it, that when I say H.P., I do not mean Hot Potato. I went there. Amazing place. That is, you'll think so. Doesn't affect me. Make a good set for a film. And George Arliss would make a good High Priest. Good actor, that! Is he still at it? I found the High Priest in a very nasty mood. Yes, a very nasty mood. Anybody can have my job of Low Priest who wants it. He didn't say anything. He's dumb—though I sometimes wonder whether H.P. doesn't also stand for Hokus-Pokus. We have a sort of deaf-and-dumb language, and it can be quite expressive. This morning he expressed a lot of things. One was—' he paused for a moment '—a state of doubt.'

'What sort of a doubt?' asked Haines.

'A doubt about Oomoo,' answered Oakley slowly. 'He doesn't seem too sure of Oomoo's authenticity.'

'That may be awkward,' remarked Lord Cooling.

'It's going to be damn awkward,' nodded Oakley. 'If he finds out there's been any hanky-panky work, it'll put the kybosh on things for the lot of you.'

Medworth stirred uneasily. It was rather painfully easy to pick out the heroes and the cowards of the company.

'You've got a—a sort of insolence I don't like, Oakley,' he muttered. 'Damn it—when you say things like that, don't you *mind*?'

Oakley answered, looking at Ruth, 'No.'

Haines frowned, but Ruth suddenly laughed.

'That's a courageous lie, Mr Oakley,' she said. 'I'm not offended.'

'Do you think I care a penny tram-ticket whether you are or not?' inquired Oakley.

'I'll spare you the answer,' smiled Ruth, 'but you can remember that I'm trying to be courageous myself.'

'You're not doing so bad,' conceded Oakley. 'Yes, it's a pity you're here, though maybe Fate's had a spot of an idea in bringing you along. Anyhow, remember what I said. Nothing really signifies. Think of yourself. Big, eh? Important? Then think of this island, full of things that imagine they're just as big and as important. Even ants, I expect. We have ants. Dear little things with teeth. Then think of the ocean round the island. Then think of the world. Then think of the sky round the world. Think of the stars. Think of the whole blamed firmament. Think of—Infinity. And then swing back to yourself, and see whether you can hold on to that notion that you're important. It's what I do every time I eat Wooma.'

'Ah! Wooma!' exclaimed Lord Cooling. 'Your philosophy comes a little late. What is Wooma? Or—don't we talk about it?'

'Wooma is just a sickening vegetable. Nevertheless, we don't talk about it. We're talking about the High Priest, and his doubts about the non-vegetable Oomoo. The H.P. isn't merely doubtful. He's jealous. He prefers the gods in their places. If they start moving about, they won't be so manageable. So—as I implied a few minutes ago—he is going to do a very, very rare thing. He is going to leave the Golden Temple at midday—'

'At noona,' murmured Lord Cooling.

'That's right,' replied Oakley, with the nearest approach to a real smile he had yet vouchsafed. 'I rather like you, Cooling. Fact.'

Smith, all for etiquette, broke in.

'I suppose it wouldn't occur to you, would it, to use his title?' he snapped.

'Sorry, it wouldn't,' agreed Oakley. 'We shed titles here. A couple of Christmas turkeys hanging up in a shop don't call each other Lady Cluck and Lord Gobbler any more. They just wait quietly for the happy day.'

Lord Cooling cleared his throat.

'I wonder, Mr Oakley,' he said, 'whether I like you as much as you like me?'

'Doesn't matter a hoot either way,' replied Oakley. 'I shall go on rather liking you. It's the H.P. you must try and make up to, though. As I said, he's going to make a tour at noona. You can thank your stars it isn't soona. When he comes—his visits are very rare—we all go into a sort of mourning. I arrive first, sounding a gong. That's the signal for retirement. Everyone else goes into his hut and lies flat on his face. Or her face. We have both kinds here, as you may have noticed. Even the Chief does it. And flat on our faces—and you, also, flat on your faces—will be the condition until I sound the gong again. I should say it will be a good hour . . . What's the excitement?'

For Ernest Medworth had given a sudden exclamation.

'I was just thinking,' he answered, 'that we might make it a *very* good hour—a very good hour indeed! But go on, go on!'

'Thanks for the permission. While you are on your faces the H.P. will examine you. Then he will go and examine Oomoo—who, of course, will not be on his face—and he will make some tests. If you feel sorry for yourselves, forget it. Oomoo is the one who is going to have the merry time. If he survives the tests—if it were anybody else I should say there wasn't a dog's chance, but this Ben fellow—well, I don't know, he seems to have something unsinkable about him. If he survives, then it's full steam ahead for the trial tomorrow, and we may be able to work it. If he doesn't, the H.P. will develop High Pressure and become a Heated Proposition. I'm rather good at initials. Used to go in for competitions in the dear old days. Do they still have 'em? You know, they give you a list of Examples, and you have to—'

'Yes, yes, we know!' burst out Medworth. 'Shut up for a moment.' He swung round to the others. 'Look here, this visit of the High Priest isn't as bad as it sounds. Don't you see, it gives us our chance! When the fellow's finished with us we'll hop off to his Temple while he's with Oomoo, and have a squint round. We might even make a start, if there's anything movable!'

'I say, you *have* got a brain!' murmured Oakley.

'Well, I'm not quite the fool you take me for?' retorted Medworth. 'You can help to make the visit a long one, can't you? Keep him busy with those tests, as you call 'em. Everybody will be inside, you say, so we can easily slip off, and—oh, what about our guards? Do they go down on their faces, too?'

'Undoubtedly.'

'Excellent! Then it's child's play! We stay at the Temple till the second gong goes—'

'And then everybody gets up and comes out,' interrupted Ruth, 'and we walk right into them!'

'Well, confound it, it's a chance!' cried Medworth, appealing to Cooling. 'Are we going to sit here and wait for it?'

'I agree it's a chance,' said Cooling after a moment's reflection. 'I also agree that we have every right to exact payment for our uncomfortable treatment. In a British Court of Law we could claim heavy damages.'

'There you are!' exclaimed Smith. 'Trust his Lordship to give us the logic. We've got to be our own British Court of Law, eh?'

'And, of course,' put in Miss Noyes, anxious to side with the majority—it was so much easier—but finding it necessary to justify herself morally as well, 'if some of us felt that perhaps we oughtn't to take the gold, we could put it to a good use when we got back. A charity, for instance. Or a Missionary Society.'

'Good Lord, can't we forget the wretched stuff?' cried

Haines. 'Let it rip! Our first job is to get away. We'll be insane to take unnecessary risks!'

'Just lunatics,' agreed Ruth.

'I'm afraid the voting is four to two against you, Miss Sheringham,' responded Lord Cooling. 'And I am convinced that our absentee, when he turns up again, will make it five to two. No, the question before the committee is not *whether* we shall enrich ourselves, but *how* we may best do it. What is your opinion, Mr Oakley? Do you advocate a trip to the Temple?'

Oakley shrugged his shoulders.

'All the same to me,' he answered. 'It'll be your funeral.'

'That is just my point. *Will* it be a funeral?'

'The betting's in favour.'

'But—from what we gather—the betting's in favour of the funeral, either way.'

'Sure. Your only real chance of saving yourselves is through Oomoo.'

'I am remembering that theory. I am also remembering that Oomoo may constitute the British Court of Law, and spare us a lot of trouble by awarding us our compensation.'

'If Medworth were Oomoo, he would,' said Oakley. 'But here's something else to remember. *Ben*'s Oomoo. A funny little chap with, so it seems, that far, far funnier thing, a conscience. Medworth thought I was wasting my time talking about his philosophy. I commend it now to your attention. Ben's going to be the fly in your ointment, and whatever the voting is here, he has the casting vote among the whites.'

There was a short pause. Then Lord Cooling said, with gentle significance:

'Excuse me, Mr Oakley—but don't *you* interpret Ben?'

'Sure I do,' answered Oakley.

'Then,' asked Lord Cooling, the gentle significance increasing, 'doesn't that give *you* the casting vote?'

'I'm alive to your meaning,' replied Oakley.

He regarded the ground for a moment moodily. Then he rose abruptly, took a sheet of paper from his pocket, and handed it to Cooling.

'Here's that glossary I spoke of,' he said. 'You'd better study it, all of you. May be helpful.'

He began to walk away.

'Hey, wait a bit!' cried Medworth. 'Where are you off to?'

'To give a spot of advice to Oomoo,' responded Oakley, without turning his head. 'If he *doesn't* pass those tests, the one with the casting vote will be the High Priest.'

The next instant he had vanished.

11

A Language Lesson

We will shortly follow Oakley, to learn in what condition he found Ben; we will also shortly search for Ardentino, who was enduring a personal experience no less nerve-racking—an experience destined to affect both the captives and the natives on the island. But first we will wait to hear Lord Cooling read the glossary which Oakley had thoughtfully prepared. He read it aloud, then studied it for a few moments, then passed it round. It ran as follows:

Hya, Hyaya	Yes.
Nya, nyaya	No.
Sweeze	Look!
Vooloo	What do you want, what is your will?
Choo	Buzz off!
Koo	Come here!
Kawa	Silence!
Kawaka	Shut up unless you want your ears sliced!

Choom	Hurry your stumps.
Hooja	What the blazes?
Kwee	More kindly exclamation of interrogation.
Koocha	Do as I say.
Koochacha	Same, with knobs on.
Mayo	Child.
Poopoo	The verb 'to speak,' complete.
Fzzz-fzzz	The verb 'to eat.' The more the repetition, the greater the appetite.
Quass	The verb 'to drink.' (Cf. "Quaff.")
Wooma	An unpleasant vegetable. Staple diet in lean times.
Quomogee	Just water.
Lungoo	Fried knuckles.
Sula	Trial.
Domo	Tomorrow.
Toree	Temple of Gold.
Holalulala	Condition of having one's eyes taken out.
Moose	Condition of having one's head taken off.
Kim	Friend.
Zoozo	Enemy.
Owlah	Raise spears! Salute!
Ong	Go flat!
Waa-lala, waa-lala Oli O li, Waa-lala	Cannibal Common Prayer.
Beebul	Chief; King.
Kooala	High Priest.

The effect of the glossary was vaguely dampening. Medworth grunted as Lord Cooling passed it on to him, and remarked that if he had ever needed proof that Oakley was a madman, this silly tosh supplied it.

'How do we know he isn't spoofing us?' demanded Smith.

'Why should he spoof us?' replied Cooling. 'The list seems to me most convincing. Well, Medworth? Vooloo?'

Medworth studied the sheet, and then let out savagely:

'Moose kooala!'

'My sentiments exactly,' smiled Cooling. Ruth Sheringham did not smile. She was looking at the word 'Child.'

12

Preparations for a Test

Mr Robert Oakley, late of Eton and Oxford, and in his mood late of the very world his feet still trod, walked through the village of skulls in a disturbed frame of mind, and it was perhaps a coincidence that, while Ruth Sheringham—partly responsible for the disturbance—was vaguely wondering why he had included the word *mayo* in his glossary, he was pausing to regard one of the prettiest children on the island. It was the child Ben himself had noticed on his journey to the Chief's dwelling.

The child was about thirteen years of age. She had been ten when Oakley's half-drowned and battered body had been washed up on the island, and she was the first pleasant thing he had noticed. Later, he had noticed a few other pleasant things. Some of the dusky island dancing girls were undoubtedly beautiful, and he had to admit they would not have disgraced a London revue. Then the Chief, at odd moments, had a quite engaging smile. Beneath the atrocious habits of the natives—their laziness, their licentiousness, their lack of party manners, and their idolatry—lurked a simple, almost pathetic sincerity. It lay behind their frenzied patriotism and religious fervours, and their unswerving adherence to the gods and the High Priest. In the High Priest alone had Oakley failed to discern any human spark.

But as time had progressed, the intolerable strain and discomfort and terror of the island had nearly completed the head-damage he had received during the wreck, and he had realised that he was on the point of insanity. He had to go mad or go numb, and just in time he chose the latter alternative. He ceased to react to his surroundings. He died, deliberately, before his death, retaining as his one possession the dry fragments of an ironic, detached sense of humour. He ceased to notice that the dancing girls were beautiful. He was no longer touched by the Chief's occasional smile. He watched the pretty child grow without interest. He smashed his fear, and in doing so everything else went with it.

It is possible that the crack on his head, delivered by a falling mast some days before he floated to the island, may have begun the ultimate damage. There was no Harley Street doctor on the island, however, to diagnose his case. The only doctor available visited his patients with coloured straws through his nose . . .

But now there was a gentle stirring again, like the impulse of life that brings spring with its glory and chaos through the frozen surface of winter. Ruth, whose voice whispered memories and whose eyes recalled old dreams, was a little itch in his mind. Ben—that miserable idiot, Ben!—gave him alarmingly friendly feelings . . . And here he was looking at the pretty little girl, and realising her charm once more.

'This won't *do,* my child!' thought Oakley. refusing to respond to her smile. 'You're only an insignificant atom like me. You don't matter!'

He walked on abruptly, with a strong desire to find a rock and bash his head against it.

The child looked after him. She liked the Low Priest, though she didn't know why.

He reached the end of the village, and entered the Chief's hut which he had christened Buckingham Palace. He wondered whether Ben would still be inside, or whether he would have fled. Staring towards the throne he beheld an odd sight. Ben was standing stiffly with arms outstretched. One arm was pointing ahead of him, the other from his side. He looked something like a signpost. Fortunately there were no eyes other than Oakley's to behold him.

'What's this?' asked Oakley quietly. 'Your daily dozen?'

Ben's arms dropped, and he sat down hastily on his seat.

'You didn't see me come in, did you?' continued Oakley, still keeping his voice low. 'S'pose I'd been somebody else?'

'Well, didn't I look orl right?' muttered Ben. 'I was practisin'.'

'What for?'

'Dif'rent posishuns. I gits stiff. And then don't I seem silly sittin' like a waxiwork and never movin'? I thort if I could find one or two dif'rent posishuns wot looked a bit noble like, it might 'elp.'

'You haven't moved from your seat, have you?' inquired Oakley.

'Well—yer saw me standin' jest nah,' answered Ben, rather uneasily.

'I mean, you haven't *left* your seat? Come away from it?'

'Oh!'

'That means you have?'

'Well—I 'ad a poke rahnd once.'

'Don't blame you. But it was a mistake. What happened? No, wait a minute!'

97

He moved towards the curtain to the inner chamber.

'Tha's right, tell 'em not ter come in fer a bit,' whispered Ben. 'I'm bizzy.'

'I've got something else to tell them,' replied Oakley. 'And to tell you, too. Sit tight for five minutes, and don't move an eyelash.'

Ben grunted, and reverted to his waxwork pose. Oakley disappeared through the curtain. In less than the five minutes he returned.

'Keep steady,' he murmured. 'You're going to see a pretty sight.'

He stood aside. Then the rush curtain parted again, and the Chief emerged. His twelve wives followed. In single file they marched across the floor without pausing, and vanished through the outer curtain.

'O.K.,' said Oakley. 'Loosen up.'

'Well, I'm blowed!' exclaimed Ben in astonishment. 'Course you're a bloomin' majishun! 'Owjer manidge to pour 'em out?'

'I'll tell you in a moment,' answered Oakley. 'But let's hear your news first, if you have any.'

''Ow long 'ave we got?' asked Ben.

'About an hour,' replied Oakley.

'Go on!' cried Ben, and then suddenly clapped his hand over his mouth. The loudness of his exclamation alarmed him. 'Wot abart the blokes ahtside?' he whispered.

'They've gone for a walk, too. We're quite alone. Do you want to stretch your legs?'

'Do dawgs like sossidges?' grinned Ben and leaped from the seat.

As he reached the ground his legs gave under him, and Oakley caught him.

'Tha's funny,' blinked Ben. 'Me knees is orl wobbly like. You know—they ain't there.'

'Run about and see if you can find them again,' suggested Oakley, releasing him carefully.

'No fear. I'd go over—I feels worse 'n I did on the ship. I b'leeve I've bust me knee-caps 'oldin' 'em tight. Or p'r'aps it's bein' 'ungry. 'Unger starts in yer stummick and then goes dahn ter yer legs.' He rubbed his knees. The blood began to circulate once more. ''Ooray! They're comin' back!'

'But haven't you had any food?' asked Oakley. 'Didn't they bring you any *wooma*?'

'Wooma! I calls it bloomer! Yus, they brought it, and I put some in me marth while they was watchin'—not quick, o' corse, but stitely like—and when I gits it in me marth I thinks "Lumme," and I puts me 'ands on me 'ead, like yer sed meant "Go away," and they goes away, and then I 'ops dahn and spits it aht in a corner. That was the time I left me seat, see?'

Oakley shook his head gloomily.

'I wonder, Ben,' he said, 'whether you're going to see this through?'

'See it through?' repeated Ben. A new look came into his eyes. 'Listen, and I'll tell yer. I've seed more things through than—than yer'd think there was. I've seed 'aunted 'ouses through, and I've seed creepin' 'ands through, and blood comin' dahn the staircase through, and I seed fices at the winder through, and murders through—not done 'em, seed 'em—and I've seed habder-cashuns through—'

'Habdercashuns?' queried Oakley.

'Yus. Them things wot one bloke steals another bloke fer a ransiom. And yer can bet yer larst button, mister, that I'm goin' ter see this through. See? Yer larst button!'

'Ben,' replied Oakley, 'I almost believe you.'

'Well, yer can,' declared Ben solemnly, 'becos' I've lived with meself orl me life and I knows meself. But I ain't goin' ter eat that blinkin' wooma! Mindjer, I'm a mug. It's a fack. Yus. I don't mind tellin' you becos' yer knows it. But there's somethink funny in me—born like, sime as Napoleon—wot carn't stop once I gits goin', and I keeps on goin' till I gits there. When things is easy, yer wouldn't notice me. Walkin' along the street in the sunshine—jest nothink. But when things goes wrong, I sticks ter it. Funny, ain't it?'

'I wish you weren't so interesting, Ben,' said Oakley. 'It's a pity.'

'Oo's int'restin'? Wotcher mean?' answered Ben. 'Oh, I see. Comic like. Well, I don't mean it like that. I'm seerious. Becos' nah I'm goin' ter tell yer somethink else—and if I'm torkin' a lot I can't 'elp it, 'cos I bin quiet so long me marth's fair bustin'. Where was I? Oh, yus. Somethink else. I'm goin' ter see this through like wot I sed, but it ain't the way yer think. I've bin workin' it aht, sittin' ere and gettin' accalermetized—'

'Accalermetized?'

'I say, yer 'ave fergot yer English, aincher? Accalermetized. Gittin' used ter a thing. Settlin' dahn like. Well, I'm settlin' dahn like, and it's come ter me—doncher larf—it's come ter me that p'r'aps is Fite. P'r'aps I was meant ter be 'ere. Look at 'em orl! Hignorosses. Don't know nothink. P'r'aps the *real* Gawd 'as sent me—see wot I mean?—ter teach 'em abart 'im, by easy stiges. Any'ow,' said Oomoo, '*that's* wot I'm goin' ter do—*that's* wot I'm goin' ter see through and *that's* wot I'm tellin' yer. Not meanin', o' corse, ter be blasfemious.'

Oakley groaned, while Ben paused for breath.

'Wot's the matter?' asked Ben anxiously. 'Aincher goin' ter 'elp me?'

'I guessed you were going to be a trouble, Ben,' replied

Oakley. 'I see I was right. You want me to help you to perform the impossible—believe me, old chap—the impossible—and I dislike effort. Particularly useless effort. Effort is energy. Energy is heat. Heat is life. Life is feeling, minding, worrying, being hopeful, being, dashed, being courageous, being afraid, being terrified—loving, hating, laughing, shrieking—joy, agony. And here, Ben—only agony. *Agony!*'

He paused. He held up his hand and regarded it. He found it, to his relief, steady.

'I don't git yer,' murmured Ben swallowing.

'Don't try to,' answered Oakley. 'Forget it. We have been having a little dream, Ben, you and I, but now it is over. Let us be practical again. You have talked quite enough, and you will now be a good chap and confine yourself to short answers. This meal of wooma. The Chief was not supposed to watch you. How did it happen that he stayed?'

'I don't s'pose I give 'im time ter go.'

'I understood that you were stately?'

'Tha's right. Stitely and quick.'

'What happened after you had got rid of the Chief—'

'And 'is wives.'

'Oh, the whole family?'

'Yus. In they comes, like a 'en with its chicks. That larst one's a bit of a mess, ain't she?'

'What happened after you got rid of them and, also, the wooma?'

'Eh? Oh! I come back to the seat, see?'

'Your knees were not so weak that time?'

'Yus, they was. It was then they starts feelin' funny. I 'ad ter come back on 'em.'

'Are you feeling any better now?'

'No. Yus. I dunno.'

'Well, can you get back to your seat now, without walking on your knees?'

'I dunno.'

'Have a shot. Or shall I help you?'

'No, let's see 'ow she goes.'

He returned to the throne shakily.

''Ome!' he announced. 'Coo, wot a gime!'

'Be careful about "Coo," Ben,' warned Oakley.

'Eh? Wotcher mean?'

'I am telling you what "Coo" means on this island. It means, "Come here."'

'Coo! I mean, Lumme!'

'That is preferable. Lumme is not down in our dictionary. Well, proceed. What happened after you had returned to your seat on your knees?'

'Well, they keeps poppin' in—not the knees—and so I keeps puttin' me 'ands on me 'ead, and then they keeps poppin' aht agine.'

'And is that all your news?'

'Yus, barrin' the gittin' stiff, and the thinkin' wot I've jest told yer.'

'But you are going to forget that.'

'No, I ain't. I've mide up me mind. Wot abart the others? Did yer give them me messidge abart the gold?'

'I implied your standpoint.'

'Wot's that? Me toes?'

'You are very trying, Ben. One of these days a tragedy will happen. You will make me laugh. I must avoid you. I told them you did not care much for their idea about the gold.'

''Ow did they tike it?'

'Two of them agreed with you—'

'I knows which *they* was!'

102

'The others gave you the veto.'

'Did they! Well, I'll give 'em one back!'

'What?'

'Wot you sed.'

'Let us start again. The others are determined to get hold of the gold if they can—or, rather, some of it—and they expect you to assist them at the trial tomorrow.'

'Oh! 'Ow?'

'By making it a divine order from Oomo.'

'They can expeck!'

'Meaning you will refuse?'

'I'm a gawd o' storm, ain't I? Not o' thievin'!'

'The storm is coming.'

'It can, fer me.'

'I anticipated your refusal. So did they. In fact, anticipating it, they suggested—'

Oakley paused abruptly. Was it expedient to inform Ben of their suggestion? It occurred to Oakley, as he watched Ben's eyes and noted the queer light in them, that it would not be expedient. If Ben proceeded with his mad ambition to reform the natives, a certain amount of licence might indeed be necessary when interpreting Oomoo's signs. Oakley's advantage would be weakened by Ben's foreknowledge of it.

'Wot did they sergest?' asked Ben.

'That they would have to do without you,' said Oakley. 'And, as I told them, you may not be in a position to help them at the trial, even if you want to—which brings me to my main point, Oomoo. I have seen the High Priest. Would you like to see him, too?'

'Wot, that bag o' black bones?'

'The bones aren't black.'

'No, but the bag is. I ain't goin' ter see 'im!'

'I'm afraid you'll have to—'

'At the trial, yer mean? Well, I ain't goin' ter see 'im, not even then.'

'How will you manage it?'

'Shut me eyes.'

'If you do that, he will grow even more suspicious.'

'More wot?'

'Suspicious.'

''Oo's 'spishus?'

'I am telling you. The High Priest.'

'Go on!' exclaimed Ben, trying not to feel a draught. 'Wot's 'e gotter be 'spishus abart? I'm doin' it orl right, ain't I? And, any'ow, 'e ain't seed me yet.'

'No,' answered Oakley. 'But he is coming to see you very soon—'

''Ere, 'old 'ard!' interrupted Ben. 'I thort yer told me 'e never lef' 'is temple?'

'I told you he rarely left his temple. He evidently regards this as a special occasion.'

'Blimey!' muttered Ben. 'Tell 'im I'm aht!'

'I'm afraid he knows you're in. He is coming at midday or, as we have it here, when the shadows are smallest—and he is going to test you.'

'Wot's that? Test me?' gasped Ben.

'To prove whether you are human or divine. It won't be fun, but—well, we'll go on hoping.'

'I'm 'oping' 'ard,' murmured Ben. 'Wot's these 'ere tests goin' ter be? Will 'e jest prod me, like?'

'I don't know. Unfortunately there's no precedent.'

'Yer mean, if there was, 'e'd stop it?'

'What?'

'Well, if there ain't a precedent, there's a chief, ain't there? Can't 'e stop it? 'E knows I'm Oomoo.'

Oakley smiled rather sadly.

'The Chief couldn't stop the High Priest. No one on the island can stop the High Priest—except Oomoo himself. So your job is to see that you remain Oomoo while the tests are going on. I'll be here, to do what I can.'

'Thank Gawd fer that! Git the Chief back, too—e's on my side.'

'That wouldn't be in the rules. When the H.P. leaves the Temple, I'm the only one who is allowed to see him. All the rest, including the Chief, have to be out of the way. That's how I packed the Chief and his wives off just now. I told them they must go at once, and got rid of them early. When I leave you, I shall walk through the village calling "Kooala"—'

'Wot's that?'

'High Priest. That will be the first warning. Then I shall meet the H.P. at the Temple and return with him, sounding my gong. There won't be a soul about. They will all be in their huts, lying flat.'

'Where'll the Chief be? 'E ain't in 'is 'ut?'

'He has a second residence where he keeps the wives he is not using. I sent him there. He'll probably come back with a new selection. The H.P. will visit the prisoners first, then come on here. And—well, that's as far as I can tell you. Maybe it won't be as bad as it could be.'

'That's nice,' said Ben. ''Ow bad could it be? 'E ain't goin' ter cut me 'ead orf ter see if it jumps back, or anythink silly like that, is 'e?'

'That is hardly likely. Especially if you adopt the right attitude.'

'Adopt a wot?'

'If you keep dignified—stand-offish—"stitely."'

'Tha's right,' nodded Ben, a gleam of hope dawning. A very tiny gleam. 'Stitely. Arter orl, if I am a gawd, I *am* a gawd, well, ain't I, and a gawd wouldn't put up with no monkey-tricks!'

'You've got the idea exactly,' answered Oakley. 'It's precisely what I was going to advise you to do.'

'Yus, come ter think of it, p'r'aps it won't be so bad,' continued Ben struggling to increase his hope. 'See, if 'e comes too close, I can stick on a nexpreshun meanin', "Go thou away!" Otherwise, 'Op it. Like this 'ere.'

Oakley studied the expression.

'That ought to send him away,' he admitted. 'The High Priest is pretty sure to try and frighten you—that will probably be one of his tests—but I'm not sure, Ben, that you won't win.'

'I'll 'ave a good shot,' Ben promised fervently. 'I got one nexpreshun even worse'n that, but I won't show yer 'cos it 'urts. Torkin' o' which—there won't be any pine, will there? Boilin' water, or stickin' yer with a knife ter see if yer squeak? 'Cos I squeak easy . . . Oi! Wot's that?'

Oakley raised his head. From the height on which the Temple stood came an ominous clang.

'Confound the fellow!' he muttered. 'That's the Priest's gong.'

'Wot's 'e sahndin' it for?' asked Ben.

'For me. I wonder if anything's happened? Or is he just growing impatient? It's not noon yet.' He shrugged his shoulders. 'Perhaps it's as well. The sooner it begins, the sooner it'll be over. I must go.'

'Oi! 'Arf a mo'!' gasped Ben as Oakley turned towards the exit. 'Do yer mean that the—the nex' time I see yer, 'e'll be along with yer?'

'That's what I mean, sonny,' replied Oakley. 'Good luck.'

'I'm 'avin' so much luck,' answered Ben, 'I don't know where ter put it.'

Oakley walked to the curtain, then suddenly stopped.

'Of course, you can take a chance and scoot, if you want to,' he said.

'Scoot yer grandmother!' retorted Ben. 'I'm seein' it through, ain't I?'

'I've a hunch you are,' said Oakley.

13

The Misery of Ardentino

The difference between Ben and Richard Ardentino was that Ben was a coward and looked it, whereas Ardentino was a coward and didn't. The advantage was on Ben's side, for he had no appearance to keep up. But Ardentino did not worry about appearances until he had put a considerable distance between his splendid frame and the unpleasant folk he was flying from. Then he paused, partly for breath, and partly to commune with himself.

The necessity for keeping up appearances came flooding back. Ardentino was never alone. There was always an unseen audience watching him, admiring him, and eagerly observing all his actions, and he now had to explain to this unseen audience why he had left his companions in the lurch and effected a strategic retreat. As, later, he might also have to explain to the companions.

He found his reason easily. He was a skilled logician in the art of self-exoneration. He had retreated so that one at least of the party would still be free to manœuvre, and to contrive the rescue of the rest.

'Suppose I had stayed?' said his thoughts to his film fans, although they had never seriously doubted him, or he their allegiance. 'What good would that have been? I should just have been caught with the others, and I should now be equally useless! Our chances of ultimate escape would have been jeopardised. No! I will go further! They would have been utterly ruined! It was my *duty* to avoid capture, even at the risk of a charge of cowardice. Observe, I face the world! Greatly as I disliked it, I had—so to speak—to run away!'

He felt considerably better. He duped himself as well as his unseen audience. He was a part in many of his films—a hero temporarily misunderstood. He was on home ground.

The whitewashing eased him mentally but not physically. Indeed, his physical plight was desperate. He was breathless and fatigued and although for the moment he was in a little sheltered, rocky bay, at any instant a native might appear, or a spear or arrow might flash into his torn shirt from an unknown source. He liked open shirts, but he felt his shirt just now was a little too open.

Hunger added its unpleasant pangs. The one advantage of freedom was that it deprived him of a prisoner's diet. Richard Ardentino was in a mood to eat anything, without inquiries.

He waited for a minute or two, under an overhanging rock. There was no sign of his pursuers. He did not know, and lost much comfort by his ignorance, that the spearmen who had defaulted by permitting him to escape had decided to assume, for their own honour, that he had never existed, and that they had had one less to guard. The startling incident of Oomoo had certainly confused the count.

Presently he left the overhanging rock, and continued on his uncertain way. In due course he would save his companions, but he was in no immediate hurry to do so. The farther away he got, the better he would be able to think how best to return.

He stuck to the coastline till the sea licked a projecting cliff and forced him inland. Trees, strange and unfriendly, rose about him. They grew thicker, and almost shut out the light. The branches were having all-in wrestling with clinging, winding, drooping vegetation. He seemed to be wandering through a dim green mist.

Through the mist, illuminated by a patch of unnatural sunlight that had somehow found and pierced an opening, some little points of red came into his vision. Berries? Yes, berries! He hastened forward, and nearly toppled into the bush. Regaining himself, he stared at the berries.

To eat or not to eat—that was the question! Hunger beat discretion, and he ate. They looked rather like raspberries, and he pretended with all his force that they were.

He wandered on a little less happily. The necessity for some plan increased with his inability to create one. Something else increased also. An unpleasant sensation in his stomach. He discovered, with a sudden terror he made no attempt this time to explain to his invisible audience, that they had not been raspberries. He sat down to think about it. Then he lay down, to try and not think about it. We will not describe the next few minutes of Richard Ardentino.

When he rose, his impotence sat upon him like a weight. He was easily the most miserable man on the island. The forest stifled him, and he groped his way down a track that, he hoped, led out of it. He longed for the sea again; felt it would refresh him. The sea had tossed him into this predicament, yet it also offered the only route to peace and familiar things. As he glimpsed a little space of blue he searched it eagerly for a ship. It turned out that he was searching the sky. But the sea came into view a few minutes later, and the track became more open and sandy. He was about to burst on to the shore—he was running without realising it—when he pulled up sharply, and his heart nearly stopped beating.

He was approaching another sheltered bay, but this time a larger one, and even more securely screened. Great, stark cliffs jutted far into the water on either side, and the only land entrance to the spot seemed to be the track he was descending. But it was not the bay itself that interested him. It was the population in it. A population he reckoned at about a hundred.

Their colour was similar to the colour of the natives he had already seen, yet there was something different about them. Even in that agonising moment of discovery, he sensed the difference. They were grouped near the sea's edge, with their backs to him, staring at a large canoe that was creeping round the right-hand cliff. It was this preoccupation that saved Ardentino's life.

Behind them lay stacks of spears and bows. Also, drawn up high on the beach, half a dozen other canoes. One appeared to be smashed. The approaching boat glided silently round the jut. The men themselves were equally silent. They made gestures. If they spoke, Ardentino could not hear them. It was the nearest approach to nightmare yet.

The boat slid towards the soft sand, accelerating suddenly and carving the water with the quick precision of a surgeon's knife. It touched the sand. Hands stretched out and seized it. Backs began to turn.

Ardentino turned likewise, and began to fly back into the forest. His legs were like lead. He hit a tree, and clambered up it. The tree was the second thing that saved his life. He

111

never knew how he managed that climb; only that he managed it, and found a leafy sanctuary. He sat down in a cup-shaped seat, formed by kindly branches, and closed his eyes. He gave up trying to be a hero, and therefore came a little nearer to being one.

'What is to be, is to be,' thought Ardentino, sinking into gloomy philosophy. 'Anyhow, there's nothing I can do now but wait.'

There was a tiny gap in his green screen, and at first he covered this with a large leaf; but presently, when the strain of hearing nothing and seeing nothing became too great, he carefully removed the leaf and substituted his eye. The canoe had now been beached, and was being carried to a sheltered spot among the rocks. The other boats were also being carried to the same spot, and soon not one remained in sight. During this manœuvre, two men crouched at the foot of the track, looking into the forest, and perfectly motionless.

Now they were joined by ten others. All had bows and arrows. After a short, whispered consultation, the ten men entered the forest, the two original sentries staying at their post. The forest track passed within a few feet of Ardentino's tree, and he hastily replaced the leaf and stopped breathing. After a while he discovered that you have to breathe to live, so he resumed the process. His breaths sounded, amid the forest silence, like those of a grampus. He shut his eyes, but it produced little consolation, for he visualised the stealthy march almost as clearly as though he were actually seeing it.

Something stirred near his head. He heard a sudden pinging sound. It was followed by a violent squawk, and the something fell with a flutter.

Then silence again.

Had the men reached the tree? Were they standing under

it? Had they gone beyond it, and vanished? So securely was he embowered that he could not answer these questions; but when he risked another glance through his peep-hole towards the beach he saw that the two sentries were still at their crouching posts, combing the track with ruthless eyes, and he knew that to attempt to change his quarters was impossible.

He wondered whether he was destined to remain in the tree for the remainder of his life—and how long the remainder would be.

And now a new terror added itself to those already existing. He began to get drowsy. Once his head nodded, and he came to with a violent start. 'My God!' he thought. 'I mustn't go to sleep!' If he slept, he would be sure to fall off his perch. But he nodded again, came to again, and nodded again. And the last time he had a dream which, later on, he rechristened a prevision.

He dreamt he was in the Temple of Gold, and that the men on the beach were attacking it.

He came out of the dream in a sweat. For a moment he did not know where he was. Then, as knowledge dawned, he struggled against it, trying to convert the forest into a bedroom.

Having failed to remodel reality to suit his own convenience, he took a look at reality. The beach was deserted. The sentries had gone. Not a living thing was in sight.

14

The High Priest Calls

Meanwhile, Robert Oakley was reaching the Temple of Gold in response to the High Priest's summons.

The High Priest's appearance was quite as unpleasant as Oakley had depicted it to Ben. Although a white robe clothed most of his skin, and his skin clothed all of his skeleton, it was the skeleton that impressed itself upon the beholder of the outer casings. But as life is mainly what you make it, so people—and even skeletons—are largely what you make them, and it was many moons since the High Priest had struck terror into Oakley's breast. He was to Oakley merely a flat picture on a canvas. Not a picture one would have chosen, perhaps, if one had been the artist, but still a picture. Two dimensional. Like everything else.

We shall presently see the High Priest through many eyes. Through Smith's and Elsie Noyes's as a nightmare to be fled from: through Ruth's and Haines's as a nightmare to be faced; through Medworth's as a damned impossibility; through Cooling's as an inconvenient reality that might be vastly entertaining in a cage; through Ben's—well, let that reveal itself. Through Oakley's he was a conception of the past. Already finished with. Poof!

It was not quite so easy to poof the High Priest on this particular morning, however, as he stood outside the Temple. His white robe glared like an evil wraith in the ruthless sunlight. His long, scraggy neck, looking somehow twisted, and partially concealed by wisps of beard (the beard's one good office), rose out of the whiteness to form a channel that was surely choked between mind and heart. Above the neck was a head that should never have existed. A mother he must have had, but she had long departed this life in shame. His eyes burned with an inherent hatred of everything saving the tortured spark that was himself. They said, 'I rule what I despise. When I am dead, my skull will be the skull of skulls.' They spoke the truth.

All these things Oakley had learned and digested. They were the familiar accompaniment to his day. Yet now as he returned the High Priest's gaze, with eyes as dull as the priest's were live, he sensed a difference. Was it in the priest, or was it in himself? He did not know, and he tried hard not to care. His thoughts crystallised themselves into three words: 'Poor old Ben!'

The High Priest made a sign of indignant impatience. Oakley pointed to the sun, not yet at its greatest elevation. The High Priest made a sign that his own height sufficed; that he, indeed, was higher than the sun, and had a greater power to burn and blast miserable mortals who kept him waiting. Oakley made a sign that, dash it all, he *was* a Low Priest, and that ought to count for something. The High Priest made a sign that it counted for nothing; less than nothing; that a Low Priest was as low as a High Priest was high. Oakley made a sign that he had been busy and that he could not possibly know that the High Priest was waiting if the High Priest did not stick to his arrangements. The High Priest made a sign that it was the duty of a Low Priest to interpret a High Priest, just as it was the duty of a High Priest to interpret Oomoo, Washa, Mung, and all the other inhabitants of the sky; further that Oakley was an earthy toad, a crawling slug, and a decaying worm. Oakley made a sign implying, 'O.K., darling,' lay on his stomach, touched the priest's toes with his forehead, resisted an almost uncontrollable impulse to seize the toes and tip their owner over, and rose.

Then Oakley took a hand-gong from a niche in a rock by the entrance, turned, and began descending the steep hill towards the village, chanting:

'Kooala—Kooala—Kooala.'

The kooala waited until Oakley was some fifty yards ahead, before slowly following, keeping the same distance between them.

The villagers heard them coming. So did the prisoners in the compound. So did Ben, on his throne in the Chief's hut. Oakley had developed his chanting to a fine art, and was rather proud of the manner in which he could make the greatest noise with the least effort. His voice penetrated to the village long before he himself reached it. When he entered the village he sounded his gong, but this was mere form, for the villagers were already in their hovels and the roads were empty.

The single file, composed of two separated men and a voice, passed the Chief's hut, but did not pause there. The Chief's hut with its distinguished occupant was the *pièce de resistance*, reserved for end. There was no pause until the village had been left behind, the twisting road beyond had been covered, and the compound had been reached. Then, as he entered, Oakley stopped, and waited for the High Priest to draw up.

The native guards were on their faces. The six prisoners, however, were erect. Oakley smiled faintly.

'Kooala coming, sweethearts,' he said. 'He won't like seeing you in the perpendicular.'

'I'm not going to lie on my face for anybody!' chattered Elsie Noyes.

'No, no, it wouldn't be British,' agreed Smith in a voice that was scarcely British.

'But it might be wise?' inquired Cooling cynically.

'Wise be damned!' muttered Medworth, and then suddenly changed his tone. 'Yes, but after all, what about it? We want to put him off his guard, you know? Throw dust in his eyes?'

Ruth whispered to Haines, 'I think Miss Noyes came out of that best!'

They remained standing, their eyes glued on the entrance. Only one more remark was made before the High Priest appeared. It was a characteristic one from Oakley.

'Any good shows on in London?' he asked.

Then the High Priest arrived.

Reaching the entrance he stopped, and regarded the prisoners; at first collectively, then separately, each in turn. It was the most unpleasant scrutiny they had ever endured. It beat Miss Noyes.

'Don't you look at me!' she gasped ridiculously, with a little shriek.

The High Priest turned to Oakley. Oakley translated the remark. The High Priest advanced to Miss Noyes, who backed into Smith. Smith grasped her, and held her firmly in front of him.

The High Priest stopped again, then made a sign.

'What does that mean?' inquired Cooling.

'It means, "Prostrate yourselves before the Chosen of the Gods, white spawn,"' translated Oakley. 'What do I tell him?'

'I should say that what you tell him is obvious,' answered Cooling. 'A little sentence of three words, the last beginning with H.'

'Weema nya stooka,' said Oakley, gesticulating to the High Priest. 'Stooka swarli.'

The High Priest's eyes blazed.

'Excuse me, but did you really tell him that?' asked Cooling a little anxiously.

'I softened the blow,' replied Oakley. 'I told him that white people never lie down unless it is to sleep.'

The High Chief was gesticulating again. He gesticulated for some while. Oakley translated:

'The High Priest warns you that if you are disobedient you will soon lie down for your longest sleep, but, for the moment, he defers to your heathenish habits. He is now about to touch you, to make sure you are real, for he finds you as hard to believe as you doubtless find him. While he touches you, you will remain motionless, and you will not touch back.'

'What would happen,' asked Medworth as the High Priest advanced again, 'if I boxed his ears?'

'It would happen very quickly,' answered Oakley.

No one boxed his ears. They submitted to the ordeal. Happily it did not take long. The High Priest only paused at Smith, whose fat flabby arm seemed to interest him, and at Ruth. That time he did nearly get his ears boxed.

'Find me interesting?' asked Ruth as he peered at her closely.

'I'd hold on to that fist of yours, if I were you,' Oakley murmured to Haines. 'It won't do any good.'

'Yes, steady, Tom,' said Ruth. 'I can stand it.'

'So can I, so long as he keeps his dirty hands off you!' muttered Haines. 'But if he starts pawing you again—'

'Shut up, shut up!' growled Medworth. 'He's getting ratty!'

Perhaps the High Priest gathered, without interpretation, the sultry undercurrent, and decided that it might be wiser to satisfy his curiosity more completely in the Temple, where he was on home ground. The natives obeyed him implicitly, but these white monstrosities were less trained. Whatever his reasoning, he suddenly withdrew, and beckoning Oakley to the entrance discoursed with him volubly by his peculiar method. The silent conversationalists were watched by the prisoners, who gathered that some little trouble was on. Oakley, for once, appeared to be objecting. At last, however, the High Priest made a gesture of finality, and Oakley shrugged his shoulders.

'Well, what was all that about?' asked Lord Cooling, admirably concealing a nasty flutter around his heart.

'Oh—just that we're going,' answered Oakley.

'Try again,' suggested Cooling.

Oakley stared at the ground for a moment, then suddenly looked at Haines.

'I still think Ben is your best chance,' he said. 'I'll know whether the chance is scotched or not in a few minutes. But meanwhile I'm taking no responsibility, and if any of you want to try a spot of *sauve qui peut*, don't say I'm stopping you.'

He swung round on his heel and vanished.

The High Priest did not follow him immediately. He stood in the entrance, with his back to them. Tom took a soft step forward. He felt Ruth's detaining hand on his arm, and at the same moment the priest's white sleeve fluttered slightly, and something long and thin it concealed slid down a little way. From below the folds protruded for an instant a sharp gleaming point.

Then the High Priest slipped out of the doorway, and vanished after Oakley.

'Well?' said Cooling. 'Are we glad he called?'

'What I want to know is what that fool Oakley meant,' exclaimed Smith a little more loudly than was necessary. But one had to do something once in a while to show one had a house and paid rates.

'Yes, and why did he look at you, Mr Haines, while he said—what he did?' inquired Miss Noyes. 'That seemed to me most odd!'

'Bah, he was tipping us the wink!' retorted Medworth. 'And *I'm* going to take it—though not in the direction he meant!'

'You're going down the gold-mine, Daddy?' inquired Cooling.

'No, up into it!' grinned Medworth. 'Who's climbing with me?'

Haines turned to Ruth, and asked her gravely:

'What do *you* want to do, Ruth?' he asked.

'Oh, I'm still betting on Ben,' she answered. 'Let's sit down and play noughts and crosses!'

15

The High Priest v. Oomoo

Ben heard them coming. He had heard them coming a hundred times, but this was the time that was *it*. He screwed up his courage, or the frozen mental attitude that was his substitute for courage, and went over his lesson. It took the form of Questions and Answers.

'Nah, then, do yer know wot yer gotter do?' began the lesson.

'No,' came the prompt reply.

It was a disappointing start. The lesson proceeded, growing quicker and quicker as the approaching footsteps grew closer and closer.

'Go on, I *told* yer!'

'Wot did yer tell me?'

'I've fergot. Oh, yus. Fust thing, yer've gotter sit tight.'

'Tha's right.'

'Yer mustn't do a bunk, wotever 'appens yer mustn't.'

'Tha's right.'

''Cos why? That'd give yer away. Gawds ain't afraid o' nothink.'

'Then I ain't a gawd.'

'Nah, then, Ben, doncher start that! Corse yer a gawd!'

'Wot, me, wot never goes ter church, and with a fice like a gargle?'

'Wot's gargle?'

'I dunno, but I bin called it.'

'Well, gawds don't 'ave ter be good-lookin'. Not your kind, any'ow. I reckon yer 'ave ter look like a gargle, and if yer looks like one then that's orl right. Say it's orl right!'

'It's orl right.'

'Agine.'

'It's orl right.'

'Agine.'

'It's orl right.'

'And stop wobblin' yer knees.'

'They ain't wobblin'.'

'Then wot are they doin?'

'That's vibrashion. You know, like when a trine runs under a 'ouse.'

'Are you goin' barmy?'

'Yus. I wanter cry. I wanter go 'ome. Lumme, it's no use, I'm sweatin', and gawds don't sweat, and when the 'Igh Priest sees it 'e'll say, "Wot, you a gawd, come orf it, yer blinkin' himpioster, come orf it an' be cut hup."'

''Ere, don't think so loud!'

'Was I?'

'Yus. Yer'll be torkin' in a minit! I'm not sure that yer wasn't, 'cos when yer thinks loud it sahnds more inside yer than when yer torks sorft. Nah, listen, quick. Yer *ain't* frightened, see?'

'Tha's right.'

''Cos yer *are* a gawd, see?'

'Tha's right.'

'Yus, but I means it, 'cos I'll tell yer why. Gawd's *mide* yer a gawd.'

''Owjer figger that?'

'Are yer arter that there gold?'

'No.'

'Do yer mean no 'arm ter nobody?'

'No.'

'Ain't yer goin' ter try and do a bit o' good?'

'Yus.'

'Do yer like children?'

'Yus.'

''Ave yer ever 'urt a hanimal?'

'Not meanin' ter.'

'And look 'ere. 'Ere's somethink helse. Do yer hever stand still, sudden like, and begin thinkin' abart things yer don't know wot they are, see? Stars, like, and 'ow fur they are away, and yer mother, yer ain't fergot 'er, lumme, I wish she was 'ere, and, well, sort o' feelin's, if yer git me?'

'Tha's right.'

'And yer knuckles hitchin' like a sign o' trouble, that ain't nacheral. They're hitchin' nah. And then seem' the insides o' people—even when you 'ates 'em. "They carn't 'elp it," yer ses, "they was born that way." Whites and blacks alike. Well, there yer are. Corse, yer ain't much, reely, but yer, well, symperthetic, not meanin' ter boast, and tha's why Gawd's chosen yer. And nah that's enuff o' that, and yer goin' ter see it through, aincher, like yer sed yer was. Aincher? Aincher?'

It all happened inside ten seconds. The approaching footsteps were now very close indeed.

'There!' concluded the lesson. '*Nah* do yer feel better?'

'No,' came the reply.

The lesson ended as disappointingly as it had begun.

With his eyes fixed ahead of him, but with eye-corners alert, Ben waited during the final agonising seconds in a state of mental incoherence. If the lesson continued, it was no longer translatable. It ceased to be a word argument; it became a battle of stark emotion, pluck struggling to conquer fear, and fear hitting back.

Then, all at once, Ben was conscious that the ordeal had begun. His eye-corners, usually unbeatable, had been cheated, and someone had slipped through the outer reed-curtain, and was standing, watching him.

He knew it was not Oakley. Ben was sensitive to auras (though he did not know what the word meant), and the newcomer's aura extended to him across the gloomy space like an evil aerial tide. It enveloped him in a spiritual, hypnotising stench. His decision not to move was superfluous. He could not move.

''E's watchin' me ter see if I blink,' thought Ben.

Life resolved itself into an effort not to blink. The result on Oomoo's physiognomy was satisfactory.

By strict rules of procedure the High Priest should not have been the first to enter the Chief's hut. Oakley should have preceded him, clearing the air of pollution. But the High Priest, with the excuse that a living, moving god formed an exception, had suddenly accelerated, passed Oakley, and reached the hut a clear winner. Oakley, swearing under his breath, and also accelerating, interpreted the manœuvre as the High Priest's determination that there was not going to be any hanky-panky.

Standing behind the priest, Oakley gazed over his shoulder at unblinking Oomoo. His faith in Ben was a trifle shaken. Surely the most heathen of gods had never stared with such ghastly intentness! 'This is going to be a war!' thought Oakley, and decided he must not delay his assistance to the weaker party.

He pushed past the priest, as though blinded to the priest's indignation by religious fervour, and prostrated himself before Oomoo. Oomoo raised a hand solemnly, in recognition of the tribute, then let it fall back into his lap. Oakley rose, stood aside, and glanced towards the priest.

Now the priest advanced. Despite his doubts, this *might* be Oomoo! In that case, even a High Priest should prostrate himself to avoid the possibility of divine wrath. Reaching the throne, he lay down on his face.

''Ooray!' thought Ben. 'One ter me!'

The one lasted a long time. The priest remained on his face. Ben wondered whether he had met seccotine and got stuck. As the seconds went by and the priest did not rise, Ben's wonder changed to uneasiness. He longed to leap upon the prostrate form and squash it. There was greater probability, however, that he would get squashed.

'I know,' he reflected presently. 'I've fergot to rise me 'and.'

It was another tickle on his nose—their number was legion—that reminded him of the omission. He raised his hand, and with a subtle thumb settled the tickle. But even after that the High Priest did not move.

On the point of glancing inquiringly at Oakley for a tip, Ben desisted. It was the position of the priest's head that caused him to desist. The head seemed stretched, the neck quietly straining. Two little bright beads, that should have been directed to the ground, were just discernible beneath the expanse of forehead.

'Blimey. 'e's squintin' at me!' thought Ben. 'Tryin' ter catch me aht! Well, of orl the dirty tricks! I'm learnin'!'

At last the High Priest rose, and slipping a long, thin blade from the folds of his robe, he slashed it in the air. The priest was wily, for, he argued, if Oomoo indeed sat upon the throne, he would not interpret such movements as a threat to himself but as a preparation for some solemn rite. The innocence of the blade, however, would take a human being longer to perceive. During the air-slashing Ben said several prayers. 'Now I'm for it,' he thought, 'but I'll 'it 'im!' He survived the ordeal, however—to Oakley's secret astonishment, for once the whirling blade came within an inch of Oomoo's nose—and prepared for the next.

The next was worse.

The blade stopped whirling, and was directed towards the priest's own arm. The point entered, and came away red.

'Wot's that for?' wondered Ben. ''Ave I won, and is 'e goin' ter commit suissicide?'

The High Priest had no such intention. He was merely going to offer Ben a drop of his distinguished blood. He had taken the drop, incidentally, from a fleshy part of his arm where blood could be spared and feeling was not considerable.

The ruddy point was held out to Ben.

'Wot am I s'posed ter do nah?' thought Ben. 'Say, "Thanks very much"?'

An idea occurred to him. Gods doubtless had different tastes. Some might not like blood. He decided to be one who did not like blood, and he suddenly donned a new expression indicative of intense aversion.

The effect was definite. The High Priest sprang back. Oakley, seizing the moment, advanced quickly and clasped his hands as though in fear.

'Oomoo poopoo, Oomoo poopoo!' muttered Oakley.

'Yus, I orter poop a bit more,' thought Ben and raised his right arm high above him.

The priest hesitated. Then did a daring thing. Possibly, for a moment, he lost his head. He advanced again, determined to make his offering, thrust the blade forward, and pricked Ben's stomach.

It was only a little prick, but for all Ben knew it might develop into the final agony, so perhaps the moment that followed was the greatest of his life. He bared his teeth and smiled.

The High Priest stood motionless. He stared, and as he stared his lamp-black eyes assumed a disquieting expression. The grin seemed to fascinate him. He dropped his blade and swung round to Oakley with a gesture of fanatical triumph. The gesture indicated, 'Lowest of the low—*he likes it!*'

Was the battle won? For an instant Ben thought so, and held on to his grin, even when the priest turned back to him and responded. But Oakley knew the priest better than Ben did; his knowledge of that twisted nature was profound; and he realised that victory as well as defeat had its dangers, and that the particular form of this victory gave the priest a deadly weapon which he was showing a disposition to take.

The priest did not want a functioning god of any kind. Without the supreme authority to which he had been accustomed, life would be intolerable. A false god was preferable to a real god, since a false god was easier to deal with and dispose of, but a real god who liked pain—who grinned at his own torture as well as at the torture of others—might also be disposed of! This very grin of Oomoo's might be a cynical invitation to conclude the encumbrance of earthly form—a humorous order to send him back to carved rock! Gods had their little jests . . .

The blade was raised again. Ben nearly swooned with disappointment. Oakley, laying his hand on the priest's arm, exclaimed, 'Nya, nya!' It was the unusual emotion in Oakley's voice—the first Ben had heard, in fact—that warned him even more surely than the priest's attitude of his deadly danger.

And then the miracle happened, shattering the plans of mice and men, and shaping astonishing new courses. A clap of thunder suddenly rent the heavens above the island.

It was, of course, a mere coincidence, and the thunder possessed a thoroughly earthly meteorological explanation, but as the priest dropped his blade and fell flat, and as Oakley's mouth opened in a sort of blank wonder, Ben's fear slipped from him like a cloak. 'Wot did I say?' he communed with himself. 'If the real Gawd ain't lookin' arter me, 'oo is?'

Ben rose to his feet, hardly knowing that he did it. A new spirit had undoubtedly entered into him. He looked at Oakley, then at the prostrate priest, and jerked his thumb towards the latter. Oakley stooped, and touched the priest's shoulder.

The priest raised his head. His eyes were terrified. Fear was the only emotion that could quell him, and for the moment he was quelled. 'Wot a miser'ble blighter,' thought Ben. 'Yer see, we can orl come ter it.' He lifted both his hands towards the roof. He waved them slowly from side to side. Then he lowered them, and sat down again.

'I dunno wot it meant,' he reflected, 'but it seems ter stamp it, like.'

The High Priest rose. He made a hasty sign to Oakley, then rapidly left the hut.

'Whew!' murmured Oakley, wiping his brow. 'He's coming back, Ben—but first round to you!'

Ben hardly heard him. He was too busy feeling religious.

16

The Transition of Ben

The unexpected clap of thunder that burst over the island like a sudden exclamation mark did many things. It sent a hundred creeping warriors leaping for cover. It gave palpitations to another hundred natives who were already under cover. It nearly shot Ardentino from a tree and Medworth over a precipice. It caused Ruth's pencil to slip, losing her a game of noughts and crosses. But its greatest work, without question, was that of establishing for the time being Ben's bona fides as a god; and you or I in Ben's place might have been forgiven for scorning the idea of the meteorological explanation.

To the stolid, matter-of-fact mind of Oakley, no other explanation occurred. A meticulous study of cause and effect had reduced mystery to its minimum and had eliminated surprise. Cannibals worshipped idols. Idols needed dusting. Heads became skulls. Wooma made one sick. Englishmen played golf. Climatic conditions caused thunder . . . So he commented, after a long silence,

'Queer that you owe your life to a variation of temperature.'

'Eh?' asked Ben coming slowly out of his reverie.

'I was remarking,' said Oakley, 'that, but for the accident of that thunder-clap—happening in just that way at just that time—you would probably be dead.'

'Haccidunt?' repeated Ben solemnly. 'That wasn't no haccidunt!'

'What was it, then?' inquired Oakley.

'Stright from 'Eving, tha's wot it was,' answered Ben. 'I'm bein' looked arter.'

'Meaning, old son?'

'Wot I ses. I'm bein' looked arter. And—I ain't sure yer orter go on callin' me "old son."'

'I beg your pardon?' murmured Oakley, raising his eyebrows.

'Not that I mind fer meself,' continued Ben, 'but it's like this 'ere. Seein' as 'ow I'm bein' looked arter—and bein' give a job—I've gotter keep up me posishun. Tike King George. Yer don't see 'im playin' marbles, do yer? E'd like ter, but 'e mustn't. 'Cos why? *E's* got a job.'

'I see,' said Oakley, stroking his forehead to make sure it was still there. 'You and King George, eh?'

'Well, that's puttin' it a bit strong, like,' replied Ben, rather doubtful as to the rightness of the collaboration. 'I was on'y menshunin' 'im as a symbiol. P'r'aps I orter've sed the Bishop o' Lunnon. Yus, the Bishop o' Lunnon. 'E carn't go foolin' abart. 'E's got wot they calls a call, and when that there thunder come along, savin' me life fer a purpuss like, I reckon it called *me*.'

A disturbing notion entered Oakley's head as he listened to Ben's earnest words. Was the poor little chap going really and truly dotty? It would be a pity, but, Oakley conceded, eminently understandable.

'Ben,' he said, 'if I may still call you that—you don't *really* think you're Oomoo, do you?'

'Oomoo,' repeated Ben as though he had heard the word for the first time. 'Let's see. Oomoo. Corse, 'e's the Gawd o' Storms, ain't 'e, and there *was* that there thunder.' He shook his head. 'No, I ain't Oomoo. Oomoo's bad.'

And he spat. Oakley stroked his forehead again.

'Look here,' he remonstrated gently. 'Don't get bats. We've won the first round, as I said, but there are some more rounds coming, and we've got to keep our think-pots clear for 'em. If I mustn't call you Old Son, you mustn't spit on Oomoo. You'll undermine him. You. Him.'

'Wot's unnermine?' inquired Ben.

'Weaken him. Render him impotent. Ruin him.'

"E's a bad 'un, ain't 'e?'

'He's doing *us* a good turn.'

"E's a *bad* 'un, *ain't* 'e?'

'He has some quaint ideas.'

'Like killin', an' torcherin', an' eatin' wot ain't s'posed ter be ate?'

'So they say.'

'Yus. Well it ain't wot *I* ses, and I'm *goin*' ter rooin' 'im.'

'Ruin him, by all means,' agreed Oakley. 'It'll be one less to dust. But don't ruin him until you've used him.'

'I don't git yer,' answered Ben.

'Be a bad god, for a bit, so that it can make you strong enough to be a good god afterwards,' explained Oakley.

'No, it don't work like that,' replied Ben. 'They sed that in the war. Kill ter stop killin'. Tell lies fer the blinkin' troof. Well, the way ter 'elp a thing, so I works it aht, is ter do the thing. It's wot yer calls fithe. Mindjer, yer don't always git me torkin' like this. I got on a tub once in 'Ide Park, couldn't think o' nothink ter say, and come dahn agine. But terday—since that there thunder—somethink's got inter me. I'm wot they calls hinsipired.'

'Poor fellow,' thought Oakley. 'Right off his dot. How the deuce can I put him back on it?' But he went on trying. If Ben could be induced to forget Higher Morality for a while and to press his advantage with conventional art, there might be very satisfactory issues. He might save his grubby skin, and the fairer skin of an attractive girl might also be saved. Oakley was quite partial to Ben's ideas, and he didn't mind the Higher Morality in the least, but one had to be practical and to keep steady. 'You say that the way to help a thing is to do the thing,' he remarked.

'Yus,' nodded Ben.

'What thing are you going to do?'

'I dunno.'

'When are you going to know?'

'I dunno.'

'You're not going to wait for another clap of thunder, are you?'

'I dunno.'

'Who, exactly, do you think you are?'

'I dunno. I feels funny. P'r'aps I'm goin' ter act funny. P'r'aps I'll go inter them trances, and then come aht fer a bit ter 'ave a bite, and then go back agine. This might be the larst time I ever torks to yer proper. I dunno. I dunno nothink, 'cept that I feels funny. Yer remember when 'e pricks me stummick? Wot did yer think I was goin' ter do?'

'Scream the place down.'

'That's jest wot I thort. I 'ad me throat orl ready. But I didn't. No. Why? I jest smiled. Yus. Why?' He rose. His eyes were slightly glazed. 'Ter mike this plice a plice fit ter live in. Ter stop thievin' and killin'. Ter mike 'em orl see light! That's why I bin sent 'ere. Me, wot's nothink, 'as bin mide somethink . . . Lumme, I'm goin' orf.'

His eyes became more glazed. Oakley got ready to catch him. He wondered whether, after all, Ben's strange condition might prove more effective than mere cleverness, and whether it was mistaken tactics to argue with him.

'Right, Oomoo,' he said suddenly. 'I'll stand by you. But just remember this—for it's all that matters. Sometimes, as a poet once said, to do a great right you've got to do a little wrong. You may find it so here. You may find that these natives won't obey you—not even Oomoo—if you don't go a bit slow with them. You may find that—that you've got to take life to save life. Are you listening? You may find that unless you act in a way they can understand, you'll get no response, and that everything will go phut.' He paused. He did not know whether Ben were listening or not. And then, into his own breast, entered something strange and new. 'Ben!' he cried. 'There's a girl on board—don't forget—and *she's* the one who's in danger now!'

There was no reply. He paused abruptly. He rounded on himself.

'Hell!' he shouted. 'What's it matter?'

Then he became quiet, and the old cynical lines returned to his face, and the light died out of his eyes.

'It'll be all the same a hundred years hence, Ben,' he said.

He sat down at the foot of the throne, folded his arms, and waited.

17

Noughts and Crosses

'That's twenty-three to me and twenty-one to you,' said Ruth, drawing a line with rather weary triumph through three crosses. 'You'll have to hurry if you want to overtake me—there's only room for about three more games.'

The pencil was Haines's, and they were using the back of Oakley's glossary to write on.

Haines did not reply. As she drew the 'board' for their forty-fifth contest, he stared at her fingers abstractedly.

'Yes, they do rather need a manicure,' observed Ruth. 'I don't suppose there's a Beauty Parlour on the island . . . What were you really thinking of?'

'Your fingers,' he replied, 'though not that they needed a manicure.'

'I was thinking of this sheet of paper,' said Ruth. 'How did it get on this island?'

'I must ask Oakley,' answered Haines. 'It's terribly important.'

'Why?'

'Sorry, Ruth. That was supposed to be humour. The best

I can manage.' He gave a sudden exclamation. 'What the deuce am I doing?'

'All you can, my dear,' she returned. 'This is one of the times when doing nothing's best. But I know it's—trying.'

'Trying!' He raised his eyes from the paper and met hers. 'Of course, you're too plucky to exist!'

'I'm nothing of the sort,' she retorted, colouring slightly. 'I'm just a girl in a mess, with a lot of other people in the same mess, and trying not to make a nuisance of myself by fainting. We'll all get through this, somehow.'

'Yes—and a lot *I'll* have had to do with it!'

'That sounds like ego.'

'It is ego—though thanks for reminding me. I'm bursting with ego! Here am I, plonked in the middle of a situation that's shouting for heroics—and all I can do is to play noughts and crosses.'

'You're not even doing that,' she reminded him. 'It's your turn to start, and it's my turn to let you win. Here's the pencil.' As he took the pencil and drew a nought she added, 'But the situation *isn't* shouting for heroics, Tom. The last thing it wants is heroics. It's begging for patience which is just what you've given it. Let's have the pencil.' He handed it back to her, and she drew a cross. 'Besides—you *are* doing something.'

'What?'

'You're making the situation tolerable. Can you imagine— can you *imagine*—what it would be like—for me—if I were alone with all those others? If you weren't sitting by me at this moment playing noughts and crosses?'

He smiled.

'They are a bit difficult,' he admitted.

'Difficult? They're hopeless!' she exclaimed. They did not

hear her, for three had departed, and the fourth was asleep. 'Smith's a blight, and Medworth's a scamp—'

'And Cooling?'

'Well, I like Cooling. Perhaps I shouldn't, but I do.'

'Why shouldn't you?'

'Because he's a scamp, too. A different sort of a scamp, but a scamp. My solicitor—'

'What, have you got a solicitor?'

'Yes. He's a sort of guardian, and looks after my money for me. He told me once never to put any money into a company Lord Cooling had anything to do with. There's a tip for *you*. "Men like that ought to be in prison," he said, "but only sometimes get there." Just the same, I like him. And if ever he does go to prison, I'll send him some grapes. Your play.'

'I'd like him better,' grunted Haines, 'if he'd drop that gold standard idea. Your play.'

'It was Medworth's idea.'

'But he's backing it. Did you ever know such fools? All three of them trying to sneak up to the Temple at this moment—unless that clap of thunder's turned them back! I'll tell you one thing that's handicapping us, Ruth—making us helpless. There's no cohesion. No unity. We don't make a team. We're all sorts. If I suggest a thing, they down it. If they suggest a thing, *I* down it. The next voyage I make we'll have ship-wreck drill! Then we'll know what to do!'

'Jolly good idea, Tom. There's my cross. Now put your nought and win.'

He put his nought and won. Then he glanced towards Miss Noyes, who was snoring gently against the hut. Then he looked towards the entrance to the compound, where the native guards lay on their faces. They, too, might have been asleep for all the movement they made. They had fallen flat the moment they had heard the gong, and had not stirred since.

'Has it struck you how extraordinarily obedient these natives are?' he said. 'Like children. There must be an amazing power somewhere on the island.'

'Of course there is,' she answered. 'We've just seen it.'

'The High Priest? Yes. I wonder whether our comic stoker is going to wrest the power from him?'

'I believe he will.'

'What makes you think that?'

'Haven't any idea.'

'And what will he do with the power if he gets it?'

'That's easy. He will raise his hand, and Oakley will tell them that means, "Oomoo orders you to let the prisoners go, and to give them your largest canoe, and to fill it with food—which *they* will select—and to wish them God speed or Oomoo speed!" Then it will all happen, and we shall live happily for ever after.'

'Yes—that's the bright side.'

'I always look on the bright side.'

'I agree with the principle. But—just in case Ben isn't winning against the High Priest—let's look at the dark side.'

'All right. What do you see?'

'A scrap.'

'I can do my bit. Feel!'

She held out her arm. He felt her muscle, and approved.

'But we'd come off second best,' he said. 'So, after all, it mustn't be a scrap.'

'What's the alternative?'

'Sheer flight.'

137

'Well, my legs are as good as my arms, and I can run even harder than I can hit. But where do we run to?'

'The sea.'

'And have a bathe?'

'No, we have a boat. That big canoe you mentioned just now. We take it without the permission.'

'Where do we find it?'

Suddenly he stared at her, and hope and shame shone in his eyes.

'My God! What fools—what mugs! Why, that's our *job*, isn't it? That's our plan! Instead of wasting this time on a mad errand to the Temple of Gold, we ought to have been searching for a boat! There must be canoes somewhere, and here's our chance to find them . . . if it's not too late!'

He jumped up.

'Do you mean—you're going *now*?' she exclaimed.

'Don't you agree?' he asked.

'Yes—of course!' she gulped. 'Only—I'll go with you!'

But he shook his head.

'I'll be better alone,' he said. 'Quicker, too.' He saw she was going to argue, and jerked his head towards the hut. 'Besides, there's Miss Noyes. Can we leave her here all by herself?'

'You win,' murmured Ruth unhappily. 'But—Tom—come back!'

'You bet I'll come back!' he assured her. 'That's all I'm going for!'

With a smile that failed utterly to convey the impression that there was no danger, Tom Haines crept towards the entrance to the compound and slipped past the prostrate guards. He wondered at the ease with which he did this.

Cooling, Medworth and Smith had wondered the same thing before him when they had slipped by with similar ease on their way to the Temple. They did not know that such occasions, when the slightest disobedience would bring the wrath of the gods and perhaps, also, the High Priest's boiling pot, were accompanied by a sort of self-protective stupor. The guards would respond to one thing only—the sound of the second releasing gong. To all else—the hardness of the ground, sharp stones pressing into their stomachs, insect bites, tickles, stiffness, aches, soft little noises creeping by them, even thunder claps—they were or strove to be oblivious. They could lie thus for hours—and sometimes did.

It was this circumstance that permitted the four male prisoners to make their respective escapes from the compound. We will shortly follow them; but first we will stay with Ruth, who found this new ordeal the worst so far endured. After watching Haines go, she waited with anxiety and envy. She was anxious about his danger, but envious of its definiteness. It was this waiting, this constant brooding expectation, this sinister silence and atmosphere pregnant with unknown things that played the devil with one's nerves, and when she had sympathised with Haines's forced inactivity, she had been sympathising with herself.

But now he was on a job. His moody eyes had leapt with sudden life, inspired by an enthusiasm far beyond Noughts and Crosses. For a few moments, foolish moments which brought self-wrath afterwards, she almost wished he had not thought of the job and that they were still playing their silly useless game. She stared at the paper with its patchwork of crowded lines as though it were some relic of the unredeemable past.

Then, 'Don't be a silly schoolgirl!' she said aloud. 'Stop thinking of yourself. Think of other people. Think of Miss Noyes!'

Miss Noyes was still snoring gently. She had not slept like this for a long time. Fatigue had beaten fear, and when she woke up she would be a little ashamed, and pretend perhaps that she had not really been asleep at all. Had Ruth been inside Miss Noyes's dream she might have envied her, too; but the snoring—a peculiarly unnerving sound, and lacking the discipline of the waking state—gave no clue to that fact that Miss Noyes was reviewing a company of black Girl Guides, telling them that it was a very good joke, but that they couldn't deceive *her* and were to go off at once and wash their faces; and by her side was Mr Smith, perfectly groomed, waiting to take her to a church and marry her. The only trouble was that Mr Smith wore a necklace of miniature skulls round his neck, looking like the relics of some former life reduced to convenient size . . . yes, she would have to speak to him about the necklace . . .

'*Asleep!* How *can* she!' murmured Ruth.

The minutes slipped by. The silence seemed to grow more and more intense. She waited for something to break it. The second gong. No, not the second gong! A bird. A flutter. Footsteps. A movement outside the bamboo wall. Tom's voice. Anybody's voice. Anything at all! . . . Of course—there *was* the snoring . . .

'I know! I'll play another game of Noughts and Crosses!' she said.

She spoke aloud. Her voice was company, and she wanted to be sure that she still had it. Her throat was getting strained and tight, like every other part of her. She was realising that she needed Tom very much indeed. She played with an imaginary Tom. She made his noughts for him. She let him win, though it wasn't his turn.

'There, that's twenty-three all,' she said. 'Well played!'

She gasped at herself.

'My God, what's happening to me?' she wondered. 'Am I really cracking up? I wouldn't have thought it of me!'

The trouble was, she was beginning to think. Oakley had made a permanent habit of numbness, but she could only numb her intelligence temporarily. She had set her soul against believing. She had tried to cheat knowledge. But now knowledge began to sweep back like a frightening tide, and reality gripped her. She fought a desire to scream.

She thought of Oakley, recalling his last remark as he had been about to leave them. 'If you want to try a spot of *sauve qui peut*, don't say I'm stopping you.' How ridiculously the man talked! A spot of *sauve qui peut*! He had looked hard at Tom while he had said it. Why was that? She knew why it was as she put the question to herself. The High Priest had conveyed something to Oakley, and it was a definite threat to—*her*! That was why Oakley had looked at Tom.

Suddenly she listened. She thought she heard a faint, metallic droning through the silence. Or was it imagination? She did not know whether she were really hearing it or not. It might be a sound within herself—the sound fear makes just before it bursts.

She turned to Miss Noyes, still sleeping and dreaming and snoring against the wall of the hut.

'I'm going to be damned mean—I'm going to wake her,' she said. 'I've *got* to have company! Even Miss Noyes's company!'

She ran towards the hut. She stretched out her hand, to take Miss Noyes's shoulder and shake it.

'No—I won't!' Her hand dropped limply. 'That would be too caddish!'

She turned slowly, and as she did so her hand went up to her heart. At the entrance stood the High Priest.

18

Gold

When Lord Cooling, Ernest Medworth and Henry Smith slipped silently by their guards and found themselves outside the prison walls, they beheld an astonishing sight. They had expected to see a few prone spearmen, but they had not anticipated thirty or forty. The obedient fellows lay on their faces like corpses on a battlefield, without any sense of formation or order. Most of them lay singly, but a few lay in small groups, sprawling over each other as though suddenly stricken down by a plague. Their disposition was eminently satisfactory to the Englishmen, but, as Cooling pointed out later, it was also rather insulting.

The beholders did not pause to dwell on the astonishing sight. They put it behind them as quickly as possible, diving down a track that appeared to be in the direction of the village and of the height beyond. The track zigzagged down into a little dip, then zigzagged up out of it. Over a brow they struck the first huts.

'We must be quiet here!' muttered Smith, making the first noise since they had started.

'Shut up!' whispered Medworth, making the second.

But their precautions were unnecessary, for the village they tiptoed through looked deserted, and if the walls of the huts had dissolved they would merely have seen a repetition of the sight they had beheld outside the compound. Only in this case the natives would not have been spearmen; they would have been women, old men, and children.

They left the village, and passed, without knowing it, the larger hut in which Ben and the High Priest were having their silent encounter. They began to ascend the track to the height on which the Temple stood. The hearts of Medworth and Smith pumped with fear, relief, and excitement. Cooling's alone remained normal.

'Charming scenery,' observed the latter when he felt it was safe to speak. Though collected, he was taking no unnecessary risks.

'Yes—reminds one of Madeira,' answered Smith, puffing, and trying to be social.

'You know Madeira?' inquired Cooling.

'Well, I've seen the posters,' replied Smith. 'But p'r'aps I'm thinking of Corsica. One of those places you cruise to, anyway.'

'I suppose it *is* wise to talk?' queried Medworth.

'Provided we continue to keep the conversation really intelligent,' responded Cooling. 'Wiser than walking so near that precipice.'

Then came the unexpected clap of thunder that nearly sent Medworth down the precipice. Smith, fortunately in the middle of the track, did fall flat.

'Going native?' asked Cooling as Smith picked himself up.

Smith wiped his brow.

'Whew!' he gasped. 'That gave me a start!'

'So I gathered, Mr Smith,' observed Cooling dryly. 'If you are not enjoying yourself, perhaps you had better go back.'

As Smith reddened, Medworth came to his aid. He had received a shock himself.

'It *was* a bit unexpected,' he pointed out.

'It was certainly unexpected,' answered Lord Cooling, with a noticeable crispness in his tone which may have provided the key to his own secret mood, 'and it will also be unexpected if we suddenly encounter the High Priest, or a native executioner, or a gorilla guarding the gold. Do I take it that you will meet such emergencies in a similar way—by leaping into the air and falling on your noses? If so, I anticipate most valuable assistance.'

Now Medworth reddened.

'No need to be sarcastic,' he muttered.

'There is every need to be sarcastic,' retorted Cooling, 'if no other means exist of bringing you back to your senses. It will be time enough to howl when we are hurt.'

'And then I expect you'll howl as loudly as either of us!' snapped Medworth.

'Possibly even louder,' answered Cooling. 'I dislike being hurt intensely.'

The conversation having taken an unsatisfactory turn they proceeded for a while in silence, but as they neared their goal they forgot their differences in the strange, compelling sight that unfolded. They had seen as they climbed the rocky wall beyond which the Temple rose. Sometimes they had lost sight of the wall as some more immediate prominence obscured their upward view, but every time they saw it again it increased in size and revealed more details. Now, as they entered their last short lap, it reared its face with sharp, forbidding distinctness. The brilliant sunlight accentuated the shadows, making the rock's uneven surface appear pocked with deep black holes and velvet cracks. The wall was a natural structure, thrown up in a past age by volcanic action, and it was a fitting preliminary to the grim glory that lay behind.

An archway, which may also have been natural, led through it, but it was blocked by a heavy wooden door. The door swung on large wooden hinges, and though a civilised carpenter might have laughed at it, it was cleverly contrived. Normally it was bolted on the inside, but since locks and keys were unknown on the island, it could only be secured against intruders when there was somebody inside to secure it. Now it was slightly ajar.

'D-do we go in?' whispered Smith.

'You bet we go in,' answered Medworth. 'That's what we've come for, isn't it?'

'The door is rather too obligingly open,' murmured Cooling. 'Still, as Mr Medworth points out, this is what we have come for. Who's first?'

'I am,' said Medworth, and gave the door a shove.

It swung inwards. They peered through into a space that had the atmosphere of a ruin without being one. It was a kind of outer chamber that led to another wall of rock, but now the sides were walled as well, and only a roof was missing. In the farther second wall was another archway, and another door.

They passed into the space, and became enclosed in a stifling atmosphere. It seemed to require a wind to clear it. The blue sky baked above them.

'Do we *all* go on?' asked Smith, 'or does one of us stay here—you know, to keep a watch?'

'It sounds to me,' replied Cooling, 'as though one of us stays here.'

'I will, if you like,' said Smith with desperate obtuseness. He was wishing hard he had not joined the party. The compound had been bad enough, but this was worse. 'Then I can let you know if anyone comes.'

'Provided the anyone who comes permits you to let us know,' added Cooling. 'Well, Medworth?'

Medworth frowned. He was thinking, with some justification, 'If we leave this chap here alone, he'll probably get the jim-jams and run away!' Aloud he said, 'I think it might be wise if we all stuck together, eh?'

'Oh, just as you like, just as you like!' growled Smith, quite aware of what Medworth was thinking. 'I was only trying to help. Tactics, you know.'

Cooling turned and examined the door they had just come through. It had a stout vertical wooden bar on the inside. Closing the door, he swung the bar from vertical to horizontal, and an end came down and fixed itself into an open-topped groove in the rock.

'Voilà!' said Cooling. 'Now the anyone cannot come!'

'By Jove! There you are!' exclaimed Smith with a spasm of relief.

'Yes, but wait a moment,' retorted Medworth. 'What you mean is that someone can't get *in*. He can *come* all right, and find the door fastened—and that'll give him the tip that *we're* inside! Wouldn't it be better to leave it as it was—and to keep our eyes and ears peeled.'

'Quite right,' sighed Cooling. 'I prefer my idea, but yours is sounder.'

He swung the bar back to its vertical position and opened the door a crack. Smith's momentary happiness vanished in a cold draught.

'And now, onward, Christian soldiers,' said Cooling.

147

They began to cross the space. Their feet made a dull clatter on the hard ground. In the middle of the space Smith suddenly stopped and wheeled round.

'My God, what's that?' gasped Medworth.

He and Cooling turned, also, and joined Smith in staring at the door. Nothing happened. Cooling regarded Smith with frank contempt.

'Nerve-storm?' he inquired politely.

'Well, damn it, this isn't a picnic!' jerked Smith. It was the first time he had ever been rude to a man with a title. 'I thought I heard something!'

'I'll find out if you did,' replied Cooling and ran back to the door.

Reaching the door he poked his head out cautiously, then brought it back again, and returned.

'Nothing,' he reported. 'Try to improve, Smith. Nerves are catching, and we don't want a panic.'

'Yes, come on, come on,' grunted Medworth.

'This place smells dead!'

Their feet resumed their soft, dull clattering. The second door was reached. Like the first door, it was ajar.

'Will you walk into my parlour?' murmured Lord Cooling and gave it a push.

The next moment they stopped dead and stared.

The Temple of Gold was no longer a phrase; it was a reality. Even Lord Cooling, who imagined he had complete control of his emotions, gaped like a schoolboy. From the roof, from the sides, from everywhere, gold exuded a strange unnatural light with an effect that was mentally numbing and physically stifling, and in the reflection of that light, which was relieved only by glimpses of sky blue that picked out a number of slits round the walls, the beholders seemed to turn yellow themselves. Their souls certainly did.

The floor was not gold. That was of rock worn smooth by centuries of grim worship. But it glowed with the prevailing colour, and the ornaments, the effigies, the seats, the vacant thrones, and an enormous pot of unbelievable dimensions, were formed out of the metal that has made monarchs and madmen and that has ruled the world with its ironic, specious value.

'My God!' muttered Medworth at last.

'Look at it!' gasped Smith.

'We seem to be doing so,' said Cooling.

Suddenly Medworth began to laugh. As suddenly he stopped. He had the sense to save himself, in the nick of time, from frenzy. The next remark of Cooling helped to sober him.

'We haven't got it yet, you know,' remarked Cooling.

'No, but we're going to get it,' replied Medworth thickly. 'Or a slice of it!'

'How?' asked Smith.

'In the absence of a removal van, the question is pertinent,' answered Cooling. 'A pity the articles are so large. I think the one I would like to see removed first is that pot.'

'What do you suppose it's for?' faltered Smith.

'If my memory serves me aright, hot quomogee,' said Cooling.

'Quomogee?' queried Smith.

'Water,' replied Cooling. 'But we will not inquire what the hot water might be for.'

Although he was discouraging curiosity, his own proved too great for him, and he walked towards the pot. Descending steps curved round behind it, he stood at the top, gazing down.

149

'See anything interesting?' inquired Medworth.

'Yes, very interesting,' replied Cooling. 'These steps appear to descend to a recess beneath the pot where a fire can be lit. The bottom of the pot is evidently of some other metal.' He paused. 'I wonder how all this gold got here? If there's a mine, they must have exhausted it.'

'Some of it may be spoils of war,' suggested Medworth.

'Very possibly,' nodded Cooling. 'But it is the gold's future, not its past, that concerns us.'

'You bet!' grinned Medworth. Looking at the grin, Cooling noticed for the first time the yellow reflection illuminating it. 'What a waste this stuff is here!'

'Yes, everything is a waste that we cannot use ourselves,' agreed Cooling. 'That happens also to be my own definition of the term. But I expect the High Priest finds it useful. It must add immensely to his influence with the natives. One can well understand their obedience to the ruler of such a Temple. Well—has anybody found the brain-wave?'

'I've got one,' said Smith unexpectedly.

'Let us hear it.'

'We get back to England, tell 'em at home, and annex the island.'

'How simple,' smiled Cooling.

'Well, I don't really see any other way, you know.'

'I'm afraid I don't even see that way, Mr Smith. How do we get back to England to tell them?'

'We've got to do that, anyway,' retorted Medworth. 'But my idea is that we'll take samples.'

'Certainly, Medworth. You take that effigy, I'll take that throne, and Mr Smith will take the pot.'

'You do love sarcasm, don't you,' grunted Medworth savagely. 'Damn it all, there must be some smaller stuff somewhere! Look, there's a door up the other end—wonder where it leads to?'

His companions followed his gaze. The door was at the far end of the Temple, in a shadowed corner. It was smaller than the door they had entered by, but it was more arresting. Hanging from a knob above it was a golden skull.

'Would that be the vestry, do you suppose?' whispered Smith.

'Go and see,' answered Cooling. As Smith showed no anxiety to do so, he added, 'Or shall we toss for it?'

'I expect it's the Priest's quarters,' said Medworth. 'That blasted fool Oakley told us he lives here. Wonder if there's any small stuff there?'

'Probably there is,' replied Cooling. 'Let us see whether we can find his golden toothbrush.'

They moved towards the door. Though they trod softly their footsteps echoed with uncanny protest against their intrusion. Their feet should have been bare and silent. Reaching the door, they stopped, and Cooling's hand rose with grim humour towards the golden skull.

'What are you doing?' demanded Medworth sharply.

'Don't we ring or knock?' inquired Cooling.

'Ha, ha! Very funny!' gulped Smith.

But Medworth glared.

'You think this is a game, don't you?' he growled.

'That is my earnest endeavour,' admitted Cooling, 'as it was of the French aristocrats who jested as they went to the guillotine. I wonder whether we are playing the game intelligently? Shall we hear the second gong while we are in there searching for the golden tooth-brush? Could we even hear it from *here*?'

'By Jove!' exclaimed Medworth.

'So you see, Medworth,' continued Cooling, 'though I have my playful moments, my brain as well as my nerve remains better than yours. Mr Smith, do you feel inclined to act upon your original suggestion, and to go to the outer gate and scout for us?'

'Eh—scout?' stammered Smith.

'Scout and listen,' said Cooling, 'and if you hear anything, come back and report?'

Smith hesitated. It had been his original suggestion, but he was not sure that he liked it so much now. To journey back alone did not appeal to him. This was one of the occasions when three were company.

'Er—well, why not?' he muttered when he could stand Cooling's cynical eye no longer. 'Yes, certainly. I—er—yes, certainly.'

He turned and left them with a palpitating heart.

'Three little sailor boys, feeling rather blue,' said Cooling, 'one watched for cannibals, and then there were two. Come along, Medworth. As we haven't got our visiting cards we *won't* knock.'

The door opened as easily as had the others. They peered through into a dim passage that turned out to be a narrow descending ledge. On the right was an overhanging rocky wall in which was another door. Ahead and on the left were tall tree-tops, those on the left rising many feet above them, shutting out light. They were on the tip of a promontory that dipped through thick forest down to the sea.

'Charming situation,' commented Cooling. 'I wonder whether the High Priest lets his villa?'

He walked forward a little way along the ledge, pausing when it dropped more steeply. Then he turned and regarded Medworth, whose eyes were fastened on the door in the wall.

'Walk in,' said Cooling. 'We know our host is out.'

'Suppose somebody else is in?' muttered Medworth.

'I have made several little fortunes in my time,' answered Cooling, 'and none without some personal risk. Your persistent courage, Medworth, shall go down in my autobiography it I am spared to write it.'

He returned as he spoke, and prepared to give the door a push, but as he did so scurrying feet caused him to pause. Smith had come back to report.

'They're outside,' came his gasping voice. 'My God! We're done!'

19

A Summons to Oomoo

The attitude of the High Priest as he stood and regarded Ruth was very different from the attitude expressed in his first visit. Then he had been aloof. Now he was burning with some inner excitement. 'Something's happened!' shot through the terrified girl's mind, and she tried not to increase her terror by guessing what it might be. No guess was likely to bring her any consolation. But, even if she had faced her guesses, she would have guessed wrong.

He beckoned to her. She did not move. Then he approached a few paces and beckoned again, more imperiously. Then, as she still hesitated, he whipped out his knife.

In spite of her terror, Ruth's mind worked quickly. If he already knew her companions had escaped, she could serve no purpose by refusing to accompany him, especially as the gleaming knife rendered ultimate refusal impossible. Perhaps he was going to take her to them; that, after all, would suit her as well as him. If, on the other hand, he did not know they had escaped, then she must postpone his knowledge as long as possible, and trust that he would believe they were all, with the exception of Miss Noyes, in the hut.

Miss Noyes was still asleep, enduring dreams which though uneasy were preferable to the reality she would presently wake up to. Did the High Priest want her, also? Ruth turned uncertainly towards the sleeping woman, but as she did so the Priest sprang forward, and now his blade was definitely threatening.

'The beast only wants me!' thought Ruth. She hoped devoutedly that Miss Noyes would continue sleeping, and that she would not wake up till she returned . . . if she returned . . .

'All right, you horrible man!' she said aloud. Of course he could not understand her, but she wanted to hear her voice. To her gratification and surprise it was quite steady. 'I'll come! But you'll find I've got a fist if there's any nonsense!'

She moved towards him. He motioned to the exit from the compound, and waited till she was by his side. Then, with the point of his knife almost touching her waist, he moved along with her.

'Sunday afternoon stroll?' inquired Ruth. 'We must look a pretty couple of lovers!'

The point pricked her waist.

'I see—mustn't talk?'

The point pricked again, answering in the negative.

Outside the compound Ruth saw the strange sight of prostrate natives viewed earlier by four of her companions, and she was led along the route that three of them had taken. In silence they reached the silent village. Once Ruth paused, but the point of the High Priest's blade urged her quickly on again.

Presently the High Priest paused himself. They stopped outside one of the huts, and he motioned her to enter. She did so, wondering whether this was to be her new prison, but a moment later she realised that it was not. She found herself in a dim chamber, in which were three more prostrate natives. One was an old man, another was a woman, the third was a child.

The Priest approached the child. Now his blade pricked the back of the child's neck. Ruth gasped, and prepared to spring at him, but before she could do so the blade was withdrawn, and the child had turned.

The Priest looked at the child, whose large, pretty eyes returned his gaze with tremulous directness. The gaze lasted for several seconds, and Ruth gained the impression that some form of silent communication was in process, and that the child was learning the Priest's wish. When the Priest stood aside, the child rose, and walked to Ruth. Her eyes were wide and solemn. Ruth quelled an impulse to take her into her arms.

Now the Priest made another gesture towards the doorway. They were to proceed again. The child moved instantly. Ruth obeyed almost as quickly, rebelling against her obedience, and also against the manner in which she, too, was learning to interpret the Priest's odious language.

They left the hut. During their brief visit, the old man and the woman had not moved an inch.

'Where next?' wondered Ruth.

They wound through the village and came to the Chief's hut. Here, for the first time, the High Priest seemed undecided as to his course of action. He stopped them again when they had passed through the encircling wall, and stood gazing towards the hut. Something was on his mind. It was Oakley. He did not want Oakley to be present at the little interview ahead. A disturbing element had entered into the Low Priest's attitude, and his presence might not assist a delicate situation. Making up his mind suddenly, the High Priest detached himself from his prisoners—for the child seemed as much a prisoner as Ruth—and went into the hut alone.

Ruth watched him disappear, then turned to the child and smiled. The child looked back solemnly. Ruth wanted to say something, though she did not know what it was she wanted to say. She was afraid, moreover, that her strange language might disturb the child and accentuate the difference between them. But a pat is the same in all languages, so she patted the child's shoulder. The child's only response was to move a little closer to her.

In a few moments the High Priest came out again. With him was Oakley. 'Thank God!' thought Ruth. A white face was what she needed to help her in her desperate struggle against this numbing sense of loneliness. But, beyond its colour, there was not much to cheer her in Oakley's face. He looked exceedingly glum.

'Well, what's the weather?' she asked, daring speech.

'Bit sultry,' replied Oakley ignoring the High Priest's glaring. 'You've got to go inside.' He added quickly, 'But I'll be here when you come out again.'

'Oh—we will come out again?' said Ruth.

'You'll come out,' nodded Oakley.

'Who will I find inside? Are the others there?'

'Others?' Oakley's frown grew. 'Haven't you just left the others?'

'Afraid not,' returned Ruth. 'I thought perhaps . . . but I see I was wrong.'

The High Priest made an impatient gesture. Still ignoring him, Oakley asked:

'Where are they?'

'Gone hunting. All but Miss Noyes. Our dear Priest seems to be bursting. Just tell me what I'm going to find, and then I—we—had better go in.'

'You'll find Ben,' said Oakley. 'But you'll find him a bit changed. Don't forget I'm outside. If there's any trouble, shout.'

Some quality in his tone impressed itself on her.

'I thought you weren't—interested?' she murmured.

'Not a damn,' he answered. 'But remember to shout.'

He turned away. The High Priest now looked more like bursting than ever. Ruth took hold of the child's hand, and went into the hut.

At first she saw nothing. She merely felt conscious of dark gloom around her. Then the bare strange chamber grew out of the dimness, with its queer occupant squatting silently in the seat of honour.

Although she had expected to find Ben changed, she stared at him in amazement. He was quite motionless, and he was gazing over her head into space. There was no flicker of recognition, no sign of the emotion that surely must reside behind his grubby exterior. Judged by his appearance, his demeanour, and his atmosphere, he might indeed have been a little god, and she a mere mortal who had come to learn his will! Of course, it was just acting . . .

The High Priest rustled by. He approached the seat, threw himself on the ground, rose, and turned, waving his arms in the direction of Ruth and the child.

Ben lowered his eyes. He came out of his trance, and actually saw the visitors for the first time. Until that moment he had been, as he himself described it later, 'in a sort of a cloud like,' and the cloud still floated vaguely before him. 'They seemed ter be there and yit at the sime time they didn't, if yer git me.'

But as the cloud thinned, and the High Priest continued to gesticulate in a manner demanding attention, the god in Ben became a little less and the man a little more. His glassy eye shed something of its fish-like quality, and Ruth realised—with relief—that she was being recognised. The relief was due to a sudden theory that madness, not histrionic ability, was at the bottom of Ben's condition. It was the child, however, who did most to bring Ben back to earth, and to destroy his resemblance to a deified haddock.

His gaze shifted from Ruth to the child, and remained on her. The child gazed back, and appeared to be reflecting Ben's own transition. Her big, awed eyes lost their fear. Her lips parted slightly . . . They were smiling at each other.

The effect on the High Priest was startling. He flung his hands into the air, as though in ecstasy, seized the child, and lifted her aside. Then he began gesticulating again towards Ruth.

"Ow was I ter know wot the blighter meant?' asked Ben afterwards.

In ignorance, he smiled at Ruth.

This completed the Priest's elation. He fell flat once more, then leapt to his feet, seized the two visitors he had presented, and drove them unceremoniously out of the hut.

Oomoo gazed after them. His soul was troubled. Something had gone wrong in these last few moments, and he did not know what it was. He needed another clap of thunder to encourage him and to dispel a sense of failure. Mind you, he *wasn't* going to fail! Not he! He was going to see this through to the end, like wot 'e'd sed, and it was going to be a happy end for white and black alike—yus, and pertickerly fer that black kid. But he would require periodic assistance, for even a little god must be backed up by a big god, and is helpless all alone . . . and, at this moment, Ben was utterly alone. He had a cannibal chief's hut entirely to himself.

'Wot I wishes,' he thought, 'is that this blinkin' hinsperashun wouldn't keep on comin' and goin' like. Why don't it stick? Wot I wants is a trarnce fer the doorashun, and then ter wike up when it's orl over. It's mixin'. Fust you 'ave 'em orl under yer thumb, and nex' they 'as you under their thumb, till yer don't know where yer are!'

A notion occurred to him.

'P'r'ps I ain't tryin' 'ard enuff?' he reflected. 'Nah, then—fergit yer Ben. Yer Oomoo, see? Oomoo! Oomoo! Oomoo!'

He murmured the word aloud, hoping it would put him into another trance, but all it did was to bring Oakley back. Well, that was something.

'Yes, we know who you are, old sport,' said Oakley. 'You needn't tell us.'

'If you ain't the bloomin' limit!' muttered Ben. 'I was jest goin' orf!'

'Going off where?'

'Eh? In a trarnce. See, I'm no good nacheral, but when I'm in a trarnce things comes ter me.'

'Well, don't go into a trance for a moment or two,' said Oakley, 'because I've got to talk to you and I've only a minute. As a matter of fact, you can stop having trances for several hours if you like. Make your next one in the Temple of Gold.'

'Wotcher mean?' blinked Ben.

'I'm arranging that the Chief won't come back here. He'll spend the night in his second retreat, where he is now, and you won't meet him—or anybody, I hope—till James calls with the carriage.'

"Oo?'

'Never mind. The point is that this hut will be taboo to everybody for the rest of the day, so, provided you don't make a noise, you can do what you like here. Stand on your head—ping-pong—Sailors' Hornpipe—or blow bubbles. I'll pop in and see you when I can, and I'll bring you your wooma.'

"Ooray!' answered Ben. 'But wot abart the others?'

'Don't worry about them. I expect you'll meet them in the Temple.'

'Yus, but where are they nah?'

'Heaven knows! Some of them appear to have taken little walks.'

'Wouldn't mind tikin' one meself!'

'Well, see you don't. If they don't come back I'll have to try and round them up, and I don't want to have *you* to chase as well.'

'Walks, eh? Wot for?'

'I haven't had time to find out yet.'

'P'r'aps I can sive yer the trouble.'

'Oh?'

'P'r'aps they're lookin' fer gold?'

'Yes,' murmured Oakley frowning. 'You may be right. Well, I must be off. See you later. Round about tea-time.'

'Oi, 'arf a mo'!' exclaimed Ben. 'I got suthing helse ter arsk.'

'Well, shoot it quickly.'

'Why did Ugly-Mug send yer aht o' the room jest nah? When 'e come in with the gal and the kid?'

'He probably thought I'd be in the way—and, I gather, I *would* have been!'

'Not in mine! I needed yer. Wot did 'e bring 'em ter me for? And the kid, too?'

'You'll learn.'

'I wanter learn now. 'E mikes signs at 'em, and then I smiles at 'em, meanin', "They're nice, that's orl right," and orf 'e bundles 'em afore yer could count 'arf.'

'Yes—I saw the end of the show.'

'Where's 'e bundled 'em to?'

Oakley hesitated, then answered:

'The Temple of Gold. And I've got to catch them up before they get there and help to show them in.'

'Wot 'ave they gorn there for?' demanded Ben.

'For the night.'

'Coo! Will they be sife?'

'Safe as houses.'

'Yus, but some's jerry-built!'

'As safe as Holloway, then.'

''Owjer know?' insisted Ben. 'If any 'arm comes to 'em—the little 'un, sime as the big 'un—Gawd, I'll rise a storm!'

'I'm sure you will, Ben,' nodded Oakley. 'But the High Priest will make it his special job to see that they are safe until—'

'Yus?'

'I've got to go, Ben. I've got to sound the second gong.'

'Until wot?'

'Until you see them again at tomorrow's sunrise.'

'Yus, yus,' said Ben. 'Go on, I can see ye're keepin' suthing back! Wot 'appens at termorrer's sunrise?'

'Sula domo toree—the trial.'

'I know that! But wot else 'appens? I've gotter be told!'

Oakley looked at him steadily, then replied:

'I haven't second sight, Ben, but I can tell you one thing that will happen—you and I will be working like hell to save their lives. So hang on to that, my love, and let the damn rest rip!'

Then he went out. Ben listened for the gong. But it did not sound.

20

To the Priest's Quarters

The reason Ben did not hear the gong was because, just as Oakley was on the point of striking it—his hand was actually raised to do so—a sudden thought came into his mind. He paused and considered the thought. He decided it was a good one. His default would mean a row, but it might save another row considerably bigger.

He hurried after the High Priest and his prisoners, therefore, without first acquainting the prostrate village of the departure. His conversation with Ben had given them a long start, and he did not overtake them until they had nearly reached the Temple. Ruth and the child were walking a few paces ahead of the Priest, and the Priest was watching them with the intentness of a cat.

Oakley watched the Priest with equal intentness. The intentness gave his mind a pain. His mind was not used to this distressing exercise, and it rebelled. 'What are you using me like this for?' it complained. 'Confound all these people! Let me go to sleep again!'

Oakley sympathised with his mind's protest, agreeing

164

with it utterly. These people were an unholy nuisance. Instead of adding to one's acceptance of life, as good pals should, they invaded philosophy and pierced the comfortable sluggishness that he had woven around his tortured body to deaden sensation. They were dragging him out of his self-protective stupor. But . . . well, what was there to do about it? If Oakley had developed his power of acceptance, he must accept even this new human invasion on his long-suffering emotions.

It was Ruth who carried the most deadly weapons. Her very back stabbed, bringing uneasy longings to starved eyes. 'That's a good back,' thought Oakley, striving callously to reduce it to the terms of a joint hanging in a shop. The ruse was completely unsuccessful. The smaller back of the child gave Ruth's a maternal quality that made her all the more distracting.

'H, e, l, l,' thought Oakley as he increased his pace, passed the High Priest—ignoring the latter's glare—and overtook Ruth. He fell into step quietly beside her till she noticed him and turned her head.

'Good-afternoon,' murmured Oakley.

'Lovely weather,' answered Ruth.

'Who's going to win Test Matches?' he asked.

'We are,' said Ruth. 'Batsman's wicket. Besides,' she added, 'haven't we got the umpires? To stop any body-bowling?'

'Body-bowling?' repeated Oakley puzzled. 'What's that?'

Ruth smiled, but the smile faded as a shortened shadow that was not hers or Oakley's or the child's crept into the corner of her eye.

'Cave!' she murmured.

'I'm cavying,' Oakley murmured back. 'Au revoir for a moment.'

He dropped behind to the advancing Priest, made some earnest signs, and then came forward again.

'I've done my little piece,' he said. 'Told the H.P. that I am giving you a few special instructions direct from Oomoo, and that I've just time to finish them before we reach the Temple if I'm not interrupted. That gives us three minutes. He thinks the instructions are to be a good girl till you see Oomoo again. Well, perhaps it's not a bad one.'

'Yes—if I am made to understand it,' answered Ruth. 'What, exactly, does "good girl" mean on this island?'

'In your case it will mean to wait obediently in the Temple till tomorrow's sunrise, when the trial takes place.'

In spite of herself, Ruth looked startled.

'Do you mean—?' she began.

'That you are not going back to your original prison?' said Oakley. 'Yes. You're changing quarters. You'll stay—with the child here—in the Priest's annex, just behind the Temple. Make a note of the geography, will you? May come in useful. Temple's on the promontory we're reaching. First comes outer wall. Then gate in outer wall. Call it Outer Gate. All gates can be fastened on the inside, but not on the outside. Wooden bars that swing round and slide. No keys on the island. Outer Gate leads to large, gloomy, walled space. No roof. Need umbrella in rain. Call this space Outer Chamber. Beyond is another gate. Inner Gate. Leads to Temple itself. At end of Temple, third gate. Small door, rather. Call it Priest's Door. Leads to a long ledge path. Don't slip. Left, sheer drop into top of forest, though the tree-tops rise above it, forming untrustworthy wall. Right, trustworthy wall of rock, with a fourth door. Call this Front Door. Door to Priest's quarters. I've never been in—yet. Note the "yet." You'll be taken there, and you'll stay there till the trial. You'll be absolutely safe—till the trial. Absolutely. Till the trial, the High Priest would defend you with his life.'

'And at the trial?' asked Ruth.

'At the trial you'll see us all again, and we'll put anything right that's wrong.'

'I congratulate you, Mr Oakley.'

'Meanin'?'

'You are a politician. You choose your words tactfully. But I'm not a politician. When Oomoo smiled at me—and the child—did the High Priest interpret that as a sign that Oomoo wanted us for—'

'Yes,' interrupted Oakley wincing. 'But please try and be a politician with me.'

'Of course, you're a fraud.'

'Meanin', once more?'

'You pretend you can't feel.'

'It wasn't pretence. It was genuine.' He raised his eyes from the ground, and looked at her for a moment. 'I suppose you know you're ruining my life?'

'I'm sorry.'

'Don't worry. I still know behind it all that nothing matters. By the way, don't get the idea that I'm paying you a compliment. Any pretty white girl would have done the same. Edna Best, Gertrude Lawrence, Tallulah—are they still queuing up for Tallulah?—Kay Hammond—I used to like Kay Hammond. Cheeky little thing. Still alive? So, you see, there's nothing in it . . . As a matter of fact,' he went on, now staring at the ground again, 'there's nothing in it, anyhow. I don't care a damn. Not a damn. Well, any more questions?'

'If there's time,' she answered.

'For about three, I should think. There's the outer wall

ahead, but don't stop to admire it. Shoot! I suppose they still say that at home?'

'First question, then. Where does the ledge path lead if one doesn't jump off into the forest on one side or into the Priest's house on the other?'

'Shoot me for a mug,' replied Oakley. 'I ought to have told you that without your asking. Meant to. Brain's rusty. Needs oiling. It leads to a beach. Pretty long walk. Priest's private beach. Taboo. No boat there. Difficult to get one there—'

'Tom—Mr Haines—is looking for a boat.'

'Is he? He won't have any luck. They were all brought in before the storm for annual repairs. It's a long path. Steep in places. Plateau halfway down. Well, second question?'

'Did you sound the second gong? I didn't hear it.'

'You didn't hear it because I didn't sound it. You told me, you remember, that some of the party had gone hunting. I want to give them all the time I can to get back. Once I sound the gong the guards will be alert again. Thank the Lord, the H.P. hasn't noticed my omission yet, but he will presently, and then I'll have to return to the village and make a din.'

'Wouldn't they hear the din from here?'

'They would but they won't, because I've conveniently lost the gong. Left it behind by mistake on purpose. That'll give me a chance to go back and find it—and to see the position. I'm *supposed* to stick around up here, you see.'

'I thought you said your brain was rusty, Mr Oakley,' said Ruth. 'It seems to me to be working quite well. One last question, if I've not exceeded my allowance. What's our plan to date—if any?'

'Our plan to date,' repeated Oakley, as they came within the shadow of the wall. 'Oh, just to save seven or eight lives, and to pocket seven or eight tons of gold, and to convert a thousand cannibals to vegetarianism. But the seven or eight lives come first, and your own tops the list. If you think that's sentimental, forget it.'

There was no further opportunity for conversation. The first gate had been reached, and the High Priest had drawn up with them again.

Oakley's brain, in spite of his doubts, was working exceedingly well. Judged dispassionately, he found the surprising fact rather interesting. He noticed that the gate was slightly more ajar than he had recollected, and he gave it a quick push before the High Priest had a chance to notice this himself.

In silence they walked through into the outer chamber. Ruth struggled hard to suppress her shivers as Oakley, obeying an imperious sign from the High Priest, closed and secured the gate behind them. They crossed the chamber to the second gate, and entered the Temple. Here Ruth stood for a moment and gasped, as three others had gasped before her. She was given no time, however, to drink in the full strangeness of the scene, for the Priest prodded her and forced her hurriedly to the third door.

But at the third door the Priest himself paused. Oakley was a little way behind, stooping, and the Priest swung round to communicate a sudden thought. Oakley straightened himself quickly, and looked inquiring.

The Priest also looked inquiring. Oakley made a sign to imply that he had experienced a sudden pain in his back, probably administered by Oomoo to punish him for some omission. The Priest, accepting this, made angry motions describing the omission. The gong—why had not the Low Priest sounded the second gong? Oakley clasped his forehead, looked vaguely around, held up his two empty hands, glanced back in the direction from which they had come, and fell upon his face. The Priest made further angry motions. Oakley's contrition, and his desire to repair his omission, became more and more evident. The Priest shrugged his shoulders, and pointed to the exit. But Oakley, who had risen, threw himself on the ground again before an effigy, and insisted on mumbling penance until the Priest, growing impatient, decided to leave him to it, opened the door to his quarters, and pushed his prisoners through.

Out of the corner of his eye Oakley watched the door open and close. He heard the wooden bar swung into its socket. He counted twenty. Then he rose, and bent once more over the real cause of his original stooping, which had not been a pain in his back, but a bit of soil.

One of his jobs was to keep the Temple spotless. He knew every smut and every stain, and conscientiously removed all that were removable. This bit of soil, he was certain, had not been on the ground when he had last been in the Temple. Had it been conveyed here recently—by a boot?

Putting two and two together, Oakley arrived at the decision that it had.

He glanced towards the door to the Priest's quarters. He listened. There was no sound. Then he advanced to the door and listened again. Silence. He tried to visualise what was happening on the other side. Emotion suddenly seized him. It was like an abruptly released tide—a tide that had been too long in check. It made him want to hurl himself at the door and smash it down. He backed away, lest he should yield to the impulse.

He touched his forehead with his finger. The finger came away wet. He stared at the dampness, almost in terror.

Then he smiled. It was an uncanny, twisted smile, and perhaps it was as well that nobody saw it. It was the smile of a sane man creeping deliberately back to mental contortion.

'My dear, beamish lad,' he murmured, 'have you forgotten that you are dead? And that, in a few meaningless years, we shall all be dust?'

In this recaptured mood he searched the Temple, and found, in the concealed recess beneath the giant golden pot, Lord Cooling, Ernest Medworth, and Henry Smith.

'Come out, dears,' he said softly.

They came out, and only Cooling managed not to look humiliated.

'Is there time to talk, Mr Oakley?' he asked.

'There isn't a second to talk,' answered Oakley.

'Then what is the order?'

'Quick march back to Holloway.'

Medworth and Smith began their quick march at once, but Cooling hesitated.

'Can we pass safely through the village, Mr Oakley?' he inquired.

'Have you heard the second gong yet?' replied Oakley.

'Thank you,' smiled Cooling. 'When we get back to England I shall allot you a thousand shares in Gold Temples, Limited. Lead on, MacDuff!'

21

In Conference

Had Miss Noyes awakened to her solitude she would probably, as she herself admitted, have run amok. 'I might even have gone out of my mind,' she confessed. But Fate was kind to her. It permitted her to go on dreaming, and she was still dreaming when the prisoners returned.

'Sleeping Beauty,' murmured Cooling. 'But where are the rest?'

Oakley had not been communicative on the way down. He had decided to postpone his news, lest it should incite hasty and unwise action, and he wanted Tom Haines at the conference. It disturbed him now to find Tom still absent.

'They're inside, I expect,' grunted Medworth. 'Billing and cooing.'

Smith, anxious to reinstate himself by making himself useful, dashed to the hut, poked his head in, and reported emptiness.

'That's not news to you, I take it?' inquired Cooling, who had been watching the silent Oakley for signs.

'No, it's not news to me,' answered Oakley. 'I knew Miss Sheringham wouldn't be there, and perhaps it was too much to hope Haines would sit and wait if he got back and found her absent.'

'Oh, they're not together, then?' asked Medworth.

'That's a smart deduction,' replied Oakley, making no effort to conceal his sarcasm. 'Smarter, anyway, than the one about billing and cooing. While you went to look for gold, Haines went to look for a boat. As you didn't know this, I suppose you left on your little tour first.'

'Both Haines and Miss Sheringham were certainly here when we left,' said Cooling. 'Where is Miss Sheringham? . . . Bless my soul, how that woman snores!'

'I'll wake her,' suggested Smith, preparing to perform a second good deed.

'Why?' asked Oakley. 'Will she be helpful?'

'Eh? What do you mean?' demanded Smith. Miss Noyes was the only member of the party he was able to impress. 'She's got more sense than most of us!'

'Then emulate her sense yourself, Mr Smith, by letting her snore on,' returned Cooling. 'I asked where Miss Sheringham was, Mr Oakley.'

'She's in the Temple,' answered Oakley, and added while they stared, 'She arrived there just before you left.'

'H'm,' murmured Cooling. 'Is that serious news?'

'Damn serious. In fact, the most serious we've had yet.'

'Explain the seriousness, please.'

'Yes, but wait a moment!' interposed Medworth, nervily postponing the explanation. 'If she's there—'

'What do you mean, *if* she's there?' asked Oakley. 'Funny, how I can't cotton to you somehow.'

'Well—we didn't see her,' muttered Medworth, reddening.

'If I remember rightly, you weren't in a very good position to see anything,' Oakley reminded him. 'You didn't see the

High Priest, either, or a native child. They crossed the Temple and went into the Priest's quarters just before I said "Cuckoo" to you.'

'That's right, make a joke of it!' growled Medworth.

'I am not making a joke of it,' replied Oakley icily. 'That is just the way I talk.' He turned to Cooling. 'There's one word I didn't include in that glossary I gave you. Mumba. It means sacrifice.'

There was a short silence. Then Cooling asked quietly:

'And, knowing that, you brought us away?'

'Knowing that, I brought you away,' answered Oakley. 'She won't be touched till sunrise—the trial, you know—and this is not a matter for a sudden rescue. It's got to be a complete rescue—and we've got to keep our heads.'

'I like you a trifle better than I did, Mr Oakley. And I agree that we have got to keep our heads. Emphatically. If we don't, we shall undoubtedly lose them. Can we trust Ben to do his bit?'

'I don't know. That's what we've got to talk about.'

'You've lost your faith in him a little?'

'In his intentions, no. In his capability—well, the H.P. scored the last point. He interpreted Ben's expression into a desire for these sacrifices. And he means to have them.'

'But, surely,' said Cooling, 'Oomoo can readjust that at the trial?'

'If I could be sure of that I wouldn't worry,' replied Oakley.

'Why aren't you sure?'

'For one thing, Ben may go pop and give the show away at any moment. He's developing trances. For another, I'm not absolutely certain that the H.P. isn't weakening already in his belief that Ben is Oomoo. He'll be in a far more dangerous state tomorrow than he's in today.'

174

'What will happen, in your opinion, if Ben makes a sign tomorrow which you interpret to the Priest as a cancellation of the sacrifices?'

'This—in my opinion. The H.P. by that time will be in a frenzy of desire for them. He will spend the whole night working himself up—though you needn't worry about the safety of Miss Sheringham and the child. They won't be touched. They're sacred. I know how these things go. But if Oomoo goes back on his word at the trial, the H.P. will feel thwarted and suspicious. He'll test Ben again—and that may be the end of Ben.'

'What would be the test?'

'Can't say. But one is pricking Ben's stomach.'

'I beg your pardon?'

'Pricking his stomach. Ben survived it last time, and gave the impression that Oomoo liked pain. I've a notion the H.P. will see just how much pain Oomoo *can* stand if things don't go the way he wants tomorrow.'

'I see,' murmured Cooling. 'Yes, I see. By the way, Mr Oakley, does it occur to us that our little stoker is, after all, something of a hero?'

'Best one I've come across,' answered Oakley. 'But, of course, not the usual type. And it's not heroism we want at the moment—it's a plan.'

'You've none?'

'I've one, if everything else goes phut.'

'What is it?'

'I'll have to kill the High Priest.'

'That sounds a very nice plan,' said Lord Cooling. 'I wonder we didn't think of it before!'

'I've thought of it twenty thousand times before,' replied Oakley, 'but it's no good doing a thing just for the fun of it.

If I kill the dear lad, that won't get us off the island. We'd have the whole island against us, led by the Chief—to a man. The Chief is simple in a great many ways, but he isn't quite as simple as all that.'

Medworth chipped in suddenly.

'Yes, but damn it all,' he exclaimed, 'why couldn't Oomoo have ordered you to kill the Priest?'

'Sounds simple, doesn't it?' answered Oakley.

'Come, come!' said Smith, backing Medworth up. 'You must admit it's an idea!'

Of course it's an idea. It even occurred to yours truly. But why should Oomoo order me to kill the High Priest?'

'Fools like these don't need reasons!' retorted Medworth.

'Wrong, as usual,' answered Oakley. 'They do need reasons. I don't say mental ones, but ones they can *feel*! A devout Catholic would need a reason for the murder of the Pope—though of course, murder isn't a part of the Catholic religion. Just the same, the natives wouldn't stand for it . . . Unless, perhaps, Oomoo killed the Priest himself—'

'Yes, why not?' cried Medworth.

'Now, that *is* an idea!' beamed Smith pastily.

'You know, you two make me tired,' complained Oakley. 'One can't think aloud without being pounced on. I'll tell you why not. Because Ben *isn't* Oomoo, and the High Priest would get in the first thrust. Yes, and that's what you chaps keep on forgetting. Ben *isn't* Oomoo. If he were he could prove his bona fides by being boiled in the pot and coming out smiling. Then the natives would accept anything he did without question—and without any intermediary. *Real* evidence of the miracle—that's what we need to help us through—and Ben can't supply it.'

'There's another point we mustn't forget,' added Cooling.

'If Ben were really Oomoo he would, I gather, require these sacrifices.'

'Indubitably,' nodded Oakley. 'You've said it.'

Medworth gave a cry of exasperation.

'Then if we can't kill the High Priest, why the devil did you suggest it?' he demanded.

'I suggested killing the High Priest because, if all else fails, I—not Ben—will certainly kill the High Priest,' replied Oakley. 'But it will have to be done by some subtle method as yet undiscovered . . . Hallo! Who's here?'

He paused abruptly as a figure slipped quickly into the compound. It was Tom Haines, excited and breathless.

'By Jove—bit of luck, getting back before that second gong—never thought I'd do it!' he panted. 'Whew!'

'Er—so you've got back, eh?' said Smith, imagining a silence of two seconds was an eternity.

'Looks like it, doesn't it?' he replied. 'I see you have, too! Find any gold nuggets? Where's Miss Sheringham?'

Oakley answered this time. No one else seemed anxious to.

'She's safe for the time being,' he remarked. 'Safer than the rest of us. Tell you about her presently. What's *your* news?'

Haines looked at him sharply. Despite Oakley's casual tone he detected the serious note behind it. Glancing round, he saw the serious note reflected in the faces of the others.

'My news waits,' he said. 'Let's hear, Oakley! Where is she?'

Oakley shrugged his shoulders.

'As you like. The High Priest has taken her to the Temple—'

'My God!'

'Don't get excited. I told you she was safe, and she is. If she weren't, I wouldn't be here. She'll be safe till sunrise—and, by that time, we'll all be at the Temple to give her a hand, if necessary.'

177

Haines controlled himself with an effort. Then he walked to Oakley, and looked at him fixedly.

'If anything happens to Miss Sheringham,' he said, 'it'll happen to the lot of us.'

'I'd agree with you if she were the only lady in the party,' answered Oakley. 'But nothing's going to happen to her if we keep steady. Will you oblige while I give you the full particulars?'

'Have you seen me lose my head yet?'

'No. You're a ship's officer.'

'I don't forget it. Carry on! Well?'

Briefly and unemotionally, Oakley related the circumstances. When he had finished, Haines stared hard at the ground for a while. Then he said quietly:

'Thanks, Oakley. Now I'll tell you my news. But, first, just repeat one thing. I don't disbelieve you, but I want it repeated all the same. Miss Sheringham is absolutely safe till the trial? You're quite sure of that?'

'Quite sure. Unless—'

'Yes?'

'Unless we create some new situation by doing anything silly.'

'Such as?'

'Rushing to the Temple and trying to rescue her without a plan.'

'I agree that would be silly. We'll find the plan. But meanwhile I'd like to know why you're so sure?'

'Knowledge of the island, old dear. Knowledge of the natives. Knowledge of the High Priest. While he's left to himself, and while he remains undisturbed and unsuspicious, he's got no cause to harm either Miss Sheringham or Yaala—that's the child's name. On the contrary, if anybody touched a hair of their heads, he'd run the person through. And now it's your turn, Haines, and I shan't mind if you look slippy. I've got to sound that second gong before 1990. By the way, I suppose it isn't 1990 yet, is it? I've gone a bit rusty on dates.'

'Well, my news is quite interesting,' answered Haines. 'I've found Ardentino.'

'Indeed?' interposed Cooling. 'Yes, that *is* interesting! Was he at the top of a tree?'

'Not when I found him. He'd just descended from one—rather too quickly. He's hurt his leg.'

'I see. And that's why he hasn't come along?'

'One reason. Another is that we decided it would be more useful to have him where he is than here.'

'And where is he?'

'Near a secluded bay. I could take you to it. In fact, I'd hoped—' He gave a sudden groan. 'Do you know, Oakley, the absence of Miss Sheringham is the worst luck that could have happened. There are *boats* in the bay!'

'I beg your pardon?' replied Oakley, raising his eyebrows.

'You didn't know, then?'

'Sure, I didn't know.'

'But this island has boats?'

'They are all in dry dock.' Suddenly Oakley looked at Haines sharply. 'By Jove!' he murmured. 'By jolly old Jove! Yes—your news *is* interestin'!'

'Exactly,' nodded Haines. 'If these boats don't belong to the islanders here, who do they belong to?'

'Perhaps you can tell us?' asked Oakley.

'I can only tell you what Ardentino told me,' replied Haines. 'While he was at the top of his tree, he saw a pack of black folk on the beach. As a matter of fact, it was the black folk

179

that sent him up his tree. They were beaching their boats and hiding them. And then they came inland, and began climbing through the forest. If my geography's right, they climbed towards the Temple from the farther side . . . Well, Oakley—how does that affect the position?'

22

Oakley Goes Scouting

Oakley walked to the exit and stood for a few moments with his back to them. He was gazing into the distance over the prostrate bodies of the guards. Nothing stirred within his vision. The brooding silence of the island remained unbroken. Then he returned, and there was a noticeable change in his manner.

'Do you feel like taking an order, Haines,' he asked, '*and seeing it's obeyed?*'

'I'll take it from you if that's a good order, Oakley,' answered Haines.

'And I will help him to see that it is obeyed,' added Lord Cooling. 'Always count on England in a crisis.'

'Oh, this is a crisis all right,' said Oakley. 'The order is to stay right where you are, and not to budge till I return.'

'When will you return?'

'The moment I can, but it won't be for a bit. Tell me exactly where you left Ardentino?'

Haines described the spot. Oakley nodded.

'Thanks. Well, I'm off,' he said. 'See you later.'

'Whoa! Wait a minute!' exclaimed Medworth. 'You can't go like that! Aren't we to know anything?'

'You'll know all you want when I come back,' retorted Oakley.

'Yes, but suppose—I mean, these other black fellows—suppose they turn up here?'

'There you are!' cried Smith. 'What do we do?'

'Hit 'em,' said Oakley, and vanished.

'That chap's a fool, if there ever was one!' muttered Smith, staring at the opening which now yawned with a terrible new significance.

'It wouldn't hurt you to try and pick up some of his folly,' suggested Haines curtly. 'I don't suppose it occurs to you that, without him, we'd be done for?'

'Nothing occurs to a vacuum,' said Cooling softly, 'beyond a permanent impulse to preserve its space. We should undoubtedly be done for without Mr Oakley. Though, frankly, I think we have a very good prospect of being done even with him.'

'Dear me!' exclaimed a long-forgotten voice.

It was Miss Noyes. She had wakened up suddenly with a start, and was flushing with shame.

'I—I think I must have dozed off for a moment,' she murmured muzzily. 'Has anything happened?'

Cooling smiled grimly.

'Now is your chance to make yourself really useful, Mr Smith,' he remarked. 'Tell Miss Noyes our bedtime story.'

Meanwhile Oakley was running. He had not run for years, and his indignant legs rebelled, as previously his brain had rebelled, against unaccustomed exercise. But, in spite of protests from both ends, he continued to slog his legs and his brain, and he reached the Chief's hut in record time.

He did not enter. He merely stooped to the spot where he had deposited the gong before following the High Priest and his captives to the Temple, picked it up, and then resumed his journey.

His next halt was at the Chief's annexe. Here, at long last, he sounded the delayed summons back to normality and activity. The Chief soon appeared, stretching his stout, stiff limbs. He was obviously pleased that the enforced siesta was over, but his beam faded at Oakley's first word.

'Choolooka,' said Oakley.

'Huh?' exclaimed the Chief.

'Choolooka,' repeated Oakley. 'Oomoo loto domo. Choolooka, choolooka!'

The Chief rolled resigned eyes, turned, and went back into the annexe. He had been informed that the god Oomoo desired utter solitude, and wished to occupy the Chief's main palace entirely by himself until the morrow.

Then Oakley sped back to the main palace, sounding the gong as he sped. He found Ben in an earthly mood, doing exercises. The particular exercise he did as Oakley suddenly appeared was a back leap towards the seat.

'Lumme, give us a bit o' warnin'!' he gasped, when he realised that the back leap had not been necessary.

'Sorry,' smiled Oakley. It was not the time to smile, but Ben always upset logic. 'Doing your daily dozen?'

'I thort they'd loosen me up like,' answered Ben. 'Tork abart stiff. Got any news?'

'Yes, I've come to tell you. The island's being invaded.'

'Eh?'

'Invaded.'

'I'm blowed! 'Oo's doin' it? The Old Country?'

'You'd hear if it were.'

183

'Not afore the Hultimitium.'

'Shut up! Listen. Some other blokes have landed from another island. It's our ruin or salvation, Ben. Probably the former. But there's just a chance, if—' He paused. 'Well, there's no time to talk now. I only dropped in to report and to tell you to sit tight. Back presently.'

'Oi!' exclaimed Ben. 'Aincher goin' ter stop ter tea?'

'Sorry.'

'So'm I! Wotcher goin' ter do?'

'Have a look round.'

'And wot 'ave I gotter do?'

'I've told you. Sit tight.'

'My Gawd! Ain't I bin doin' it? I'll 'ave it wrote on me grive-stone! Wot 'appens if one o' the black blokes pips me with a poisoned arrer? Do I still sit tight?'

'He won't—'

"Owjer know? Lumme, I do like islands! Oh, I see, yer mean 'e wouldn't shoot a gawd. Yus, but s'pose these new 'uns don't know I'm a gawd? I better pint meself up a bit. Wot abart blue rings rahnd me eyes? Or trihangles, eh? They'd look more 'orrerble—'

'Shut up, shut up!' interrupted Oakley. 'That wasn't my reason. What I meant was that the attack hasn't actually started yet, and I don't think it will for a bit. I'll bring you more information when I get it. Meanwhile, don't worry.'

'Corse not,' answered Ben. 'Me 'eart's goin' pitter-patter with 'appiness!'

'Well, keep it pitter-pattering,' said Oakley, turning.

'It does that without my tellin' it,' retorted Ben as he disappeared.

The village had come alive again as Oakley walked through it. It was alive with sound as well as with movement. The hive-shaped huts emitted a strange buzzing, as though bees were actually in occupation, but many of the bees had issued into the road and were producing their queer music in little groups. They were performing the overture to a concert that would last for many hours—unless there were some unforeseen interruption—and that would culminate in the grand finale at the Temple.

Some of the natives were squatting on the ground, beating small drums. Others were merely squatting and swaying. Others were chanting, while others were on their feet executing a dance that, to the uninitiated observer, had no form, but that had been danced in exactly the same way for countless generations. When the dancers grew tired they squatted on the ground, and others rose to take their place. The proportion of drummers, swayers, chanters, and dancers always remained approximately the same.

One hut was silent. Oakley obeyed an impulse to pause and peer in. A woman and an old man were sitting side by side, staring at the opposite wall.

'Yaala toree,' said Oakley.

They turned to him, with solemn, submissive faces.

'Oomoo kim Yaala,' said Oakley.

The old man raised his head sharply, and the woman murmured:

'Kim?'

'Hyaya,' nodded Oakley. 'Kim. Oomoo kim Yaala.'

They stared after him as he left them, and then at each other. If Oomoo required the sacrifice of Yaala, how could he be, as they had just been told, Yaala's friend? Of course, to be sacrificed was a great honour, provided the person sacrificed did not belong to an enemy tribe, like these white folk. It ensured eternal joy in the life to come, cleansing the

185

soul of sin . . . Yes, the Low Priest must have meant that. He was reminding her. Mothers were apt to forget.

'Oomoo kim Yaala!' chanted the woman, with tightened lips.

'Oomoo kim Yaala!' cackled the old man.

Oakley passed through the village and beyond it. When he was out of sight of the last hut he began running again. He kept his eyes skinned while he ran, and presently, when he neared his destination, he decreased his pace once more to a walk.

He knew the geography of the island thoroughly. He knew the tracks to take, and the tracks to avoid. He knew that he was now in a region that was taboo, the region he called the Priest's Preserve, and which included at its extremity the private, cliff-bounded bay and the precipitous path up to the Temple. The only other land route to the bay was through the densely overgrown forest path he was now traversing, and which Ardentino had traversed before him. The fact that he met none of the invaders on this path confirmed his certainty that their sole objective was the Temple.

The end of the path was almost blocked by bushes. One could just slither one's body through them. Before performing this prickly act he paused and peered at the clearing beyond. The clearing was bounded on one side by rock, and on the other by the last trees of the great woods that sloped up to the Temple and through which the Temple track ascended. Satisfied that none of the invaders were about, he parted the bushes and emerged into the clearing. He looked towards the beach.

A head peeped cautiously over the rock, then disappeared precipitately. It was not a native head. Oakley marked the spot, took one more glance in the opposite direction, and made for it. Climbing over the rock he peered into the darkness of a cave.

'Mr Ardentino at home?' he inquired softly.

The head reappeared. It looked like a wraith half-developed in black shadows. As the wraith did not answer immediately, the visitor continued:

'I'm Oakley.'

'Er—yes,' murmured Ardentino. 'So I gather. But—where are the others? Couldn't they get away?'

'They're still in quod.'

'Oh! I'd hoped—'

'They might have got away if Miss Sheringham had been with them, but she isn't, and of course it's a case of all or none.'

'Well, naturally—'

'I'm glad you agree, Mr Ardentino.'

Ardentino frowned.

'Meaning?' he inquired.

'Afraid there isn't time to exchange personal opinions,' replied Oakley.

'Or, apparently, to form them correctly!' retorted Ardentino warmly. 'I know perfectly well what you meant! But if I'd been fool enough to be caught with the rest, how could I have done my—er—scouting work?'

'We'll leave it at that,' said Oakley. 'Anything happened here since Haines left you?'

'I'm not keen on your tone, Mr Oakley,' snapped Ardentino.

'A good scout doesn't waste time,' answered Oakley. 'Anything happened?'

'No.'

'Seen nothing?'

'No.'

'Heard nothing?'

'No.'

'They went up that track there, didn't they?'

Oakley pointed towards the Temple path.

'I believe so. I didn't see—yes, I think they must have.'

'Any idea how many there were?'

'Not the slightest.'

'Fifty thousand?'

'Of course not!'

'Two?'

'Two thousand?'

'No. Just two.'

'Don't be an idiot.'

'Between two and fifty thousand. Might we say a hundred?'

'About that, I should think.'

'Good. We're getting on. Now see if you can give me the next information more quickly. Know where the boats are?'

'Somewhere round that jut over there.'

'I wonder if they've left a guard round the jut, too,' murmured Oakley. 'I'd better go and see.'

'My God, be careful!' whispered Ardentino.

'Who isn't careful sitting on a bomb?' retorted Oakley. 'But if you sit too long you go up!'

He fell on his face and began to crawl away. Ardentino watched him till he vanished round a boulder.

'Damn my leg,' muttered Ardentino. 'I wish I could go with him!'

The insincerity of the wish hit him in the middle. He saw himself with painful clearness, and the sight was so unpleasant that he actually made an effort to follow Oakley. The next instant he sat down promptly. His injured leg had given under him.

Oakley returned in five minutes. He looked grim.

'Find the boats?' asked Ardentino.

'*And* the guard,' replied Oakley. 'Luckily there was only one guard.'

'Was?' repeated Ardentino, noting Oakley's tone.

'Was,' nodded Oakley.

Ardentino gave a little gulp.

'I—I tried to follow you,' he muttered, thanking heaven that he had.

'Good man,' said Oakley. 'I apologise.'

He held out his hand. Ardentino took it. It gave him a novel sensation.

'How did you do it?' murmured Ardentino, suddenly wondering whether the hand that gripped his had last gripped a neck.

'I found the fellow asleep,' answered Oakley, 'but fortunately he woke up.'

'Fortunately?'

'Well, killing always seems to me a fairly sickening business at the best of times, but to kill a chap while he's dreaming must be quite nauseating,' explained Oakley. 'He heard me coming, sat up just before I reached him, and whipped out a knife. He missed me by half an inch, and when I got hold of the knife I aimed better . . . Well, the battle's begun, Mr Ardentino, so my next step is to do a bit more scouting after the main army. Your leg's bad, isn't it?'

'Yes, but I've got one left,' replied Ardentino.

'You'll need to keep that to hop to the boat with later on. So long. See you later—perhaps.'

'Wait a moment!' exclaimed Ardentino, grabbing his sleeve. 'Look here, this isn't *our* war! Why not let them get on with it?'

'By all means let them get on with it,' said Oakley, 'provided

189

we can get out of it. There's something you don't know. That track they've gone up leads to the Temple, and also to the spot where Miss Sheringham is—so I've *got* to go and see what they're up to, haven't I?'

'But—my God—you can't—'

'Kill the lot? I'm not D'Artagnan. But I can do a bit of good old British spy work to confirm my impression of the position—which is, and has been all along, that the Big War won't commence till to-morrow. Yes, Mr Ardentino, and if my impression is right, and if the plan I am hatching is right, we shall escape from this island under conditions more astonishing than any film you've ever figured in.'

'Suppose your impression isn't right?' queried Ardentino.

Oakley raised his eyes and glanced towards the towering forest, at the invisible crest of which stood the Temple of Gold.

'Suppose my impression isn't right,' he murmured. 'Well, in that case, we'd never have had any chance anyway, so we needn't feel responsible. And, in that case, I may not be coming down again.'

'Look here!' exclaimed Ardentino, as Oakley disengaged his arm. 'You're not going up there alone!'

'Why—can you come with me?' asked Oakley.

'I can have a shot?'

'And what good'll you do? Just hamper the retreat. No, you stay where you are, and if you hear an unholy row going on, hobble to a boat and paddle quietly back to Hollywood. So long.'

Ardentino stared after his departing figure. Oakley was quite beyond his comprehension. But so, for that matter, were his own emotions.

If Oakley had been cautious before, he proceeded now

with trebled caution, moving up the Temple track like a creeping though somewhat solid shadow. The few sounds he made were no louder than the sounds of birds or of a breeze gently stirring branches. After he had covered about a third of the distance to the top he paused. The path had grown narrower and steeper, as though already struggling to shake off the lower forest region and to prove its supremacy before its time. Its final victory however would not occur till it had lost its gradient over the edge of its present horizon, straggled across a tangled space of unexpected flatness, and conquered the dense upper forest region beyond.

It was in the tangled flat space that Oakley expected to find the enemy, and his surmise was correct. He did not prove this by continuing along the track to where it tipped over into the plateau. He proved it from a tree. The enemy had established its camp on the flat, sheltered ground, and was performing preliminary manœuvres which Oakley watched with an experienced eye. The manœuvres were silent but warlike. In the middle of a ring of warriors were six giants who struck belligerent attitudes and donned ferocious expressions. They were rehearsing war, and gaining enthusiasm by the rehearsal. Their utter silence, which was itself a military precaution, added to the horrible grotesqueness of the scene.

But Oakley's eyes were not interested merely in the men. He noted, also, stacked spears and stores, and preparations for a meal. Neither did his vision, developed to almost painful keenness, miss a carved wooden pedestal on the top of which grinned a bright red effigy. Near the effigy stood an old man with a long beard.

He had seen all he needed. Slipping down from the tree, he crept back to the track, and descended swiftly to the bottom.

Ardentino's face registered relief as Oakley clambered over the rock.

'I thought you were never coming back!' he said.

'I warned you I mightn't,' answered Oakley. 'But, you see, I have.'

'What did you find?'

'Just what I hoped—and expected. Unless I'm a mug, which is always possible, there won't be any fighting till sunrise tomorrow.'

'Then we'll pray you're not a mug. But—did you come upon them?' Oakley nodded. 'Then how do you figure it out?'

'Item, they're in camp. They wouldn't be in camp if this was a rush attack. Item, they're war-dancing. That's a lengthy proceeding. Item, they've brought one of their gods, which implies a religious ceremony. Don't forget, I'm a nut on signs. A religious ceremony before a fight is another lengthy proceeding. Item, these two lengthy proceedings will take them till dusk. Item, they won't attack in darkness. Item, they won't go back in darkness. They prefer to do their navigating in the daylight. Item, because of this, sunrise is the most popular time to attack a neighbouring island. It gives the attackers the longest stretch of daylight for the return home afterwards.'

'That sounds good logic,' agreed Ardentino. 'I hope it's as good as it sounds.'

'Yes, but there's another item,' said Oakley. 'I've recognised the tribe. I recognised it—knew my guess was right—the moment I spotted that bloke by the boats. They paint large red squares on their chests. Two of the tribe drifted here in a storm about four months ago. They were taken to the Temple, and one of 'em was boiled in hot water at sunrise. The other escaped. Get me?'

Ardentino shivered slightly.

'Perhaps I do,' he replied, 'but I'm not as good at guessing as you are. What happened to the chap who escaped?'

'Well—if I'm as good at guessing as I think I am—this is what happened to him. He got back to his people. He told 'em about the fate of his companion. He told 'em about the Temple of Gold. That'd explain why they've come along, wouldn't it? Revenge and greed. These attractive qualities are not monopolies of civilisation, you know.'

'I see,' murmured Ardentino.

'There's one thing you don't see,' answered Oakley. 'The final argument in favour of the sunrise attack. These natives have a neat sense of justice. Almost poetic. I've noticed it time and time again. An eye for an eye. A head for a head. A skull for a skull. A boiling for a boiling. If you kill my brother at midday with a poisoned arrow, I shan't be quite happy if I kill you at 3.37 by breaking your back. What I shall sweetly dream of is killing *you* at midday with a poisoned arrow—or as near the time and the process as I can devise. Just to bring memory boomeranging back to you at the crucial moment and to prove to you that your demise isn't a happy accident. Now, the Red Square was done in at sunrise. See the point? Add it to the others, and tack on what I've just witnessed half-way up the hill, and the arguments in favour of a sunrise attack become fairly conclusive.'

'Are you descended from Napoleon?' inquired Ardentino.

'I hope not,' replied Oakley. 'He lost Waterloo. But now I'm going to try to be an imitation of Wellington—so lend me thine ears, Mr Ardentino, and pay heed to what I'm going to say. No, wait a moment. We've got a bit of time, so there's something I'd like to ask you first.'

'What is it?' answered Ardentino.

Oakley turned his eyes for a moment towards the sea beyond which lay the world of fading memories.

'If, through a spot of anything I do, we escape from this Isle of Loveliness,' he said bringing his eyes back to Ardentino's, 'do you think you could wangle me a signed photograph of Greta Garbo?'

23

The Plan

'Can I come in?' asked Oakley.

Ben sat up with a start, and stared towards the reed curtain as Oakley pushed his way through it.

'Sorry I always make you jump,' said Oakley, 'but I did try to give you a warning that time.'

'I suppose yer thinks I was asleep?' inquired Ben, rubbing his eyes.

'I received that impression,' admitted Oakley.

'Well, I was.'

'Forgive me for waking you.'

'That's orl right, I was tryin' ter wike. See, I was playin' skittles with the 'Igh Priest and the balls was skulls. Wot's the noos?'

'I've come to tell you. Do you think you can listen to it without interrupting?'

''Oo's hinterruptin'? Let's 'ave it!'

For the third time—the first to Ardentino, the second to the prisoners in the compound, and now to Ben—Oakley related his discoveries and conjectures, while Ben listened in silence with a solemn face. At the conclusion of the recital, Ben said:

'It's a mess!'

'It is going to be a very nasty mess,' nodded Oakley.

'I 'ates blood.'

'I'm not enamoured of it myself, and plenty will be spilt tomorrow, I am afraid—'

'If we don't do nothink,' interrupted Ben.

'Yes, if we don't do anything. The Red Squares will burst in upon the Temple a few minutes after the trial has begun, and there will be a general massacre.'

'Then we gotter do somethink!'

'We're going to do something—'

'Cos we can't 'ave no blood.'

'I beg your pardon?'

'I ses we can't 'ave no blood. Or Oomoo ses it. Sime thing.'

Oakley frowned at him.

'My dear Ben, or Oomoo, sime thing,' he said. 'Are you really suggesting that two hostile tribes—one about to attack the other—can meet without hurting each other?'

'Well, they've gotter, ain't they?' retorted Ben. 'That's wot I'm 'ere for. Gits pliner and pliner, don't it? Why aintcher told our blokes abart these other blokes—the Red Squires, as yer calls 'em? Corse, it might be a good idea ter wait a bit, but wot's the reason?'

'I have told our blokes.'

'I mean our black blokes.'

'Oh, I see. Well, if I told our black blokes about the other blokes, there'd be a bust up at once, and we don't want a bust up at once. We're not ready for it. Heaven knows what would happen! Moreover, the fight would take place in the worst possible spot for us—'

'Where's that?'

'In the track along which Miss Sheringham has got to escape to the beach—and the boats.'

'Yer mean she might, well, trip over the cashilties, like?'

'She would probably become a casualty herself. But those are only some of the reasons,' said Oakley. 'Do you think you could be a good, quiet boy again while I tell you our plan?'

'Oh, yer've got a plan, then?' queried Ben.

'Of course. Didn't we agree that something had to be done?'

'That's right, on'y I didn't know yer'd thort o' the somethink.'

'Well, I have, Ben. And they've all agreed to it, so what you've got to do is just to listen, and then do your bit—'

'If *I* agree to it,' murmured Ben, 'which I ain't doin' if they're still arter the gold.'

Oakley smiled grimly.

'Oomoo,' he said, 'do you realise the position?'

'Wotcher mean?' answered Ben.

'I mean that we are between two hostile tribes who will shortly be at each other's throats, and that although we are planning to escape from the sandwich, and are going to have a jolly good try, our chance of success is about one in a million. I'm asking you if you *realise* it?'

'Well, nah yer menshuns it, I dunno if I do,' replied Ben. 'See, I gone sort o' benumb.'

'I believe you have.'

'It's me forrid. It ain't be'avin' nacherel. Orter be runnin' rivers, but it ain't, ain't it?'

'Looks perfectly waterproof to me.'

'Eh? And then me 'eart. It ain't jerkin'. And then me knuckles. They ain't hitchin'. 'Ere I am, sittin' like we might be torkin' abart the weather instead o' running abart like a jelly. That's right, I've gone benumb.'

'Yes, and if you *weren't*—benumb,' interposed Oakley, 'you'd realise that your friends are not thinking of gold any more, but simply and solely of their own skins.'

'And the reason I've gone benumb,' Ben went on, paying no attention to Oakley's remark, 'is becorse Gawd's sent me perteckshun so's I can do wot I got ter do. See, if I wasn't benumb I couldn't do it. Wunnerful 'ow it works.'

'But don't you want to know what you've got to do?' inquired Oakley patiently.

'I'll know when the time comes,' returned Ben staring ahead of him.

In a firm voice Oakley retorted.

'You're going to know now, and if you start going into a trance I'll give you a wallop that will end your benumbness for ever more! For heaven's sake, man, forget your part for a few moments and listen to what I'm saying!'

''Oo ain't listenin'?' answered Ben. 'Let's 'ear the plan.'

'Right!' said Oakley. 'It's this. It begins as soon as I leave you. You may not know it, but you are telling me at this moment that you want the trial to commence an hour earlier than at present arranged—an hour *before* sunrise. I shall broadcast this new order from Oomoo to the Chief and to the whole village, saying that the reason for the alteration is that you have a matter of vital importance to communicate to them at the Temple.'

'Wot'll that be?' asked Ben.

'I'll tell you in a moment,' replied Oakley. 'Don't interrupt! I shall not broadcast the information to the High Priest till considerably later. He might raise objections, and there are not going to be any objections. In fact, he won't be told until you all arrive. Then I shall communicate with him by means of our special contrivance used only in emergency—I call it our burglar alarm—'

''Ow's it work?'

'Is that important?'

'Yus. I may 'ave ter use it meself!'

'You won't have to. Still, you can hear how it works. I think I've told you I am never allowed in the Priest's quarters, so when I am in the Temple and need him badly I pull a skull that hangs over a door. The skull is connected by a cord that runs through holes with another skull in the H.P.'s house. When my skull comes down, his goes up. And along he comes. Of course, there's a penalty for pulling the communication cord without sufficient reason, but there will be quite sufficient reason this time. He will find, to his astonishment, that the Temple is filled not, as he usually plans, with the Chosen Few, but with as many of his flock as can pack into it. And they will all be armed . . . I wonder if you begin to get the idea?'

'No,' said Ben. 'Wot 'appens next?'

'The H.P. is informed of the alteration in the time—too late for him to object—and then you make your communication. You will gesticulate as you have never gesticulated before. And I, interpreting your signs, will look more astounded than I have ever looked before. Because you will have informed me of the attack that is about to be made on the Temple at sunrise, and by this uncanny knowledge you will prove, beyond doubt, that you are indeed Oomoo, the God of Storms, who not only sends storms, but who knows when they are coming. Well, Ben, what do you think of it—so far?'

Ben was impressed.

'It don't seem so bad,' he admitted, 'on'y I don't see why

they've brort their weppins—yer sed they was harmed—when they didn't know abart the attack.'

'That was your order, Oomoo. Don't worry about these little details.'

'Oh! Well, wot 'appens next?'

'Having given them this vital information, and having saved them from massacre, I am banking on the hope that they will do anything more you tell them.'

'Wot more do I tell 'em?'

'You tell them to curb their impatience and not to rush out to slaughter. You tell them to retire to the outer chamber, and to wait there. You will tell the High Priest that you yourself desire to wait, with him, with me, and with all the prisoners, in the High Priest's quarters. If the High Priest objects, and suggests that the prisoners are left in the Temple to be the first victims, you will inform him that the prisoners are to be your own victims, not the enemy's, and that they are to be preserved in the High Priest's house till the battle is over. Then they will be sacrificed, to celebrate victory—'

'Wot's that?' interrupted Ben. 'Sakerficed?'

'That, Oomoo, is what you will *tell* the High Priest,' answered Oakley. 'He must have something to pacify him. Otherwise your orders may not be obeyed. Assuming that they are, the natives will retire to the outer chamber, ready to pounce upon the foe when the foe is trapped. We shall retire—by the opposite door—to the Priest's house, the only evidence of which is a small door in a rocky wall. I mention this, Ben, because the Red Squares will have to pass that door when they enter the Temple at sunrise. The door will be in deep shadow at that time, and will probably not be noticed. That, again, is a hope. Anyhow it will be secured on the inside, and since the door to the Temple itself will be immediately ahead of the Red Squares, their eyes will be fixed on that. They will enter the Temple. They will find it empty. They will begin their work of vengeance—smashing—pillaging—looting—what a scene, Ben, eh? Shall we pop our heads in, and see it?'

He paused. Ben was gazing ahead of him, picturing the episode, and completing the picture in his mind even as Oakley supplied the final touches . . .

'No, Ben, we will not pop in and see it. The people who will pop in will be our islanders, from the other side. But, first, *we* shall have popped out of the Priest's house—after the last Red Square has gone into the Temple—and we will have barred the door so that they cannot come out again. And while two tribes are slaying each other, we shall be leaving the Priest's house, and descending the track up which the Red Squares came—descending past their camp—where they are now at this moment, Ben, while you and I are talking—past that spot, and down to the beach, where we shall find Ardentino waiting in the best boat, and the best boat packed with supplies.'

He paused again, but Ben did not ask the question he had expected. Ben was visualising the battle in the Temple, and was unable to tear his mind away from the horrible picture.

'Of course, I shall have been working on the boat and the supplies during the night,' said Oakley, answering the unasked question. 'That will be my job after I have given out the news of the advanced time of the gathering in the Temple. In fact, I hope to start forraging in about an hour from now, and maybe I shall be able to find some of the supplies that tipped out of the boat you arrived in. Anyhow, that's up to me. We are assuming that I have filled the boat with all that is necessary for our long voyage—and the voyage itself is in God's hands.'

Ben jerked himself out of his reverie.

'It seems ter me,' he muttered, 'that there's a lot in Gawd's 'ands.'

'That is true, Ben,' nodded Oakley solemnly. 'I have told you what I *hope* will happen—but you will remember I prefaced my remarks with the observation that there is about one chance in a million that all the plans will go as arranged. Or, let us be optimistic, and say one chance in five hundred thousand. I believe in looking on the bright side of things.'

'Oh,' said Ben. 'Do yer call it the bright side o' things a lot o' blokes killin' each hother?'

'It is the bright side for us,' answered Oakley. 'The occupation will be so intensive that no one will think of us till it is all over—and till we are well away.'

'"Ave *you* gorn benumb?'

'I am endeavouring to recapture that enviable condition.'

'Eh?'

'Ben,' said Oakley sharply, 'are you still thinking about the impossible?'

'Nothink's himposserble when Gawd's be'ind yer.'

'Then why does God permit wars? If—as you think—God's hand is in this, don't worry about the method, but be grateful that God is giving us a slender chance to save Miss Sheringham. Be grateful that the bloodthirstiness of warring tribes, which is a natural instinct you can't prevent, and have no obligation to prevent, happens on this occasion to give Miss Sheringham a chance of going on living! Do you understand what I am talking about, or am I using too long words?'

'I unnerstan' wot yer torkin' abart,' replied Ben, 'but you don't unnerstan' wot I'm torkin' abart. Mind yer, I ain't sure I unnerstan' it meself, but I've jest got a feelin' that somethink's gotter be done, and that I'll know wot it is when the time comes, like wot I sed. And any'ow, there's one thing yer've fergot.'

'What?'

'The kid. Wot 'appens to 'er?'

'We might take her along with us.'

'Yus, that's a nidea! P'r'aps I could adop' 'er. I've always wanted one. But there's another thing yer've fergot, too.'

'I dare say there are plenty of other things,' replied Oakley, 'and that one of them will trip us up. What is this particular other thing?'

'The 'Igh Priest. Wot's 'e goin' ter do abart it, when we wanter pop orf from 'is 'ouse?'

'The High Priest is one of the things I have *not* forgotten, Ben,' answered Oakley gravely. 'To use your own phrase, we'll know what to do with the High Priest when the time comes.'

'Kill 'im?' asked Ben bluntly.

'What, kill that darling old gentleman, Ben?' exclaimed Oakley. 'My lad, how could you even *suggest* such a thing?'

They stared at each other. From the distance sounded the pom-pom of the villagers' drums.

'Course,' said Ben, 'the kid 'd feel a bit 'ome-sick in Lunnon. I wunner if the hother kids 'd go fer 'er?'

Oakley smiled despairingly.

'That's one thing I can't stand,' said Ben, 'people goin' fer each hother. I seen a lot of it.'

'If you're going to reminisce, I'll be off,' replied Oakley moving. 'Well, glad to have met you, though you're the rummest ass I ever struck, and I give you up.'

'That's where yer keep on goin' wrong,' retorted Ben. 'This *ain't* me!'

203

24

Blessings Before Battle

Ben's conviction that he was not himself increased as the hours of strange loneliness slipped by. No one came near him to remind him of his true identity. Oakley had ensured his solitude, and was himself too busy elsewhere to pay any more calls. Thus, in an atmosphere appropriate to the transition, the little stoker imagined himself slipping more and more certainly out of his familiar form and assuming a shape beyond mere physical dimensions.

For a long while after Oakley left him he sat and thought. Or, more correctly, he sat and let thoughts come. His 'benumbness' seemed to have removed the material barriers that might otherwise have prevented the entry of a spiritual guide, and he was quite convinced that from now onwards he merely had to be obedient to superior direction. Even when he left his seat at last and walked to the curtained exit, he believed that his legs were being propelled by a force considerably greater than the force of unadulterated Ben.

He stood by the curtain and listened to the queer noises that rose from the village.

Pom-pom, pom-pom, pom-pom, sounded the drums.

Waaaaaa—waaaaaa, chanted the voices.

Pom-pom, waaaaaa-waaaaaa, pom-pom, waaaaaa-waaaaaa, pom-pom, waaaaaa-waaaaaa . . .

The uncanny music, with its monotonous endlessness, added its hypnotic influence to Ben's metamorphosis. The old Ben would merely have been astonished or terrified by the unnatural din. The new Ben accepted it, and hardly felt it, indeed, to be unnatural. He did not visualise a band of strangers doing incomprehensible, idiotic things. He visualised a band of fellow-creatures, including pretty children who could smile, doing sad and pathetic things. He visualised them pomming and waaing in the afternoon sunlight feeling as normal to themselves as folk-dancers in an English village; and then retiring to their huts to sleep (unless they kept this up all night?); and then, in the cold grey hour before dawn, marching up to the Temple, in obedience to his, Oomoo's order; and then—conflict and bloodshed, shrieks and agony, death . . .

The horrible picture came to him with stark vividness. For a moment the soul of the little god dissolved while the soul of the little stoker took its place again and reeled. But Oomoo materialised once more, and gave Ben 'what for.'

'Wot are yer worryin' abart?' demanded Oomoo. 'When it ain't goin' ter 'appen? When yer goin' ter stop it?'

'That's right,' apologised Ben. 'I fergot.'

'Well, doncher fergit no more,' instructed Oomoo, ''cos if yer does yer mayn't do wot I tells yer ter do when I tells yer ter do it.'

'When's that goin' ter be?' asked Ben.

'In the Temple,' replied Oomoo.

'Wot are yer goin' ter tell me to do when we're in the Temple?'

'Do yer want ter know?'

'No.'

'Then wot did yer arsk for? It wouldn't be good fer yer ter know. Wite fer it! It'd hupset yer ter know afore'and.'

'That's right. But wot abart givin' me somethink ter do nah—somethink small—jest ter tike me mind orf, like?'

''Ave yer stopped bein' benumb?'

'P'r'aps jest a bit.'

'Well, that won't do. You git benumb agine. You go 'ome. There ain't room fer two of us inside yer.'

'All right, I'm goin'. But if yer could give me somethink ter do nah—'

'I was goin' ter give yer somethink ter do nah, but yer've no right ter arsk, see? I'll tell yer without no arskin'. Go inter the Chief's 'arf o' the 'ouse, and find some pint.'

''As 'e got any pint?'

'Will yer stop torkin'? Of course 'e's got some pint. 'Ow does 'e pint 'iself if 'e ain't got no pint? Go and find the pint, and pint yerself. Gold, if there is any. Course, *you* know I'm inside yer, but the hothers 'ave got ter be kep' hup ter it, and yer've got ter look proper when them Red Squires sees yer.'

'Oh—the Red Squires are goin' ter see me, are they?' said Ben.

'Ain't yer goin' ter stop the fight?' demanded Oomoo. ''Ow are yer goin' ter stop it if they don't see yer?'

'That's right,' said Ben. 'I fergot.'

The depressing conference over, he turned and walked mechanically towards the inner portion of the hut, and as he walked his calmness began to return. These mental conversations were a nuisance. They came periodically when some incident or thought hooked his drowning personality to the surface. But they were growing less frequent, partly through a subconscious process of self-hypnotism, and partly through the drugged atmosphere, and he hoped that when he had obeyed this spiritual instruction to paint himself, he would paint Ben completely out of recognition and leave Oomoo in undisputed possession.

It troubled him a little that Oomoo himself had not a really respectable history. A god who produced storms and who fattened on sacrifices was hardly the happiest instrument of moral progress. But if Oomoo was transforming Ben, so Ben was transforming Oomoo, and a higher power than either was directing them both towards humane ends.

He passed through the inner curtain, and trod new ground. He had not been in this half of the hut before. The silence here was utter, for he no longer heard the faint music from the village. He had expected to find another large chamber beyond the partition, but instead he found a network of irregular cubicles, and he was amazed at his lack of panic as he groped around them with stately indecision. 'It's orl right, I'm losin' meself agine,' he reflected gratefully. 'Waalaala!'

A few seconds later his gratitude became emotional. He came to a cubicle which appeared to be the Chief's beauty parlour. It contained four tub-like receptacles, each half-full of thickly-coloured fluid. Red, blue, brown, and yellow. He stared, fascinated, at the yellow.

'That's me, ain't it?' he muttered. 'Yeller. Gold like. Yus, that's me.'

He dipped a finger in the yellow tub. He brought it out and stared at it. The paint looked more gold-like on his finger than in the tub. 'P'r'aps me and that mikes gold?' he wondered, vaguely recalling some childhood lesson about pigments.

Well, his finger was already transformed. How to transform

the rest of him? The method was obvious, if the prospect made one pause. But one did not pause long, for the method was appropriate as well as obvious—a sort of religious ablution—and the sooner it was begun, the sooner it would be over. Ben climbed into the tub and stooped.

As his body went down, the yellow fluid came up. It rose to his neck—he felt it rising like a thick ascending coil of cold—and at neck-level he stopped stooping. That was enough for the moment. One needed a breather.

He knew, however, that he would have to complete the job, and that the final portion would be the least pleasant. He wondered for an instant whether he might omit it. But the humanness of his natural head would be too glaringly apparent above his unhuman body, and there was no honourable escape. So, taking a deep breath, and closing his mouth and his eyes more tightly than he had ever closed them before—he closed his mouth so tightly that he bit himself—he ducked, counted four, and came up again.

Then he left the tub, and returned glistening to his seat to dry.

If the effect of his bath on his body was considerable, it was even more considerable on his mood. As his golden casement hardened around him, he felt as though he were being armoured against terror, and also against the material oppressions that gave terror birth. It was now impossible for anyone to treat him as an ordinary human being. He could not even treat himself so. Within this new skin of startling splendour he could function clearly and authoritatively, provided his general attitude were of the same colour. Yes, until his job was done there must be no further undermining conversations, either mental or actual. He must keep others in their place, to keep himself in place

. . . to seal the dignity that would make him supreme in the Temple . . .

While revolving these matters in his elevated mind, an idea dawned which proved by its very audacity how definitely he was feeling his wings. In his right colour the idea could never have occurred to him. Even now it had to form the subject of a mental conversation, despite his vow to veto such things; but the conversation was no longer undermining. On the contrary, without interfering with Oomoo's dominance (for, as he explained later when attempting to elucidate his condition, there was only a very little bit of Ben left, and it was this little bit that put the questions to the big bit), the discourse and the manner of it added a touch of distinction to the proceedings.

'Should I go and show meself, O, Oomoo?' asked the little bit.

'Why not, O, Ben?' answered the big bit.

''Jest ter see' ow they tikes it, O, Oomoo?'

'Why not, O, Ben?'

'Fer a dress re'ersil, like, O, Oomoo?'

'For the third time, O, Ben, why not, O, Ben?'

'That means, Yus,' reflected the little bit.

He rose from his seat, and walked slowly and with dignity to the exit. It was Oomoo's walk, not Ben's. Ben's walk was quick and jerky. Out of the corner of his eye he detected yellow flashes. They were his own moving limbs. Ben would have poked his face all over himself in amazement at his transformation, but Oomoo, taking it for granted, refused to pry upon himself, kept his eyes fixed ahead, and contented himself with these vague and accidental glimpses.

The music from the village of skulls rose up to him once more, borne through the heavy evening air.

'*Pom-pom!*'
'*Waaaaaa-waaaaaa!*'
'*Pom-pom!*'
'*Waaaaaa-waaaaaa!*'

This time he did not pause to listen. With measured steps, he walked out into it.

The first native he came upon was a young man standing by himself and beating his chest. The young man was so intent on this occupation that he did not notice the approaching wonder till it was right up to him. Then he raised his eyes, and stiffened in terror.

Ben stopped and regarded him. Ben, a miserable stoker, put fear into the heart of a cannibal. The cannibal was looking as Ben himself ought to have looked! ''E 'ad one o' them Gawd-'elp-me expreshuns,' Ben related afterwards. Well, here was a god, ready at hand, to help him. So why not?

Ben extended a yellow hand and placed it on the young man's head. Then he risked a smile. A short one, that leapt for an instant from the godly mien and then leapt back again. The young man's terror changed, and he fell upon his face and rubbed it on Ben's feet.

'Lumme, 'e's ticklin'!' thought the lesser part of the god, and he proceeded on his way before the weakness of the flesh undid him.

The young man rose behind him, and followed at a distance.

Then he came upon a group. There were about a dozen, half of them squatting on the ground and beating their little drums, the other half chanting and swaying. Seeing Ben, they ceased, and stood transfixed as the young man had stood.

Now a humble stoker was striking terror into the hearts of *twelve* cannibals!

Ben did not hesitate. He had settled his simple routine and

he walked slowly round the circle, giving a pat and a smile to each member. And while he smiled, noting the various receptions—one old woman, he believed, smiled back—an illuminating thought came to him. 'This is the langwidge we orl wants,' ran the thought. 'It don't need no hinterpreter!'

When the ceremony was over and he strode towards the next group, the group he had just blessed, joined by the original young man, followed him.

The next group stood silently while he approached. He became aware, all at once, that there was now silence everywhere. With the swiftness of wireless, the news had travelled. He blessed the second group, and passed on.

He came to a line of huts. Little children were outside each hut, saving one. He paused before the hut that was childless.

'I—wunner?' reflected the smaller part of the yellow god. The greater part did not interfere.

He stared at the entrance. Behind him, the crowd waited. In the dimness of the interior he thought he vaguely saw a form. He walked to the entrance and went in.

An old man and a woman gaped at him. 'Wash the old bloke's fice,' thought Ben, 'and I seen a chap like that once diggin' pertaters.' He went to him, and touched his forehead, and smiled.

Then he turned to the woman. 'And I seen people like you,' thought Ben. Her eyes were wet with her personal tragedy. They had no right to be, but they were. She was not a perfect heathen. After putting his hands on her head, Ben put both hands on her shoulders and gave her a longer smile. Suddenly the woman threw herself on the ground and began jabbering.

The old man looked frightened. He muttered to himself, and then sprang to the woman, and heaved her up. The woman shook him off, turned again to Ben, and beat her breast. She seemed to be imploring him. She twisted round, pointed to a little bundle, then beat her breast again. 'She seems ter be offerin' 'erself like,' thought Ben as she fell once more upon her face.

Ben looked at the little bundle. He came to the conclusion that it was some form of doll. He bent down, touched the woman's back, and helped her to her feet. Then he walked to the doll, took it up, patted it, smiled at it, and put it down again. The woman stopped protesting, and was crying quietly when he left.

He continued his queer journey until he reached a point where the village ended. He gazed into the woods beyond, wondering whether a track he saw led to the prisoners' camp. But he decided not to take it. He was playing a lone hand, and he did not believe he could give any assistance to his companions until he met them on the morrow at the Temple. Moreover, he had done as much for the moment as his mind could stand.

So he turned, and retraced his way through the village, while the villagers processioned after him at a respectful distance.

'Are they goin' ter foller me orl the way 'ome?' he reflected. 'We don't want that, do we?'

When he came to the last hut he paused, turned round slowly, and raised a hand like a golden policeman. The natives immediately halted, and fell on their faces. He completed the last stage of the homeward journey alone.

As he resumed his seat of honour, he heard the village music starting up again.

25

Through the Night

The sun slipped below the clear-cut horizon of the sea and dusk crept over the island. The brilliant shore lost its colours. The tree-tops were no longer distinct, yielding their outlines to the shadows. The huts became grey blotches, and the natives retired into them. Acutely conscious of the coming of night, the scattered white folk wondered what the morrow would bring. More than one wondered whether, for them, there would be any morrow.

'The whole thing seems a mess-up to me!' muttered Medworth, gazing out into the gathering gloom from the prison doorway. Like the natives, the prisoners had retired indoors. 'Waiting like this—when we could slip off almost at once, if we decided to.'

'And leave Miss Sheringham behind?' exclaimed Haines sharply.

'I didn't say that,' retorted Medworth, although in his heart he had meant it. It wasn't sound mathematics to risk too many skins for the sake of only one—provided that one were not his own. 'But we could have found some way of getting

213

her if we hadn't left matters to the three most incompetent fools in the place.'

'Well, I—I rather agree with you there,' said Smith with a glance towards Miss Noyes, who was no longer protected from painful knowledge by slumber.

'The three fools being Oakley, Ardentino, and Ben?' queried Lord Cooling.

'Obviously!' snapped Medworth.

'I seem to remember that the first of the fools has got us out of several scrapes—including, once, death by pressure in a very confined space in a temple,' replied Cooling. 'I was being slowly and surely flattened when Oakley came along and sounded the "All clear." I am not sure whether I have completely filled out again yet . . . The second fool, one admits, did not begin well, but at least he found some boats, while we, Medworth, were looking for gold—'

'Yes, and we've made no provision for carting away any of *that*!' interrupted Medworth savagely.

'Perhaps we shall manage a few handfuls in passing,' suggested Cooling.

'The third fool could help us there, if he had a mind!'

'The third fool, Ben? Yes, but unfortunately Ben does not seem to have a mind—'

'No, a vacuum!'

'Undoubtedly a vacuum. Yet there is something in the vacuum that defies description. He ought to be given over to Sir Ernest Spilsbury for analysis when we get back.'

'*If* we get back,' corrected Medworth.

'*When* we get back,' responded Cooling. 'I still retain my confidence in our mindless third fool.'

'You're sure *you* oughtn't be given over to Sir Ernest

Spilsbury when we get back?' inquired Medworth, while Smith looked shocked.

But Lord Cooling merely smiled.

'You and I will call on him together, Medworth,' he said. 'Meanwhile we are not committed to the Three-Fool-Plan if we can produce a better. Produce it, Medworth, and we are yours!'

'Provided you don't leave Miss Sheringham out,' added Haines.

'Who's leaving anybody out?' growled Medworth. 'But what I say is this. With the whole night before us, and boats all ready, we ought to be able to fetch Miss Sheringham along so we could be well away by morning.'

'That's a hope, not a plan,' commented Cooling. 'Still, while we get to the boats and wait, Medworth, if you like you can just slip up that track to the Temple, tread over an army of black warriors with red squares on their chests, break into the High Priest's house, rescue Miss Sheringham, carry her down—treading again over the Red Square Army—and rejoin us. Only, of course, if you don't rejoin us, we'll gather that you didn't tread quite lightly enough, and so we will have to push off without you.'

'Being funny again?' inquired Medworth.

'No—quite serious. It is you who are developing into the comic turn. Of course, there is an alternative to the simple little plan I have just suggested for you. You may prefer to climb the road to the Temple—don't wake any of the villagers, will you?—and break open two doors—no, three—don't make a noise, will you?—no, four doors, I had forgotten the final door to the High Priest's palace—hit the High Priest on the head, and then carry Miss Sheringham back through the village, or down past the Red Squares—whichever route of the two most delights your fancy.'

'Oh, shut up!' exclaimed Medworth.

'Certainly,' answered Cooling, 'if it's to be a fifty-fifty arrangement. Personally, I am all for sitting here quietly and enjoying this perfect night.'

In another prison high above them Ruth Sheringham sat staring out of a slit window over softly waving tree-tops.

She was alone with the child, and had been for several hours. After conducting his captives into a small chamber, the High Priest had paid them two very short visits, and had then left them to themselves.

On the first visit he had brought them a large bowl of food. The child had eaten her share at once; Ruth had eaten hers after hesitation, to find it surprisingly pleasant if a little rich. It appeared to be some vegetable concoction—reserved, possibly, for prisoners of distinction.

On the second occasion the High Priest had brought in a thick dark mass of some compressed substance, had fixed it in a deep socket in the wall, and had lit it. It smouldered slowly, emitting considerable heat and a sweetly, sickly odour.

The odour had a soporific effect, and as she now sat by the window she was fighting it. Once she had attempted to extinguish the smouldering substance, but as the ignited surface covered a large area and the heat penetrated downwards as well as outwards, she had merely scorched her fingers.

'Well, I don't care!' she muttered. 'It's *not* going to send me to sleep!'

As though in answer to this boast, she became suddenly conscious of the child's weight against her. The child had already yielded to the fumes.

She took the child in her arms, partly through sympathy, and partly for the comfort of feeling something solid. Solidarity was slipping away . . . 'But I'm not going to sleep!' she thought. 'I'm not, I'm not, I'm *not* . . .'

On the unseen beach below the Temple, Ardentino and Oakley worked throughout the night. Oakley had examined and bound Ardentino's foot, and fortunately, although the film star could just hobble, his duties did not involve much moving about. Once the boat had been selected and shoved into the required position for launching on the early morning tide—it was the largest of the war canoes, with more than enough room for its intended new crew—he merely had to assist with the loading and the storing when Oakley made his periodic visits. If Oakley expended the more physical energy, Ardentino had the more nerve-racking job—or so he declared. Sitting alone in the darkness during Oakley's interminable absences, with the knowledge that not far above him on the heights was a camp of bloodthirsty warriors, Ardentino died countless deaths, all equally unpleasant.

'What I can't understand,' he whispered once as Oakley was about to leave him to another lonely vigil, 'is why there aren't any scouts poking about!'

'They left one with the boats,' Oakley reminded him grimly.

'Yes, and now they seem to have forgotten all about him,' replied Ardentino.

'A scout reports to an army, not an army to a scout,' said Oakley. 'Just the same, I agree that these fellows are a bit over-confident. So are our chaps when there's a war on, for that matter. Primitive emotions go to extremes, you know—exaggerated cowardice, exaggerated courage, exaggerated everything. When they fight they deal with the exaggerated cowardice by working themselves up to the exaggerated courage. That's how they lose their natural caution. Queer—but *we* needn't worry about it. It's all to our advantage.'

'Then you—you don't think there's much chance of any-one popping down from the camp?' asked Ardentino.

'Not much chance,' answered Oakley, 'though, of course, nothing's certain.'

'No. They may upset our plans by invading the Temple before sunrise.'

'They may. But I've never known a night attack yet. They want to see what they're doing, and to have light for the get-away.'

'Some of them will get away anyhow, and follow us.'

'Not the Red Squares. I know the direction they've come from, and we shall take one exactly opposite. Anyhow, I'm not sure that any of 'em *will* get away, after the surprise attack, and with their only exit barred against them. If any do, it'll be *sauve qui peut* with them. They'll be thinking of their own skins, not ours.'

'But the conquerors—the natives here?'

'If our plan works, it'll keep them busy for all the time *we* want. Keep your pecker up.'

'So simple!' murmured Ardentino. 'Are the others keeping their peckers up?'

'Haven't had time to inquire.'

'Not even of the stoker?'

'Not even of the stoker. When Oomoo and I get together we just go round and round. So does the inside of my head. I've decided not to have any more mental revolutions with Oomoo until just before we all go up to the Temple—which, incidentally, will be after a couple more visits to you here, by my present reckoning. I think I can finish by then, and it'll be about time to begin the fun. Well, so long. I must be off. Keep the eggs warm.'

Oakley's reckoning proved correct. Two more journeys to

the boat completed the preparations, and he found that he had worked almost exactly to the time-table he had set himself.

His next visit was to the Chief, whom he instructed to form the procession and to lead it to the hut where Oomoo and the Low Priest would be awaiting its arrival. Then he went to the hut, and received the shock of his life.

'My God!' he gasped, staring at the transformation. 'But—I say! It's *great*!'

26

The Yellow God

The yellow god stared back with the expressionless fixity of an idol. Then he said, and Oakley noticed a change of voice as well as of appearance.

''Ow long 'ave we got, O, Oakley?'

With quick intelligence Oakley decided not to interfere with the god's poise. He replied, in kind:

'The procession will be here in a few minutes, O, Oomoo. Say, five.'

He hoped his solemnity—and in truth he felt solemn enough, in spite of the grotesqueness of the situation—would assist Ben to maintain his own. If it *was* Ben? In any case, whether Ben or Oomoo sat before him, the unique atmosphere he pervaded was too valuable to be disturbed.

'And wot 'appens ezackly, O, Oakley, when the perceshun comes?' inquired the yellow god.

'You will be carried on the golden litter, borne by six men, to the Temple, O, Oomoo,' answered Oakley. 'The Low Priest will walk on one side, the Chief on the other. Behind will be torch-bearers and armed men. In the middle of the line will be five of the prisoners. Of the other two, O, Oomoo, one is at the boat, which is ready and provisioned for its voyage, and the other, as you know, is in the Priest's house.'

'And wot 'appens ezackly, O, Oakley, when we *gits* ter the Temple?' continued the yellow god, after a pause during which he considered the details he had just learned.

'If your will is obeyed, I summon the High Priest. And I am beside you to obey your will. He comes. You inform him, through me, of the enemy outside the gate. You order the prisoners to be sent into the High Priest's house, under my escort. You order the rest to retire to the outer chamber, there to wait. You join us in the High Priest's house. At sunrise, the enemy pours into the Temple. We secure the door so they cannot pour out again. And by these means, O, Oomoo, you save many lives, including that of a very gracious lady. Thinking of this lady, O, Oomoo, you will decide that nothing shall be allowed to interfere with this plan. No other consideration will weigh with you, O, Oomoo. You will think only of the lady, so that she may meet life instead of death.'

Now the yellow god removed his staring eyes from Oakley's for the first time, and turned them upwards. 'Poor chap,' thought Oakley, 'I really believe he is quite, quite mad—and I don't wonder.' He waited anxiously, and Oomoo's next words increased the theory of madness.

'Do yer ever 'ave vishuns, O, Oakley?' asked the yellow god.

'I think we are best without them,' replied Oakley apprehensively.

'I'm 'avin' one now,' said the yellow god. 'It's a vishun of the boilin' pot. It's a very big pot.'

'Very big indeed,' answered Oakley. 'It has to be.'

''Oo 'eats the water?'

'The High Priest keeps the water warm all night. The Low Priest brings it to boiling point. The High Priest waits till the steam issues from the hole in the lid.'

''Oo goes near the pot, beside them two and the victims? There ain't nobody else in my vishun.'

'Nobody else goes near it. It is taboo.'

'I don't see no fire in my vishun.'

'Nobody can see the fire from the Temple floor. Only I can see it. It burns beneath the pot, and the recess is out of sight.'

'That is a good answer, O, Oakley. Are you seein' my vishun, too?'

'I don't know, O, Oomoo.'

'Do you ever chinge the water?' continued the yellow god, after another short session at the ceiling.

'The water is holy,' replied Oakley, 'and is always changed after contamination.'

'When's contermashun?' inquired the yellow god. 'One o' the Fite Days?'

Oakley swallowed. He was feeling a little dizzy.

'It occurs after each ceremony,' he said.

''Ow do yer chinge the water? I don't see no bale in my vishun.'

'There is a hole at the bottom. I remove a plug.'

'Does the water go quickly?'

'Very quickly.'

'And quietly? I don't 'ear no noise?'

'Very quietly. Apart from the final moments. But if one put the plug in and left, say, a depth of one inch, the final sound would not occur.'

'Could one tell when ter do it?'

'One could, for there is a soft warning that precedes the final violence.'

222

'O, Oakley,' said the yellow god, 'do yer see my vishun a bit pliner?'

'I see it plainer,' said Oakley, 'but I do not see the use of what I see. Our plan does not need it.'

'Our plan does need it, O, Oakley,' answered the yellow god, 'so now yer knows wot ter do when ye're told ter bring up the fire.'

'But the High Priest will not now tell me to bring up the fire!'

'No, Oomoo will tell yer ter bring up the fire—and yer'll know wot ter do when 'e tells yer. Yer'll put it aht, and let the water aht. And when yer comes hup from doin' it, yer'll tell the 'Igh Priest that Oomoo ses 'e's not ter go near the pot, becos' it's bein' got ready fer—somethink speshul—something 'e's never seed afore—somethink nobody's never seed afore! A mirrercle, wot's goin' ter mike Oomoo so grite 'e'll be able ter do wotever 'e likes!' The yellow god's voice became, for the first time, a little emotional. 'Do yer know, O, Oakley, that Oomoo's begun 'is good hinfluence orlready? Do yer know, O, Oakley, 'e went fer a walk larst night through the villidge?' Oakley opened his eyes in astonishment. 'Do yer know, O, Oakley, 'e give 'em orl 'is blessin', and 'ad the 'ole lot follerin' 'im when 'e walked back? *Now* will you trust Oomoo, and do orl 'e tells yer?'

The sound of softly tramping feet fell upon Oakley's acute ears. Nothing more. No drums, no chanting this time. By Oomoo's orders.

'I'll trust you, Oomoo,' said Oakley quietly. 'But if you have any more orders, you'll have to be quick.' To himself he thought, 'Lunacy's catching—now there are *two* madmen in this room!'

The little god also heard the tramping. He relapsed into

his stolid calm as he concluded the interview with two requests.

'I'll want a fag and a box o' matches in the Temple—can yer get 'em orf one o' the prisoners?' was the first.

'If they are to be got, you shall have them,' answered Oakley. 'I believe Medworth has a secret hoard. That all, O, Oomoo?'

'No, one thing more, O, Oakley,' replied the little god, and made the second request. ''Ow do these nitives kiss each hother?'

'I beg your pardon?'

'Wot I sed.'

'They rub noses.'

'Go on! I mean, is that so? 'Ave they a spechul one?'

'Yes. If they raise their right hands afterwards and repeat the process, it means everlasting friendship.'

'Ah,' murmured the yellow god. 'Everlastin' frien'ship!'

The tramping reached the hut, and stopped.

27

The Flaw in the Plan

The procession moved silently up the hill like a long black snake with an illuminated golden head. The head was the yellow god on his raised litter, gleaming in the light of the foremost torch-bearers, and at intervals down the snake's long line were other torch-bearers, making other bright points that culminated at the end of the tail. The chanting sounds that should normally have accompanied the snake's progress would have been eerie enough, but the silence, broken only by the soft, slow tramp of naked feet, seemed even more eerie than sound.

Not a word was spoken during the journey. Thought loomed supreme. When the outer gate was reached, it was silently opened by Oakley, and after a momentary halt the procession passed through, and on to the second gate. Then, after another short halt, it flowed into the dark space of the Temple.

The Temple had not been illuminated, and the torches of the bearers provided the only light. They picked out garishly the most prominent and brilliant spots, and left the rest in deep, flickering shadow. It was a scene to make one gasp, and some of the prisoners did gasp. Even the three who had already seen the Temple gazed at it with fresh wonder in this new awe-inspiring aspect. But Ben did not gasp. He had seen it all before in his vision; or he believed he had. The impressive throne towards which he was being borne—he had seen that. The great pot, with its sliding, perforated lid—he had seen that. The steps that led downward, behind the pot, to the hidden recess beneath it—the effigies—the gold-streaked columns of rock—the one column of pure gold—the high, domed roof—the little door that led to the High Priest's passage at the far end of the Temple—he had seen them all, and although Oakley in a later discussion denied the possibility of this, Ben held on to his conviction.

But one fact was beyond discussion. The yellow god did not behave as Ben, in his right mind, would have behaved. His mouth did not open. His eyes did not stare. He did not exclaim, 'Lumme!' He accepted the terrible grandeur as a natural environment for the events to come, and he moved from the litter to the throne with a dignity that fitted the occasion.

Oakley, by now accustomed to Ben's attitude and appearance, was able to detach himself sufficiently to glance towards the prisoners to whom the transformation was new, and to note their emotions. Indeed, Ben was quite as astonishing to them as was the Temple. Smith's eyes were very nearly out of his head. The lips of Miss Noyes appeared to have become permanently parted. 'I can't understand why I'm not fainting!' she thought. 'Really, I can't understand it! Perhaps I have fainted? If not, I soon will!' Medworth's amazement had a flush of indignation in it. He was striving to be angry at the outrageousness of it all to bolster up his courage.

There was no anger, however, in the breasts of Haines and Cooling. On the contrary, the sight of Ben, and of the reverence of the natives, stirred them with new hope.

Oakley was particularly conscious of this reverence. He was conscious of the personal note in it . . .

For a few tense seconds after Ben was seated on his new throne, nothing happened. The stage wait was due to the absence of the usual producer. The Chief looked around for the High Priest.

'Kooala!' he muttered glancing at Oakley. 'Kwee? Kooala?'

Ben heard the mutter, and, staring at Oakley, pointed to the Priest's door. Oakley walked slowly to the door, grasped the skull that was suspended above it, and pulled it down. Then he returned to the throne.

There was another tense pause. All eyes were turned to the Priest's door. The minute that passed seemed like ten. Then the door opened, and the High Priest entered.

As his eyes fell upon the crowded chamber, the torches, the gleaming spears, the assembled prisoners, and Oomoo already seated on his throne, an expression leapt into his eyes that, to some of those who saw it, was unforgettable. The surprise in it was swamped by savage indignation and hatred. The little god was yellow, but the High Priest at that instant was yellower.

But the instant passed. Intelligent instinct burned behind those baleful eyes, and he would never lose his power by a momentary passion. Something had gone wrong. Those responsible should, in due course, receive the complete gift of his venom. But, first, the cause would have to be discovered, and it could only be discovered by, at this early stage, apparent acceptance. Rulers may deal out surprises. They must not let it appear that they themselves can receive them.

The High Priest advanced slowly. His eyes moved from Oakley to the little god. The eyes of the little god stared back with unquenchable purpose. Before the High Priest reached him, Oomoo was giving his next order. He was pointing to the great pot.

The High Priest paused. This should have been *his* order! And it should not have come just yet!

The Low Priest made no inquiry into the High Priest's state of mind. There had been moments in the Chief's hut when the High Priest had dominated him, but now he was slave only to Oomoo. As soon as Oomoo pointed to the pot, he prostrated himself, and then, taking a taper from the wall, and lighting it from one of the torches, he moved to the descending steps and disappeared.

A curious thought came into the mind of Ernest Medworth. 'Oh, so *that* wasn't why he wanted my silver lighter!' He had yielded it to Oakley unwillingly, with his last cigarette, before the procession had continued on its way from the Chief's hut.

Now all eyes were turned towards the spot where Oakley had vanished. The assembly awaited his reappearance. He was away a long time, and the High Priest began to grow impatient. But when he made a movement towards the steps, Oomoo gave another order, this time directly to the High Priest. He waved him back, and pointed to a spot beside the throne.

The High Priest hesitated. He noticed the expressions of the nearest spearmen. These men, obviously, had no doubts as to the authenticity of Oomoo. The High Priest could not quite understand the expressions, but he decided to be guided by them. He bowed his head, and stayed where he was. Before long he would have an understanding with Oomoo. Yes, undoubtedly, he and Oomoo must get to know each other better. But the improvement in their relationship would be established when they were alone. Quite alone.

At last Oakley reappeared. He walked back to the throne

slowly, made a motion with his hands, and once more prostrated himself. Ben found himself immensely interested in the hands, and as Oakley rose he stretched out his own hands. For a moment their hands met. Ben's came away clenched, Medworth's lighter in one, and his last cigarette in another.

The necessity of keeping his fists clenched and of camouflaging the true reason expedited Ben's next move. He began suddenly to gesticulate on a grand scale. The clenched fingers supplied a usefully bellicose touch, but as the gesticulations were unique in the language of signs, no one could possibly have interpreted them without a foreknowledge of their meaning. Oakley, however, possessed this foreknowledge, and after he had removed himself to a safe distance he watched the extraordinary performance with the required expressions of astonishment and incredulity.

His mouth opened. His eyes dilated. He turned to the High Priest as one amazed, and then repeated the performance to the Chief. Then he stared at the Priest's door, and then he did a forbidden thing. He sped to the door and disappeared beyond it into hallowed territory.

But he was back again before the Priest could make his indignation coherent.

'Zoozo!' he cried. 'Zoozo! Choom! Zoozo!'

The effect was instantaneous. Everybody stiffened, and the Chief leapt into the air.

'Oomoo poopoo! Oomoo Hoohaa! Oomoo Hoohaa zoozo! Owlah!'

At the last cry every spear was raised high, and the Chief darted towards the door. But Oakley jumped in his path exclaiming, 'Nyaya! Sweeze!' and pointed to Ben again.

Once more, Oomoo gesticulated. This time his gesticulations were in the opposite direction. He waved towards the gate to the outer chamber, while Oakley watched him intently, as before. When he thought he had done enough, Ben stopped, but Oakley wanted a little more. He pointed to the prisoners. Ben swept his arm towards the Priest's door.

'Hya, hya, Oomoo,' muttered Oakley. 'Hyaya!'

He interpreted the order. Only one man hesitated to obey. It was the High Priest.

He stood without moving, while the natives crowded into the outer chamber. Before following them, the Chief darted an inquiring glance at him, but he paid no attention. His eyes were on the prisoners, who were being marched by Oakley into his private preserves.

As the last one passed through—the last one was Cooling—Oakley paused. A vital moment had come, and all might depend upon it.

'Oomoo!' murmured Oakley.

It was an inquiry. An invitation for him to move. Oomoo remained as motionless as the High Priest.

'Oomoo!' repeated Oakley.

The little god still made no response. The three were alone in the Temple, and now that the natives had gone the only light was a faint grey glimmer that entered grudgingly through the Priest's open door.

The Priest moved suddenly. He slipped to the pot and touched it with his fingers. The side was lukewarm. It should have been hot. The next instant he had darted, out after the prisoners, and something gleamed as he went.

'Damn!' thought Oakley. 'I didn't think it could last!'

He followed him. Ben heard the door being bolted. He found himself alone.

28

Ben Plays the Joker

Then, in the dim loneliness of the Temple, the worst happened. Ben had a brainstorm.

He never knew what produced it—whether it was the diabolical intention written on the High Priest's face as he had slipped out of the door, or the sound of the door being bolted after Oakley had slipped out after him, or the sudden deathly silence and solitude that followed, with unseen slayers on either side, and the Temple as their intended battle-ground. Or was it just the snapping of a simple mind torn between two personalities? Whatever the cause, the result was shattering. With a sensation that he had been deserted both spiritually and materially, Ben fell from his perch with a bump and became the frightened stoker once more.

No longer was he 'benumb like.' Reality came sweeping back, bringing its shocks and its agonies. He felt as though he had been walking stiffly through a dream which had suddenly dissolved and left him protectionless.

How had he duped all these savages? How had he faced them without swooning? How had Oomoo's spirit entered into him, if it had, or how had he imagined that it had if it hadn't? The questions were unanswerable. He had no idea. He had been shoved off his pedestal—out of his illusory sanctuary—and he couldn't find his way back again. Literally he had been shoved off, because when he emerged from the first convulsions of the brainstorm he discovered, to his astonishment, that he was on the floor.

"Ow did I git 'ere?' he wondered.

He had got there in one leap.

He clasped his stomach to diminish its wobbling—the effect, was merely to communicate the wobbling to his hands—and crept to the Priest's door. He just dodged the hanging skull in time to avoid kissing it. Unnerving things lay on the other side of the door, but Oakley was among the things, and he wanted Oakley. He wanted him very badly. The door however was barred.

To smash it was as impossible as ungodlike. To shout would be definitely human. He might give the skull a tug. Yes—what about giving the skull a tug? Would it bring anybody? If so, whom? He was trying to work out whom, with his hand preparing to make a sudden grab at the skull, when his ear caught a sound. It was a faint cry.

Ben had heard many cries in his uneasy life, and not all of them faint, but he thought this was quite the nastiest of the lot. All one could be thankful for was the faintness.

Another sound followed it. A distant crash. Then other sounds. Swift—confused—undecipherable. 'Orrerble!

They were so 'orrerble that Ben retreated from the door. He wondered whether they had been heard by those who were waiting behind the other door, and as he turned his eye was attracted by something glinting from the ground. It gave him another little start, because he was convinced it had not been on the ground all along. It looked like a silver optic.

But when he drew cautiously closer he found that it was nothing more harmful than the silver lighter. He had dropped it during his leap from the throne. Yes, and he had dropped the cigarette, too. Where was the cigarette? He must find it. The lighter was useless to him alone. He began groping around for the cigarette.

He found it in the shadow of the great pot. It had rolled there, almost prophetically.

He crept to it, stooped, regained it, rose, and bumped his head. He stared at the pot. He touched its cooling side, to find out what protuberance had struck him, and his hand came against a knob. At the pressure, the great lid swung slowly open.

'Crikey!' he gasped leaping back.

When he had slightly recovered from the shock he advanced again, cautiously mounted four steps that led up the side of the pot, and peered over the rim. The curved interior yawned up at him like a hungry mouth. At the bottom gleamed a little dark water.

'Wot's left o' the gargle!' thought Ben.

He toyed with the notion of climbing into the pot, curling up in it, and trying to go to sleep till he died. He resisted the doubtful temptation. He hadn't finished his job yet, and even without Oomoo's assistance he supposed he would have to finish it. 'Arter orl, why not?' he queried, lugubriously. 'Everythink's ekerlly 'orrble!' His decision not to enter the pot was reinforced by the open lid. Uncovered, the pot would make a feeble funk-hole!

'Yus, but there must be some way ter close it,' he reflected. 'Let's find it.'

He brought his inquiring head out of the pot, climbed down, and pressed the knob again. In response, the lid swung slowly back into place.

The next moment he forgot the pot. Fresh noises were sounding outside the Priest's door.

His heart stood still, but his legs carried on. They carried him back to the throne. If he had left it like a rocket, he returned like a meteor, and almost before he knew it he was on his seat once more, listening to the creeping feet. He knew they were creeping feet. He had spent half his life among creeping feet, and he could recognise the sound upside down. Once he had actually done so, when he had sought sudden shelter by diving into a cupboard the wrong way up.

'Wot I carn't mike aht,' he thought, while the creeping feet grew closer, 'is why they don't give us the vote if we wants ter be born or not? I knows which way I'd 'ave voted. It'd 'ave bin narpoo! Funny 'ow it works—yer don't wanter be born, but yer don't wanter die. Wot do yer want?'

He had never found out.

Now the creeping feet reached the Priest's door. The front ones stopped, but others crept up behind, whispering their way forward.

'Give me boots hevery time,' muttered Ben trying to quell his ungodlike shivers. 'I 'ites feet niked!'

He heard the wooden bar being softly shifted. He felt like the very small contents of a large dark sandwich. The sandwich was now in process of manufacture, and in a few moments Fate would clap the two black slabs together, with himself in the middle, and take a munch . . .

'Wot I ses is this,' was Ben's last reflection before the door opened. 'When yer dead yer dead. Well, I mean, aincher?'

The Red Squares came in like a shower of rustling leaves

propelled suddenly by a strong wind. They blew without pause half-way across the Temple floor. In the dim dawn admitted by the open door and beginning to percolate through the slit windows they resembled fierce phantoms with gleaming eyes . . .

But although their spears were raised to attack, they found no foe. All they found was a small yellow god who sat and stared ahead of him with a frozen smile.

They stopped abruptly. Swung round. Gazed at the unexpected sight. One warrior poised his spear to throw, but before the spear could be released it was struck down by another warrior, who issued a swiftly muttered order. The second warrior was the tallest man Ben had ever seen. He was well over seven feet; and as, while the rest waited in obedience to his command, he wheeled towards the raised throne on which Ben squatted, the red square on his chest was on a level with Ben's eyes and the polished head towered above him. Encircling the giant's neck was a necklace of human bones.

Ben kept his eyes unwinkingly on the red square. Possibly his yellow paint saved him from immediate extermination. If he did not feel like Oomoo any longer, his appearance remained unique even in the annals of the Pacific, and the leader of the Red Squares could not dismiss this unusual spectacle without preliminary examination. Commencing at a distance, the examination got uncomfortably closer, and an old man with a long beard and a longer pole joined in warily. On the top of the pole was a small carved effigy, adding its evidence to the theory that, in cannibalistic conception, ugliness is next to godliness.

Ben concentrated desperately on his effort not to wink. He was convinced that gods did not wink—not, anyhow, at a first interview—and that his time on earth would end as soon as his strained eyelids met. It was amazing how they longed to meet. They positively ached for the encounter. He denied them as long as he could, but when the giant, having now reached the throne, bent his great head forward and downward so that it almost touched Ben's, the situation became too unbearable, and Ben ended it in a way that surprised both the giant and himself. Responding to a sudden inspiration, he bent his own head forward and upward till his nose touched that of the giant.

The giant was too astonished to move. It was Ben who caused the separation. He withdrew his head, raised his right hand, and then applied his nose a second time, waggling it up and down at the renewed contact. This, he recalled, was Oakley's formula for undying friendship.

Now the giant fell back. His eyes rolled in incredulous wonder. He appeared overwhelmed, and he turned to the old man with the long beard. The old man seemed equally astounded.

There was a whispered consultation. The upshot was a decision that the old man should try his luck, and the veteran approached none too willingly. He was, in fact, a very careful old man, and he held his pole in front of him as he advanced so that it should stand between him and any tricks. Thus the effigy reached Ben first.

Again the yellow god bent forward, treating the effigy as the giant had been treated. He rubbed his nose against the protuberance in the centre of the carved face, withdrew, raised his right hand, repeated the nasal salutation, and sat back once more.

The effect of this meeting of gods on the company was so engrossing that no one noticed that the door to the outer chamber had been quietly opened, and that the salutation had been witnessed by a second audience—an audience no less impressed. Ben was the first to see the island Chief standing in the doorway. The Chief gripped a huge spear, but he seemed in no hurry to use it, while behind him crowded his army waiting for the delayed order to fall upon the foe.

'Lumme!' thought Ben, his brain reeling. ''Ave I done it?'

Suddenly the leader of the invading party leapt round. He saw the Chief, with the massed spears behind him, and while the two enemies stared at each other they were obviously baffled by their inaction. They should have been at each other's throats. Their war-like instincts were in a fog.

But after a few seconds they began advancing towards each other, watched tensely by their respective followers. They held their weapons firmly clenched, to imply that, although they were postponing battle, they were taking no chances. They did not stop until they were face to face, their bodies almost touching. Then they halted, and stood regarding each other like a couple of huge fighting-cocks, each waiting for the other to make the first move.

Suddenly the leader of the invaders made a move. It appeared to Ben to form the culmination of some silent communication that had been passing between the two. The giant sprang back, and pointed an accusing finger towards the pot.

His gesture was approved by a low, ominous murmur from his men.

'Lumme, I don't believe I 'ave done it!' thought Ben.

The Chief also drew back, and his eyes became less passive. He uttered a word which seemed to carry its own accusation, and now his followers took it up, repeating it menacingly.

Spears became restless. The giant again pointed to the pot, and his expression grew more forbidding. He raised his spear and shook it. The island Chief raised his spear and shook it. All the spears were raised and shaken, and fierce mutterings from both sides began to rumble through the Temple, like war-drums.

'I 'aven't done it!' thought Ben.

A spear flashed through the air, embedding itself in the Priest's door. In another moment the Temple would be transformed into a hideous charnel house and not even a god would be able to divert attention from the frenzied business of slaughter. Ben acted just in the nick of time. He had played all the cards he possessed but one; he rose now to play the joker.

Only a movement from Oomoo could have stayed the attackers' murderous rush. Poised for it, they held back while Oomoo left his throne and descended to the floor with slow, dignified steps. They watched him advance to the island Chief, who himself watched as hard as any.

Reaching the Chief, Ben waved towards the pot, as though inviting him to enter. The Chief's mouth opened, while a shout of savage triumph came from the thick lips of the giant. This was retribution! But the Chief, for once, was disobedient, and as he retreated Ben turned to the giant and repeated his gesture to him. Now the giant's triumph evaporated, and *his* mouth opened. Like the Chief, he refused the invitation. Then Oomoo walked to the pot himself, pressed the knob, and mounted the steps while the lid swung open.

From the steps he beckoned to the Chief. The Chief, after a moment of hesitation, crept forward as one mesmerised. Taking the Chief's hand, Oomoo directed it towards the knob.

'Hya, hyaya!' mumbled the Chief.

Satisfied that he had been understood, Ben climbed into the pot, and a moment later the lid swung back above him.

Once more all thoughts of battle were suspended while astonished eyes fastened on the lid. No sound came from the voluntary inmate. No gasp or shriek or wail. A miracle was occurring. It held the company spellbound.

Soon, from the hole in the top of the lid, a thin grey wisp emerged. It ascended, spread a little, vanished. Another wisp followed. Thicker. Like the first, it ascended and melted away. Then came another, thicker still, and coiling. Then a ring. A low murmur greeted the ring. The ring was succeeded by more rings, curling after each other to the roof. Then a steady column . . . divine breath belching upwards from the surface of boiling water.

For five minutes the strange spectacle was watched with trance-like attention. Then, suddenly, the Chief gave a great, booming shout.

'Oomoo! Oomoo Mumba! Oomoo! Oi!'

He fell flat. His army fell flat. What a chance for the foe! The giant looked at the old man with the beard, and the old man fell flat. The giant fell flat, and his warriors followed suit.

Into this strange scene, from the Priest's doorway, entered a white-robed man. The white-robed man did not fall flat. He stared at the prostrate figures, and over them to the pot with its steadily ascending vapour. Turning his head, he looked at the empty throne. He appeared to endure a moment of dizziness, but he quickly conquered it, and he made his way to the pot, treading quickly but carefully so that he would not disturb the network of humanity that carpeted the ground. Reaching the pot he hesitated, then pressed the knob.

Ben, staring upwards, saw the lid slide open, and he sent the last puff of his cigarette into the face that peered down at him over the rim. It was the face of Oakley.

''Allo,' whispered Ben. 'I'm goin' ter fint!'

'Not before you show yourself, old dear,' Oakley whispered back.

He lifted Ben out. As he did so, the giant raised his head. Oakley pressed the knob hastily, and while the lid closed the giant rose. The Chief, sensing happenings, rose also.

Oomoo just managed to remain erect. His stifled mind was struggling to remember something. Some last job he must perform before he gave way . . . It had been pretty bad in that pot . . .

'Oh—corse!' he suddenly recollected. 'Nosey-posey.'

He beckoned solemnly. The two men approached him, awed. They stood before him, side by side. They bent their heads cautiously to examine him, and when their heads were within reach of Oomoo he raised his hands, placed one behind each head, twisted the heads towards each other, and brought them together. The warring generals found themselves rubbing noses.

They sprang apart, in amazement not unmixed with embarrassment. Oomoo raised his right hand. After a moment's hesitation, they followed suit. Then they sprang together again, and this time their noses met voluntarily.

'Owlah!' roared the island Chief. 'Owlah! Owlah!'

The natives leapt up. Spears were held high, no longer in menace. They were raised to the little yellow god who had just emerged unscathed—and not even wet—from a boiling bath, and who had united two belligerent tribes.

But the yellow god did not see the raised spears. His eyes were closed, and, as the new High Priest explained to the company, he had gone into a trance of divine ecstasy that necessitated his immediate solitude.

29

For the Duration

When Ben opened his eyes he found himself back on the throne, but the first thing his eyes fell on was a streak of sunlight. It lay on the floor of the Temple like a bar of gold that had come to life, and he kept his eyes on it for a while, feeling that it was bringing him back to life, also. Though whether he desired to be brought back to life was, for the moment, mere conjecture.

Near the streak of sunlight squatted Oakley, adding another touch of brightness to the scene. Oakley was still wearing the white robe in which he had re-entered the Temple to rescue Ben from the suffocating pot.

'Take your time,' advised Oakley, watching Ben recover.

"Ave—we got it?' mumbled Ben shakily.

'All we want,' replied Oakley. 'It's going to be a fine day. There must be an anti-cyclone off the north-west of Ireland.'

"Ow did I git 'ere?' asked Ben.

'I carried you here,' answered Oakley, 'after the guests had departed.'

"Oo?'

'Never mind. How are you feeling?'

'There ain't no word fer it. Wot's 'appened?'

'Well, quite a lot of things. But do you feel up to hearing them?'

'Gotter some time, ain't I?' muttered Ben feebly. 'Where's the hothers?'

'Which others? White or black?'

'Eh? Oh! Let's 'ave the white fust.'

'Right. The white folk are legging it across the Pacific.'

'Go on!'

'Are you surprised? Isn't that what we've been working for?'

'Yus—corse it is. But—'

'Why didn't they wait for you?' interposed Oakley. 'Don't forget, you did rather insist on staying behind, didn't you? And, afterwards—well, here's the story. Beginning from where I left you alone in the Temple—'

'And locked me in!'

'No, Ben, I didn't lock you in. The High Priest did that. As a matter of fact, it was the H.P. who started the whole ball rolling—by eventually rolling himself off the edge of the ridge and falling through the tree-tops bang into the camp of the Red Squares.'

'Go on!' exclaimed Ben. ''Ow did that 'appen?'

'Well, I am afraid he received a little assistance over the edge,' murmured Oakley. 'You see, he whipped out his knife—I saw him doing it as he left the Temple—and he wanted to take the law into his own hands . . . Nasty bit of work, I'm afraid, but it just had to be, old sport—it just had to be. Couldn't let him run amok with that knife, could I?'

'I 'eard 'is cry,' said Ben. ''Orrerble!'

'It wasn't pretty,' answered Oakley. 'It worried some others, too. Of course, his abrupt descent brought the invaders up, but by that time the rest of us had got into the Priest's house—my God, what a hovel, I shall have it spring cleaned!—so they didn't spot us when they trooped into the Temple here. Pretty narrow squeak, though. Some of our party lost their heads, and nearly scotched the whole thing. If Haines and I hadn't lugged 'em back they'd have dashed straight down into the lion's mouth. That's how *you* got overlooked till it was too late, though I don't suppose you'd have come away anyhow till you'd done your good act, would you?' Ben did not answer. 'Stout feller, eh? And Haines is another stout feller. I expect he'll pair up with Miss Sheringham . . . Not that it matters . . . where was I?'

''Idin' in the Priest's 'ouse,' prompted Ben.

'That's right. So I was. With the rest of them. We found Miss Sheringham in there, of course.'

'And the kid?'

'Eh?'

'The kid? The black kid? Yer fahnd 'er, too?'

'Yes—she was inside. Neither hurt. But—well, dazed to the world. The hovel they'd been shut up in stank with sickly incense. Whew! It's used to dope the privileged victims. I admit I slipped up in my predictions there. I knew the H.P. wouldn't hurt them, but I'd forgotten the possibility of the dope. Of course, it complicated things.'

''Ow?'

'Don't ask silly questions! How could Miss Sheringham walk when she was in that condition?'

'Oh! Well, 'ow did she git away, then?'

'Haines accepted the situation without any noticeable complaint, and carried her.'

'Dahn ter the boat?'

243

'Yes.'

'And I s'pose you carried the black kid?'

'No, I—er—carried Miss Noyes.'

'Wot, did she pop orf, too?'

'It was more of an ooze than a pop. She just oozed away.'

'Oh. Then 'oo carried—'

'There was, as you can imagine, some confusion. There was, in fact, nothing but confusion. It reached its height when, just as we got to the boat, an arrow sailed through the air, missing Haines by three inches.'

'Lumme!'

'So I thought myself.'

'And 'e was carryin' Miss Sheringham!'

'Yes. It was a nasty moment. You'll realise now, Ben, that there wasn't much time, and that some of the party got quite out of hand.'

'Yus, but 'oo—'

'Shot the arrow?'

'No, 'oo was carryin'—'

'A Red Square shot the arrow. He must have overslept, or risen late. Or maybe he was left at the camp to keep guard there while the rest came up to the Temple. Anyhow, he spotted us going down, and followed us. He sent about a dozen arrows in all, but only two did any damage.'

'Crikey—'

'Medworth has a sore foot, and Smith has a sore thumb. Personally, I'm not grieving. They were only slight grazes, and the arrows weren't poisoned—I proved this afterwards by examining one that had not found its mark. Both the casualties will live to tell the tallest stories, and I think it quite pleasant that they should take little souvenirs back with them to England. Let us hope they will smart in damp weather.

But I didn't want any more souvenirs, so I gave the boat a shove, and away she glided on the tide.'

Ben had been gazing at the ground while picturing the departure. Now he shifted his eyes to Oakley.

'Why didn't you go orf with 'em?' he asked.

'I always thought you were a spot of an ass, Ben,' answered Oakley. 'Now I know it.'

There was a short silence. The Temple had a long lurid history, most of it forgotten and none of it recorded, but within the past hour it had surpassed itself in the range of varying emotions it had witnessed. After the silence Ben said:

'Seems ter me, Mr Hoakley, yer a bit of orl right.'

'That, coming from Oomoo, is a compliment,' replied Oakley gravely. 'But, don't forget, there was plenty of clearing up to do yet, and I never make a journey till I've ticked off all the items on my list. One item on my list was that arrow-slinger. I had to settle with him, didn't I?'

'And—did yer?'

'I did. Odd, isn't it, that among all these bloodthirsty blighters, the only killing during the last dozen hours should have been done by peace-loving Robert Oakley! Don't think I like it.' He regarded his right hand with disapproval. Then went on, 'And another item was that other little person you've been inquiring about so persistently. The black child—'

'Wot!' exclaimed Ben. 'Wasn't she with 'em?'

'No. In the confusion she got left behind. Cooling would have carried her down, I expect, if he'd realised . . . but, after all, it's just as well, isn't it—as matters have turned out?'

'Wotcher mean?'

'Use your ha'p'orth of sense, lad. Where is that child's danger now—with the island in charge of Mr Benjamin

245

Oomoo and a new High Priest? You note, of course, that on my way up I stepped into the High Priest's raiment?'

Ben did not answer. He was thinking hard.

'Yes, it's rather an interesting position, isn't it?' said Oakley. 'You and I make quite a useful combination. Especially after the amazingly good work you did in here while I was messing about outside. Of course, I didn't know that. That miracle in the pot just about completed the trick—with, I admit, a few final touches of my own. After you went into your last trance—'

'Oh, trarnce, was it?'

'Bens pop off, but Oomoos go into trances. *You* ought to know that! And when Oomoo was in this trance, communing with Hojak, Mooane Kook, and Gug—Gug, you recall, is the God of Eatables—we'll tell him about Eustace Miles, eh?—I bundled the company into the outer hall and had a little pow-wow with them. I explained that Oomoo had caused the High Priest to leap to his death as a penalty for once having slain an innocent Red Square. I explained that the High Priest had committed other misdeeds the full particulars of which would in due course be communicated to them by Oomoo, divine brother of the Red Square's Chongchong—who I understand you kissed when he was presented to you by the Red Square's High Priest. I told them that one of the misdeeds was an attempt to exterminate two loving tribes who were destined by the gods to be blood-brothers, and that it was actually to put an end to the High Priest's evil acts that Oomoo had sent his last storm and had come in person to the island. And then, Ben, I told them to run away and play. They are having high jinks at this moment down in the village.'

'Coo, yer've got a brine!' murmured Ben.

'Well, I'm doing my best to take it out of cold storage,' responded Oakley.

'But wot abart them Red Squires wot you've finished orf? Won't that mean a bit o' trouble?'

'Oh, no, Ben. I haven't finished any Red Squares off. Don't you know Bob Oakley better than that? The High Priest finished them off. Killed 'em in the night. Really that H.P. has an awful lot to account for!'

'Oh! So that's 'ow it's goin'?'

'That is how it is going.'

'Well—wot abart the boat wot's gone, with—'

'With the white folk whose deaths were *not* required by gentle Oomoo? And whose lives on this island would have been just as useless? Oomoo's orders, Ben, Oomoo's orders—carried out by Oomoo's right-hand man, the new High Priest.'

'Lumme!' gulped Ben. 'Yus—we *do* mike that there comber-nashun you spoke of jest nah! Do yer suppose—'

'What?' inquired Oakley as Ben paused.

'I was goin' ter say—do yer suppose we could keep it up?'

'We might, Ben.'

'It'd—be funny, wouldn't it?'

'Unique.'

'U 'oo?'

'Unique means unprecedented in the annals of Wells's *History of the World*. Or, to put it more simply—unusual.'

'Unushel? Ah, I git yer. It's a fack! But when yer come ter think abart it, well, we might do a bit o' good 'ere—like wot I sed?'

'Like wot you said, Ben. It was all your idea.'

'The hidea wouldn't 'ave bin no use if you 'adn't bin 'ere ter 'elp it along,' said Ben. 'Yus, but—well—would it be fer hever, like?'

'Is anything for ever, like?' inquired Oakley.

'So it ain't!'

'It undoubtedly ain't. You, I, the natives, Oomoo, Haines—Miss Sheringham—all the people who are alive today, all who were alive yesterday, all who will be alive tomorrow—this Temple that has stood so long and that looks so solid, the world, the silly little sun . . .' He snapped his fingers.

'I wunner!' murmured Ben. 'But wot abart 'Eving?'

'Ask me another,' smiled Oakley.

'Well, I believe in 'Eving,' said Ben, ''cos if there ain't no 'Eving, wot the 'Ell do they mike yer go through 'Ell for?'

'Perhaps Oomoo will help you to get into Heaven?'

'Eh?'

'When St Peter asks you at the gate, "What did *you* do in the Great War, Daddy?" you could answer, "I taught some cannibals to live on cabbages."'

'Corse, the way yer tork mikes me feel funny, but I see wot yer mean. But—look 'ere—mightn't wot's-'is-nime say, "Yer did it by cheatin'!"'

'Cheating?'

'Yus. I ain't Oomoo really—though, mindjer I thort I was fer a bit—and you ain't no 'Igh Priest. So wot I ses. It'd be cheatin'.'

'It won't be the first time Religion has cheated, Ben,' answered Oakley. 'It's always cheating—'

'Go on!'

'—pretending to knowledge it hasn't got. Every religion can't be right, can it? Protestants, Jews, Catholics, Buddhists, Confucians—'

'Oo's Confusions?'

'Shut up, Oomoo, I'm talking! After years of numbness and silence, I'm saying things! . . . Methodists, Christian

Scientists, Heathens, Atheists—the whole shoot! And countries, too, each imagining itself the only one that matters, and forming God in its own image—just as these gods are formed here. After all, what *is* truth? Does anybody know it? Will anybody ever know it? We're talking of cheating, but truth isn't just saying that Y e s spells Yes and that N o spells No. Listen, you blinking owl—why shouldn't there be a bit of God in you—and of High Priest in me—if we chuck the spelling and try to do a spot of work we think God might like?'

He rose suddenly, and turned towards the open doorway to the sea over which virgin sunlight was dancing.

'Yer mean, lend a 'and,' said Ben, 'and let the rest go?'

'That's just what I mean—lend a hand in the muddling struggle towards happiness. Our souls can remain truthful even if our lips have to spell backwards.' He thought of the little boat, somewhere on that sparkling expanse—speeding away in the tide towards a continuation of that muddling struggle in another spot. Then he added, abruptly, 'Of course, Ben, we needn't stay here. We can go down to the beach now, if we like, get another of the boats, take our chance, and follow them.'

There was no answer from the throne.

'I told Haines we'd follow them before I shoved their boat off. He didn't like leaving us, but with all those arrows flying, and for all we knew the worst happening up here, it was just *sauve qui peut*. "Meet you in London," I said to him. "If not, I'll come back for you," he answered. "Not till you've seen Miss Sheringham safely home to Piccadilly Circus," I told him, "and she won't get home if we stop to talk." He understood. And then came another arrow . . . Well, what about it? Do we follow?'

'Come back fer us,' murmured Ben, 'might they?'

'They might,' nodded Oakley.

'P'r'aps we could show 'em a surprise when they come?'

'P'r'aps we could.'

'And then, corse, there's another thing,' said Ben. ''Avin'
got so fur, like, with these black blokes 'ere, wot's goin' ter
'appen to 'em if we goes and leaves 'em, like?'

'Do you mind what happens to them, Ben?' inquired
Oakley.

'I mind wot 'appens to that kid!' answered Ben. 'Where is
she?'

Oakley smiled, moved to a spot behind the throne, and
returned to Ben with the black child in his arms.

'I thought she'd had enough of the stuffy atmosphere in
the Priest's house,' he said, 'so I brought her in here.'

Ben stared at the child. Her eyes were closed. She had long,
pretty lashes.

'My Gawd, she ain't dead?' gasped Ben.

'Just asleep,' replied Oakley.

Ben held out his arms, and Oakley placed the sleeping
child in them.

'Might as well stay—doncher think?' muttered Oomoo,
rather unsteadily. 'See, I sorter promised 'er mother.' He
lowered his nose and touched the sleeping child's. 'Lumme—
tork abart feelin' foolish!'

THE END

250